She desperately wanted what he offered, but to accept it would surely get them both killed . . .

"Please tell me what is going on here," Nicholas urged her, a look of profound earnestness in the depths of his dark eyes. "This is not a normal existence for a lady as fine as yourself. You deserve so much more than this. What is the nature of your business, Delphinia?"

The warmth of his words made her stiffen. She tried to conceal her defensiveness and failed. Flustered by emotions that were unclear to her, she took a step back from him. The slight distance could not keep her feelings at bay.

"I live a very private life here, Nicholas," she said in a quiet tone. "I would like to tell you more, but I cannot. I hope one day that I will be at liberty to do so. Perhaps you do not know that I am a reserved person by nature."

A laugh escaped him, spontaneous and pleasing in its sincerity. "There is nothing naturally reserved about you." The gentle merriment in his eyes almost made her smile in spite of herself. "You are outspoken and painfully honest in all you do and say. If you are a private person, I believe it is because you have been forced into isolation against your will."

"No one forces me to do anything," she argued as he reached for her hand to prevent the words of denial he must know were forthcoming, "except you. You force me into foolish conversation when I merely wish to go riding."

Nicholas squeezed her small hands in his large muscular ones, refusing to let them go. "Even though you have made it clear that you are anxious for me to leave, I had always hoped we might come to know each other better." His sea-green eyes bored into hers with an intensity she tried to avoid but could not. "I want to know you without the superficial wall of privacy you have built around you."

She froze at the force of his words. This was the first she had heard of any of this. What was she to make of it?

She laughed shortly. "That can never be."

"Why?" he persisted, his lips close to her ear. "Why can there be nothing between us? Give me a reason."

"Your ankle is better," she observed quietly. "Soon there will no longer be a reason for you to remain here. Your carriage will be repaired, and you will be on your way."

"Yes," he admitted frankly, in a tone of exasperation. "And I won't be coming through these parts again, if I can help it. I'd sooner be back at the helm facing the Spanish, even Admiral Gravina himself, than to be lost on those moors again." His gaze becom͏ more serious, he paused, as if giving her time to absorb the wo͏ ͏ ͏ ͏ ͏ ͏ ͏ to ignore. "Is that what you want, Delphinia?"

To Gail Eastwood-Stokes, Blanche Marriott, and Pat Piscopio,
my friends and first readers,
for the memories and dreams we share.

Other Books by Karen Frisch
Coming Soon
A Regency Yuletide

Lady Delphinia's Deception

***

Karen Frisch

Forever Regency
a division of ImaJinn Books, Inc.

Lady Delphinia's Deception
Published by ImaJinn Books, Inc.

ISBN: 978-1-61026-004-6

10 9 8 7 6 5 4 3 2 1

PUBLISHER'S NOTE:
This book is a work of fiction. Names, characters, places and incidents are products of the author's imagination or are used fictitiously. Any resemblance to actual events or locales or persons, living or dead, is entirely coincidental.

Books are available at quantity discounts when used to promote products or services. For information please write to: Marketing Division, ImaJinn Books, Inc., P.O. Box 74274, Phoenix, AZ 85087, or call toll free 1-877-625-3592.

Cover design by Josephine Piraneo
Cover Credits:
Kirby Hall copyright Andrew Taylor
Beauty in Medieval Dress copyright msdvn
Candle By The Window copyright Martin Green

ImaJinn Books, Inc.
P.O. Box 74274, Phoenix, AZ 85087
Toll Free: 1-877-625-3592
http://www.imajinnbooks.com

Chapter One

Lightning ripped a path through the night sky, allowing Captain Nicholas Hainsworth a glimpse of the moorland that stretched around him. Rain pelted his unprotected head, for his beaver had long since blown off, an offering to the storm in which he and his companions had been walking for what seemed hours.

"I'm certain we passed that gnarled tree before. And that slope looks familiar." Shouting over the gale, Nicholas tried to inject some humor. "Trafalgar required lesser strategies, Harry, than getting us off these wretched moors will."

The only thing Nicholas knew for certain was that they were lost. Forming a chain, each hand gripping the next in line, these friends and servants were not the complement of sailors he would have chosen in war or peace. Thus far the six stranded travelers had maintained a spirit that would have made the toughest regiment proud. Yet with injuries of undetermined severity Nicholas wondered how long they could continue.

He would not be surprised if his palm bore permanent scars from Lady Nettleton's fingernails digging into his flesh. Clutching his other arm, Mrs. Herbert tried valiantly to maintain the pace but failed, slipping and catching her cloak on brambles. He was grateful neither the ruin of her pelisse nor the loss of her dignity appeared to alarm her as much as the storm did.

Nicholas had spent too much time aboard a cramped man-of-war in Nelson's fleet to be bothered by a bit of unpleasantness. The dark and discomfort did not concern him as much as the safety of his companions and the fierceness of the storm that checked their progress. With only jagged flashes of lightning to guide them they faced little chance of locating a safe haven and a far greater likelihood of coming to harm. Every step held danger in the flooded hollows of the rolling moors.

"Only a little farther," he shouted without conviction.

Yet what purpose would it serve to move forward without direction? They had not passed another vehicle even before their accident. He berated himself for not heeding his coachman's wisdom in suggesting they take rooms at the inn they had passed at the Somerset border. Despite his aged eyes Hobbs had driven through Devonshire too often to be deceived by darkness.

Nicholas studied the moors grimly. They were most definitely going in circles. Once the border of hedgerows had ended and the storm worsened there was no telling how far they had strayed from the high road. He saw no sign of the horses. His chestnut bays had managed to free themselves from the broken traces and bolted in terror when the barouche overturned. Without even a hayrick for shelter the ladies had insisted on making the trek as well.

"This deluge has me drenched to the skin," complained Rowena Herbert to his left. "How can you know it isn't much farther?"

Nicholas remained silent, unable to dispute the truth of her words. His ankle twisted with pain as his stride faltered. He concentrated on the more pressing problem of distance, his sense of time distorted by the unfamiliar terrain.

"I'm thinking we should have gone the opposite way, Harry," he called to Lord Nettleton at the far end of the chain.

Thunder rattled the ground beneath them while above their heads nature raged in defiance of their predicament. The gorse tore at his bare leg, exposed by a rip in his breeches. In the deluge Exmoor had become a menacing wilderness. Lady Nettleton loosened her grip on his hand, peering at him through the wet.

"Your forehead is bleeding again." Her tone was more frantic than he might have wished. Until now Marion had coped admirably with their plight. "We must get help."

"We shall, and soon," he promised. "Come, this way."

It was not his head Nicholas worried about. With every step his limp grew more pronounced and the pain more excruciating, but he ignored his torment to contend with his disorientation. He wished he might help his valet and Harry who struggled with the physical weakness of Hobbs, the coachman. They were aided by Marion's maid, whose truculent stride showed no hint of the infirmity of which she had routinely complained since they had left London.

"God help us, Nicholas!" Harry cried out as Hobbs stumbled. "How much further?"

Squinting through the torrents into blackness, Nicholas had no reply. Harry's words mirrored his own growing pessimism. Despite his weariness he was gripped with an overwhelming sense of responsibility. He had allowed Harry to persuade him to continue traveling despite his better judgment. In doing so he had led his friends to certain injury if not death.

His cough started up again, violent and uncontrollable, so like his father's last year. Cynically he considered his fate. The thought of his mother made him regret having disappointed her in myriad ways. She would be far more fearful if she knew his current plight. It would be the final indignity if he, the Earl of Greymore, heir to Tregaryan and the other Greymore estates, were to die of pneumonia like his father, all because of an inflated self-confidence that led to his wayward ramble across these blasted moors.

With every peal of thunder Nicholas's sense of adventure waned. The chill filled him with uncharacteristic desperation. Brushing aside uncertainty, he summoned strength from determination. Forgetting his pain, he rallied the group toward a hillock they took with a burst of speed. Atop the rise he paused to steady Rowena Herbert as she sagged against him. The torrent merciless now, he shadowed his eyes with his hand. Was he imagining it? Through the rains that stung his face he could make out a pair of flickering lights, distant but real. Lightning revealed the outline of a crenellated roof against the sky. His senses had not failed him. He broke into a laugh.

"To our right, Harry." His voice was barely audible in the wind. "A light. Push on!"

The ladies cried in exhausted relief while Harry made a gargantuan effort to support Hobbs. Adrenaline propelled Nicholas forward. A sharp descent lay before them, steep and slippery, before a final climb would bring them to their goal. Patches of scrub made the ground deceptively uneven, jarring their stride. Thrown off balance, they wrenched forward toward an invisible source of hope. Was it still there? Yes, faint but discernible.

Gripping Marion's arm as she tripped over his foot, Nicholas could see the silhouette of a fortress of sorts looming on the hilltop ahead, imposing but welcoming. There appeared to be a light glinting by the door and another in a window.

He barely heard the savage wind in his ears, nor did he feel the pain that seared his ankle. He saw only shelter as he stumbled blindly toward the glow in the upper window. His pace increased as he drew near, limping, dragging the others with him.

Twenty yards from the door his strength gave out. He felt his knees buckle as he sagged to the earth, his head slamming against the ground. Having delivered his friends to safety, he allowed himself to descend into unconsciousness.

The last thing he remembered was seeing the thin flame waver in the far window as a hand drew the draperies aside.

* * * *

Were there six or seven? Gazing through the raindrop pattern coursing down her window, Lady Delphinia Marlowe could not tell.

She released the draperies and let them fall back against the pane to muffle the howling of the wind. She had wondered if she might have visitors even before she heard the cries beyond her window, and long before the butler would come to rouse her. This was not the first time travelers had sought shelter here.

As familiar as she was with the darkness, she did not need candlelight to dress. Yet she had set a lighted candle in the window, as she always did on these nights. Soon Childers would be welcoming guests downstairs, his expression as neutral as if he were receiving callers from the parish, although he was getting on in years and not as agreeable to having his sleep disturbed as he once was. Delphinia's own habits made her accustomed to getting by on little sleep, for her existence was nocturnal by necessity.

Until a short while ago she had been reading by the fire. Despite the number of storms she had witnessed on Exmoor she felt unusually anxious tonight. Her keen sense of sound told her no ship had been wrecked on the coast as sometimes happened. Yet, this storm was particularly violent and reminded her of one years earlier, one so powerful the memory of it had kept sleep at bay.

She arranged a light shawl over her woolen dress as the fire spat a dying ember across the floor, awakening the aging dog who had been snoring gently in its dim glow. Her mastiff, accustomed to her frequent rising in the night, thumped his tail and laid his heavy head back down after lifting it slightly, content to remain by the warmth of the hearth.

Delphinia scratched him briefly before she closed the doors of the armoire. The weight of her onyx hair hung like a cloak down her back, and she decided to truss it quickly before going downstairs. The tail thumped again as she walked to her dressing table and drew a ribbon from a japanned box.

"A night like this is not for you, Brutus," she murmured.

It was in a storm such as this Brutus had first appeared at her door, scratching and begging entry. She had invited the thin bedraggled creature inside and nursed him back to health, earning her his unconditional loyalty. His companionship had brought new happiness to her long and often quiet days at Briarcombe.

Tonight new guests would arrive, she mused, less welcome ones. Inviting strangers into her home now could lead to complications she preferred to avoid. The dilemma frustrated her, for it robbed her of the joy of regular company. Yet she sensed these travelers posed more of a danger than a stray dog did.

Nervously she tapped her fingers on the mantel. What choice did she have but to offer them room? In the past she had withstood unexpected visitors. She would survive this as well.

The voices outside became more distinct, the quality of their diction setting them apart from the locals. Delphinia moved to the window in time to see two men carrying a third. She heard the sobs of the women, the cries of the men, and the urgency and relief in their voices at having reached safety. Hers was the only home for two miles. Yet March was an odd time for visitors.

The commotion below told her they were being brought indoors. She had no doubt Briarcombe's staff would have the situation in hand without her direction. Ivy, dear troublesome Ivy, would be at the heart of the activity. Her younger sister was only too delighted to receive guests at any hour.

As slow but steady footsteps neared her door she stepped over Brutus, who remained undisturbed by the noise. She opened the door before the butler could knock.

"Thank you, Childers." She took the lantern from his outstretched arm. "What have we this time?"

"Lost travelers, it would appear," he replied.

Emerging from her room, Delphinia surveyed the confusion from the landing. Her effervescent sister, still in her robe and nightdress, had not been able to move the guests any farther than the foyer, even with the staff's help. Their footman and a servant she did not recognize stumbled toward the library, supporting a heavy man who groaned in anguish. A slender woman with delicate features knelt before another woman who looked remarkably like herself, rubbing the other's hands despite her own shivering. At the foot of the stairs, attended by a gentleman and an older woman in servants' clothing, a man lay still.

Delphinia froze at the image. This can't be happening again, she thought dazedly, staring down the staircase. Was the man alive? From this distance she could not tell.

Stunned by the quantity of blood that had pooled and spattered on the flagstone floor amid the puddles, she collected herself and went to Ivy's aid. Her sister and their housekeeper Sophy scurried between guests, at a loss as to how to proceed.

"These people have come all the way from London." Ivy's tone mixed anxiety with excitement. "They became lost on the moors."

Delphinia finally found her voice. "That man. Is he—?"

"He struck his head when their carriage overturned." Ivy's eyes widened with new alarm. "Should I summon the doctor?"

"I'll take care of it. Did I see Clennam taking someone to the library?"

"Yes. I believe there is an injured coachman."

Still shaking, Delphinia turned to the handsome man who lay unconscious on the floor. With his wet blond hair falling over his forehead and his breathing regular, he appeared to be asleep. Kneeling beside him, she saw the dried blood on the right side of his face had come from a scalp wound. This man was the source of so much blood, which had sprung not from one wound but from many.

As she assessed his injuries she was greatly relieved that he was still alive, not only for his sake but for her own. The last thing she wanted was to have the police visit Briarcombe. With luck this man would recover.

She was about to rise when she felt a gentle pressure on her fingers. As his grip tightened, the man slowly opened his eyes, looking straight into hers. His were a startling shade of green, bright as polished sea glass despite his weakened condition. He spoke so softly she was forced to bend down to hear his words.

"Forgive . . . self," he murmured. He stroked her fingers with his own before lapsing back into unconsciousness.

Startled by the unexpected intimacy of his touch, Delphinia drew her fingers away as his hand fell across his chest. What had he meant? It was the last thing she expected to hear from a man so seriously injured. Were the words intended for himself or for her? No, he knew nothing of her background. She rose to her feet and turned to the two women who appeared to be his companions.

"This head gash appears deep," she said, taking a closer look at her guests. "I shall have one of our servants fetch the doctor at once and let him know it is urgent."

The thin woman stepped forward, lowering the drenched hood of her cloak. Her hair clung to her cheeks. "I am Lady Nettleton. My husband has gone into the library to see to our coachman Hobbs. I think he might be most seriously injured after Nicholas. This is the Earl of Greymore who lies on the floor before you."

Delphinia acknowledged his title with unease but remained too preoccupied with her guests' comfort to give it further thought as she dispatched a servant to summon the local doctor. For the next few minutes the staff busied themselves with the familiar preparations of accommodating unexpected visitors. Sophy seemed to go in several directions at once while Ivy waited with the other woman, offering tea and comfort. Delphinia had barely laid eyes on Childers since he had called for her. Now her butler led the way upstairs as servants carried first the earl, his clothing tattered and bloodstained, and then the coachman, to separate quarters.

Lady Nettleton brushed away a tear, succumbing to fear as Delphinia returned to her. "We were traveling to Cornwall, to the earl's home in St. Ives, when our carriage overturned. We became lost in the storm. These last hours have been terrible. I thank you for your kindness in taking us in. I don't know what we would have done if we had not quite literally stumbled upon your home."

"Please do not distress yourself further," Delphinia consoled her. "You're suffering from exposure and in need of rest. Give the servants a moment to prepare the rooms, and then you shall all be up to bed."

"You have not met my sister, Rowena Herbert." Lady Nettleton turned as Ivy helped remove a dripping cloak from a woman in such disarray she barely acknowledged the introduction. "Perhaps this is not the time. There will be time for introductions later."

Studying the wet, weary faces with concern, Delphinia turned to her housekeeper. "Sophy, our guests will need dry clothes. See that hot tea and biscuits are delivered once a fire is prepared in each room. Let me see, there are seven of you," she reflected, addressing her guest. "Is your sister married to the earl?"

"No, my sister—they are not married, although I admit the thought is an appealing one. They will require separate rooms. And this is my maid, Mrs. Nelly Brigham." Lady Nettleton indicated the servant beside her. "Somehow she helped Harry carry Nicholas indoors. Thank you,

Nelly."

"No thanks are needed, ma'am," Nelly Brigham said magnanimously, breathing deeply from her broad chest. She looks, Delphinia thought, as stout as any man about the township. I could find work for her to do.

"It grieves me to put anyone out on a night such as this," Lady Nettleton said shakily, "at an hour when any self-respecting person ought to be abed. But I do think Nicholas needs to be seen by a doctor right away."

"I have summoned Doctor Goodwin," said Delphinia. "You might all require his services. As for the hour, it will soon be dawn. Rest assured you are not interfering with our sleep."

With a deep sigh Lady Nettleton closed her eyes briefly. "You have been most kind. We are indebted to you, Lady . . ."

"Lady Delphinia." She chose to omit the surname that was still revolting to her. "You can be assured that our staff will see to your every comfort while you are here. This is not the first time we have been awakened by someone looking to escape a storm."

"We never have guests from London, only the locals," added Ivy. Knowing her sister had been waiting for a chance to speak up, Delphinia hoped Ivy would refrain from pursuing a friendship with the visitors. They were overnight guests at best, with no interest in a lasting relationship. While she did not want to encourage them to linger, Delphinia did not want to see Ivy hurt. She stepped back to include Ivy as she introduced them.

"Have you met my sister, Lady Ivy Herrick?"

"Yes, the charming young girl who welcomed us so warmly." The fondness in Lady Nettleton's tone surprised Delphinia, but perhaps under the circumstances it was not unexpected. Ivy would have offered them a more enthusiastic welcome than anyone.

A stout gentleman with graying whiskers who reminded her of a well-nourished cat made his way downstairs, his pace slowed more from exhaustion than from age. Drawing himself up beside Lady Nettleton, he introduced himself as her husband, the Baron of Edgecroft. She referred to him affectionately as Harry.

"Bad spot of luck." He shook his balding head. "Don't know how we can travel with Nicholas in such a frightful condition."

"Please do not trouble yourself with that now," Delphinia reassured him. "We have more than enough room here. If need be, you can stay as long as necessary to recuperate."

She thought of events only a week away and wondered what she would do with a houseful of guests were they not up to traveling by then. Still, she could hardly turn away the injured group.

"I think a warm bed will do us more good than anything." Rowena Herbert, who had been resting, rose shakily with the help of Nelly

Brigham. "I'm so chilled I hope you will not think it rude of me if I retire to my chamber."

"Of course not. Tea should have arrived in your room by now." Delphinia felt momentarily grateful she had not forgotten the social graces during her isolation in Exmoor.

The pale woman laid her hand on Delphinia's. "You are truly an angel," she murmured before being led away.

Delphinia started, unaccustomed to such frank esteem. Lord Nettleton turned back to her. "As Marion said, we cannot thank you enough for your kindness."

"It is no trouble," Delphinia said sincerely. "We are happy to be of help until you are safely on your way."

Which should be no more than a matter of days, she told herself. With a bit of good fortune they would reach Cornwall before their presence need concern her.

"Why speak of farewells when you might need to bide with us awhile?" Ivy said brightly. "We are rarely treated to company."

Delphinia felt her color rise. Her sister had chosen a most inconvenient time to be generous. It was not Ivy's place to extend such an invitation. It was her place to listen, which she infrequently did.

Lady Nettleton smiled, obviously touched.

"It is very thoughtful of you to offer," she said gently.

"You must feel free to linger," Ivy continued, "since you were lucky to find us, and we are so lucky to have you."

Without so much as a backward glance at Delphinia, whose pulse raced with consternation, Ivy linked her arm companionably through Lady Nettleton's. *Of all the impudent things,* Delphinia fumed in silence, shooting her irrepressible sister a black look. The look was wasted on Ivy, who did not even look her way. Smiling at each other, Ivy and their guest walked arm in arm to the staircase, heedless of Delphinia's growing despair.

Ivy, she fretted, did not realize what she had done. It was dangerous to have people staying at Briarcombe now. And at the moment there was little Delphinia could do but remain silent.

* * * *

Fever and chills alternately ravaged Nicholas's body as he lay in what felt like a very narrow bed. If he was on board a ship again, why did he not hear the voices of the sailors? Why had no one come to rouse him? Was Delderfield still alive, or had the captain died from his wounds by now?

Overcome by nausea and dizziness, he struggled to regain his memory, but dreams confounded his sense of reality. Somehow the ship disappeared, and he was on the moors again, reaching for a hand he could not grasp. He heard the terrified whinny of the horses and saw the windows smash as the carriage overturned, the motion slowing painfully in his mind, as if he were a spectator rather than a participant. He felt the crushing jolt of bodies hitting.

His eyes flew open, giving him a view of a detailed cornice edging the ceiling. These dreams were all too real. There was that throbbing again, a pressure in his leg that would not subside. It felt as if someone had struck his ankle repeatedly with a razor-sharp rock and now tried to tear his foot off. The pain made sleep a welcome relief. Familiar images swam together in his confusion. His father was alive again, battling his final illness. His mother's face hovered over his own, wasted from worry, looking as she had when his father was dying. That was how he felt now.

Death would find him on these Godforsaken moors. Suddenly his vision cleared. He felt himself sweating. Proof, he thought, that he was still alive. The moors had been real, he was certain, but where was he now? There was the familiar ceiling cornice again.

The fear on the faces of friends came back to him. His mother would have a thing or two to say about travel in inclement weather. She had never approved of his friendship with Harry. If anything were to happen to the baron now, especially if Nicholas were at fault, would she feel mollified or relieved?

Sleep overtook him again as the chill returned. He recoiled when he felt someone applying compresses as sharp as ice shards to his fiery forehead. The warm stillness of the room was a blessing after the rainy, windswept moors. He woke to see a maid replacing a ewer on the bureau.

"Oh, sir, you're awake! I shall fetch Lady Delphinia at once," she announced and swept out of the room.

He must have returned to sleep, for he awoke suddenly to find himself more alert than he had been in days. The servant was gone. He lay in some sort of sickroom. His eyes adjusted to the mellow light as his surroundings came slowly into focus.

He realized after a moment he was not alone. Close to the bed a woman stood with her back to him, wringing out a cloth over a basin of water. Judging from the room's old-fashioned furnishings and the cut of her dress, he might have been in a time ten years previous. He wondered if his mind were playing tricks on him.

The woman rested her hands on the small of her back and stretched her torso upward in a gesture of weariness. His gaze followed the pleasing contour of her profile. She ran an idle hand along the back of her neck where her hair was caught up, not in the fashionable ringlets of the day but in lush, dark masses. As he rubbed his eyes in an effort to awaken fully she turned to him without smiling, her face so serious he wondered if she had come to lay out his raiments for the grave.

The outmoded gray work dress and carelessly gathered hair had not prepared him for features of such beauty. Her delicate oval face was highlighted by a patrician nose, moist lips, and the loveliest violet eyes he had ever chanced to gaze upon. They were a color he had seen only once before in his mother's garden. The woman moved to the bedside with considerable grace, taking his hand, which hung off the bed, and placing it firmly by his side.

"You will want to be careful of this shoulder," she warned. "You have a few bruises from the carriage accident." She regarded his cautiously. "Do you recall the accident?"

"Yes. And I think I have more than a few bruises." His eyes closed heavily, unable to remain open despite her beauty. "I was led to believe Devon possessed the finest weather in all of England. Based on my experience, I am inclined to disagree."

He opened his eyes in time to see her softly rounded lips part in a smile that enhanced her countenance tenfold. *Do not turn away,* he begged silently. Even in shadow her smile did much to encourage his sense of vitality.

"March is a fickle month in Exmoor." Her tone casual, she seated herself by the bed, taking some towels to fold in her lap. "Just as spring is settling over most of the land the cold returns to us. You chose a most unpredictable time to travel."

Nicholas grimaced. "After a brief respite in Combe Martin we would have been safely on our way to Tregaryan, my family home in Cornwall, and free of this miserable season but for this storm." Memory began to creep back with a rush of anxiety. "My horses," he said abruptly.

"They are safe," she assured him. "Your valet found them. They had taken shelter in an abandoned barn."

"I wonder we did not have the fortune to find that same barn when—when was it? How many nights ago?"

"The night before last. Do you remember the doctor coming?"

"No. Wait, I remember vaguely." He stiffened as pain shot through him. "Hobbs. How is he?"

"Your coachman is recovering. But with a broken leg and injured arm he will not be able to drive for some time."

"His leg did not have to be removed then."

"No more than your own foot need be," she said candidly, rising to soak some washcloths in a basin. "And Harry and Marion and the others? How are they?"

"The rest of your party was fortunate to have escaped with minor injuries. They have spent the past two days resting."

He listened with relief as she tallied their injuries from cuts and bruises to stiff backs and sprained shoulders. Her description made it sound as if they had come out of the adventure in rather good shape. Better than he had, he reflected. The warm wet cloths she applied to his shoulder made him wince.

"First you chill me, then you burn my flesh," he complained.

Her amusement at his reaction annoyed him. "You have no idea how vigorously I am trying to make you well, Captain. The cold on your forehead will bring down the fever, but your shoulder requires heat. Doctor Goodwin's orders, I'm sorry to say."

He noticed a darkening patch of gray outside the window. "What time is it?"

"Nearly four o'clock. You have slept the day away."

"I have lost a whole day—no, two." Nicholas turned in the uncomfortable undersized bed and sat upright. "If you will excuse me, I've got to get up."

"If you try," she said sharply, stepping aside with the washcloth, "you'll find your leg will not support you."

He gripped the headboard as his foot caught in the sheets, sending pain shooting through his lower leg. "Dash that ankle. What does the good doctor say is wrong with it?"

"It is quite badly twisted, according to Doctor Goodwin. In addition, you suffered a concussion, a shoulder injury, and what appear to be some rather painful head wounds. And, of course, this fever." She bent closer to him, the soft wool of her dress brushing his arm as she laid a cool hand on his heated forehead.

"We were exposed to that wind and rain for so long," he murmured. "I'm surprised we did not all contract a chill."

"Yours was the worst. The doctor wants you to rest quietly. You lost a great deal of blood and are weaker than you realize."

Her sober tone and the expression in her clear violet eyes made her concern apparent. Nicholas was touched by her interest in him until the next remark which she uttered with some alacrity.

"You might find yourself confined to our home longer than either you or I might wish."

Chapter Two

Alarm swept through Nicholas at her words. "How long am I to remain here?"

"As long as need be, Captain," she said softly, averting her gaze as she folded the washcloth.

He brushed his hand across his eyes, confused. "What place is this? Where am I?"

"At Briarcombe, in Exmoor. We are about two miles from Lynton and two and a half from Countisbury."

"Too far from St. Ives for my liking. Much too far." He frowned, irritability stirring within until he remembered he was at the mercy of this woman. "What year is this?"

"It is 1816, and the soldiers who returned from the war last autumn are still unemployed." He saw a look of bitterness settle briefly on her face. "Had you forgotten?"

"I was confused by your dress." Even in his weary state he noted the simple line of her dress, much like a servant's, yet admired how well it suited the curve of her figure. He had been observing his nurse carefully. Her noble bearing betrayed her breeding and background, for she was surely more than a maid in this house. "I have not seen that style on a lady of quality."

"The latest styles mean little on this remote coast," she said simply, resuming her seat.

"If that is the effect of indifference then others should disregard fashion as well. It flatters you beautifully." The exertion of paying such close attention to his attractive nurse took its toll. He fell back against the pillows, overcome by weakness. His head began to throb again before other concerns returned. "What of Lord and Lady Nettleton's valet and maid? They were traveling separately in an open carriage. I hope they had the sense to remain at the inn after dinner, as I advised them."

"They were indeed prudent enough to take your advice." She smiled at him, but it was a smile of efficiency rather than warmth. "I hope that puts your mind at ease."

"Thank heaven." Satisfied his entire traveling party was accounted for, Nicholas relaxed, enjoying the softness of the pillows despite the stiffness in his limbs. He regarded her anew. "You know my identity though I haven't the advantage of knowing yours. May I know to whom I am indebted?"

"I am Lady Delphinia, Captain Hainsworth."

Her brevity amused him and piqued his curiosity. "Have you a surname?"

Her eyes were focused on the towels in her lap, which she continued to fold although she had already completed a neat pile.

"My father's name is Herrick," she said casually. "He is well known on these shores. My husband drowned in a shipwreck. His name was Marlowe." She glanced up at him. "I understand you were traveling from London. Perhaps you have heard of my father. He spends most of his time there."

"I know the name. It is highly regarded in Parliament." But it was not her eminent father he was thinking of. It was the late Mr. Marlowe's beautiful widow who had captured his interest.

"You have a keen eye for the prevailing taste in clothing, Captain." Rising, she dipped a wash rag into one of the basins and turned her eyes to him. They were a soft delphinium-blue in the waning light. "Your wife must be among the most fashionably dressed women in London."

"My mother is the one and only Lady Greymore. I have sisters who would be scandalized to have to dress in anything below the height of fashion." He shook his head with distaste.

"They are no different from most women whose attention is consumed by fashion." She shrugged. "It seems a colossal waste to me though I fear I am out of step. Indeed, I know I am."

Nicholas wished he knew what did consume her interest. He knew no other woman so striking who did not give a fig for her attire. Moving toward him, she laid a wide cloth on his forehead that obscured his vision and made him shiver. She must have bent down to adjust the bed coverings, for as they tightened around him he caught the delicate fragrance of rose water. He drew a breath involuntarily as a silken drape of hair brushed his exposed shoulder before the clink of porcelain told him she had moved to the bureau.

"A damp washcloth and basin are within reach if you need them. If you have no further needs at this time, Captain Hainsworth, I will let you rest."

Nicholas lifted the wet cloth from his forehead in time to gaze once more into her eyes, gray-blue now in the dusky twilight. "You are most kind to stray travelers, Lady Delphinia."

"Consider yourself fortunate, Captain. There have been many accidents on the moors. Yours was far from the worst."

So much for sympathy, he thought as she closed the door behind her, the light from the hallway silhouetting her form for a mere second. He tried to rise to a sitting position, but pain robbed him of breath and made him cringe. He collapsed back into the sheets with an utterance that was half groan, half growl. Good thing my charming nurse has gone, he mused, or she doubtless would make me feel more the fool for daring to complain.

"Damn this ankle," he muttered. It was useless to him like this. Had Harry not been so eager to reach the Pack of Cards Inn they might even now be sharing a brandy and talking of last year's shooting match at Epping before Tregaryan's inviting hearth.

Nicholas sighed, closed his eyes, and thought of St. Ives. He pictured his sister scolding her children ineffectually as they ran willy-nilly over the flower beds. Sylvia and her husband Joshua were expecting him. Would he even recognize his nephews? The boys must have grown so since he had seen them last. Sylvia would forgive his tardiness, if the news of his accident did not turn her hair gray with worry first.

The throbbing in his ankle resumed, stronger this time, and exhaustion at last got the better of him. He fell back into the pillows his captive hostess had plumped for him and dozed off.

* * * *

It was after eleven that night when Delphinia was finally able to return to her chamber. At the first opportunity that presented itself she had chastised her sister soundly for usurping her authority and inviting the visitors to tarry at leisure. Ivy had smiled with a dazzling sweetness and promised not to encourage them further.

"I couldn't help myself," she had confessed. "I've been so lonely here. And you must admit it's delightful to have guests, if just for a bit."

In her heart Delphinia could not blame her. Until eighteen months ago Ivy's greatest excitement had occurred in the London schoolroom. The remoteness of the moors was particularly hard on her. Ivy was social by nature and craved more companionship than the sheep and horses could offer.

But visitors posed problems. Next week Delphinia would have business to attend to that demanded privacy. The guests would be no trouble if they rested as the doctor had prescribed. Having them less sedentary could prove problematic. Delphinia did not wish to seem inhospitable, but she fervently hoped those who had regained their strength by then would depart so her plans could proceed uninterrupted.

She was not concerned about most of the guests. She knew Ivy would be happy to entertain them once they were well enough to make their way about. The difficulty lay with Captain Hainsworth. Delphinia was not prepared for a lengthy stay on his part. In good conscience she could not turn an injured man out, nor could she make his injuries heal faster. Yet she feared the shrewdness she sensed in his manner. If he was this attentive in a weakened state, how significant a threat would he pose when healthy?

Setting aside worries that might amount to nothing, she turned her attention to matters within her control. She delved into the bottom drawer of her bureau, withdrawing a packet of correspondence written in a man's hand. For the next two hours she pored over papers she had found in the cellar, rereading the documents in her desire to find even a shred of incriminating evidence. Each time she met with failure.

In frustration she changed from her work clothes and dressed for bed. Her thoughts strayed to Captain Hainsworth, no doubt already asleep down the hall. She had never met a man with such a commanding presence. Naval veterans were common enough along the coast, but Nicholas Hainsworth possessed an extraordinary degree of self-reliance and determination. His ability to navigate his way across harsh and unfamiliar territory in such a violent storm made him precisely the kind of man England needed in her military—and the last kind Delphinia wanted under her roof.

Their conversation had convinced her he was anxious to move on to St. Ives, as were his fellow travelers. She hoped their desire to travel would hasten them back to health. Until then the presence of strangers would force her to keep up her guard.

* * * *

Having lain awake in uneasy speculation much of the night, Delphinia rose later than she intended the next morning and felt tired and listless. After selecting a garment and dressing without ceremony she headed for Ivy's room, Brutus padding after her on the carpet. She was surprised to find the bedroom door ajar. Hearing muted voices, she tapped and opened it farther.

The spectacle within stunned her. Ivy sat at her vanity, still in her nightdress and robe. Her shiny black hair was massed in ringlets that framed her oval face. Clustered about her were Lady Nettleton, Rowena Herbert, Mrs. Nelly Brigham, and even Sophy, who had better places to be and knew it. Sophy at least had sense and respect enough to flush as Delphinia glared at her.

"Don't our Ivy look beautiful, miss!" she gushed.

Spying Delphinia's reflection in the mirror, Ivy turned to her and smiled radiantly. Delphinia caught her breath. Her sister was a true beauty, fashionable and sophisticated even in her innocence. The transformation pained Delphinia. Overcome by emotion, she remained speechless. Ivy would soon make her debut in London where the whirlwind of the Season would sweep her away from Briarcombe, perhaps never to return. Ivy waited for her reaction.

"Delphinia? You have not said what you think." With the girlish eagerness of youth Ivy anticipated praise. "Mrs. Herbert did my hair. I think the style suits me."

Rowena Herbert's reply held a hint of confidentiality that Delphinia resented. "I imagine the gentlemen in London will think so as well."

"We have been dressing her hair all morning," Lady Nettleton said with a smile. "Every style flatters Ivy. She has a classic beauty that will make her the envy of the *ton*."

Ivy beamed with a look of utter gratitude that held no trace of conceit. Delphinia sensed that if she could, Ivy would hasten the day a month from now when her life would change and her attention would turn to London. Her focus would stretch beyond Exmoor, and the tenuous alliance that defined their relationship might end forever. Delphinia was powerless to stop the course of Ivy's life of privilege, for she understood all too well what it meant to be a young girl coming of age.

Returning their attention to Ivy, the women turned from Delphinia and edged closer to her sister with encouraging words, admiring her natural grace and taking pride in their efforts at advancing her suit. Delphinia watched helplessly, unsure how to participate while genuinely sharing in their enthusiasm. No words could express her sense of loneliness. Beside their joy her fear of losing Ivy seemed selfish and made her feel old, as if being on the shelf were something she cared a whit about instead of being relieved to be rid of men.

She saw the hope on Ivy's face in the mirror and forced a smile.

"You look enchanting," she replied honestly.

Concealing her misery, Delphinia closed her eyes and slipped from the room. As she shrank into the shadows of the corridor, she knew no one would miss her while they attended to Ivy. Mentally, she cursed the arrival of the female guests and the potential consequences of their visit on her sister's life.

She had too many tasks ahead of her to dwell in self-pity. Another trip to the cellar was out of the question with so many people about. Setting aside her frustration, she went downstairs to consult her cook on the state of the larder. With company expected for dinner every night now, the pantry consumed more of her attention than usual. She felt at ease leaving kitchen matters in the hands of Agnes, whose culinary skills were incomparable.

Next she checked with her groom on the status of the horses in the stable, where she stopped to admire Captain Hainsworth's chestnut bays. If there is one advantage to having him here, she thought, it is that I will be able to spend some time with these magnificent animals. The man possessed exquisite judgment when it came to horseflesh.

With some trepidation she hoped his judgment was not so keen when it came to her behavior.

* * * *

Delphinia saw little of Ivy during the day and assumed her sister was spending her time with their guests. No doubt they were filling her head with notions of society life. A note her housekeeper delivered to her that afternoon, as she was reviewing household accounts in the library, failed to lift her spirits. "It's from Martinhoe, miss, from Mr. Wainwright," Sophy announced blandly, handing Delphinia the missive she would have preferred not to see.

She broke the seal slowly, wondering if her staff could read her dislike of the man in her face. As she had expected, Percy expressed concern about the party of seven she was forced to host so unexpectedly. He hoped they were not too much of an inconvenience, he said in the terse note, and would enjoy meeting them when he joined her for dinner that evening.

Savagely she tore the note into pieces which she fed to the fire. His concern for their welfare was prompted only by concern for himself. Percy cared nothing for her visitors, whose presence these three days had been so uplifting to Ivy and so worrisome to herself. She stood at the window contemplating the vastness of the moors, realizing the danger her guests unwittingly faced.

If only they knew the truth. Delphinia wished briefly that Ivy might go with them when they left Briarcombe. It would break her heart to part from her sister, but if it would ensure Ivy's protection, how could she deny her a safer haven?

* * * *

The staff prepared for the evening's dinner party, Delphinia noted with surprise, with as much excitement as they had displayed when preparing for parties in her mother's day. With Delphinia supervising, Agnes spent the afternoon preparing a brisket of venison with a chutney accompaniment she had been waiting to try on just such an occasion. She added cabbage and woodcock and dried salmon from Lynmouth weir to the menu before she even began to consider the other courses.

To escape the clatter in the kitchen, Delphinia scoured the moors with Sophy for flowers to create the perfect centerpiece. Reveling in the spring air and the quiet of the countryside, they wandered in the protected valleys where celandine, primroses, and white violets were hiding, proceeding afterward to decorate the table in as merry a fashion as she could recall.

When, she wondered, had she ever become so bound by other obligations that she began to neglect the life she once loved? Receiving callers had been such a joy before the demands of her current lifestyle had made entertaining too risky.

Once she had attended to every detail, Delphinia began to feel confident about the evening. In her wardrobe she discovered a dress of periwinkle blue velvet she had worn in London. It set off her violet eyes to perfection and had been her favorite. It was no longer the height of fashion, as it had once been, but she decided impulsively to wear it anyway. After five years it still fit, she observed, as she adjusted the shoulders and slipped her mother's cameo around her neck. She fixed her unruly trail of hair as best she could, wondering, with a touch of sarcasm, if she should enlist Mrs. Herbert's help.

When she was done with her ministrations she felt her time had been justly spent. She might as well make the best of the evening, she rationalized, knowing Percy was bound to make it as unpleasant as possible.

Delphinia greeted her guests in the drawing room by a toasty fire, with the exception of the immobile Captain Hainsworth. Ivy was in close attendance, resplendent in peacock blue silk with green accents and an emerald choker. The brilliance of her outfit made Lady Nettleton and Rowena Herbert look pale by comparison in their respective pink and lavender.

"What an absolutely charming room," Lady Nettleton marveled, settling into the cream-colored gilt and velvet sofa. "I feel quite at home here already."

Pleased by the compliment, Delphinia gazed at the room as if she were seeing it for the first time. She had forgotten the inviting warmth of the rose silk draperies, the walls of sea-green damask set within moulded white panels, and the marble chimneypiece with its Grecian design of urns and garlands. It truly was, she reflected, an unfortunate consequence of circumstance that she could not entertain more frequently.

"Our mother would be pleased to hear you say so," she said sincerely. "She selected all the furnishings in the room, though being so isolated the house had few visitors in her day."

"Can't say I'm surprised," Lord Nettleton replied over his pipe. "It's jolly good luck the *Times* is delivered to this secluded region so one is still able to feel civilized."

"We are not so far from civilization that we cannot read of acquaintances in London," Delphinia countered.

"Indeed that is so," Rowena Herbert agreed. "Why, since my husband's death six months ago, the social column is one of the few ways I have of keeping up with news of old friends."

Delphinia politely refrained from choking on her brandy, but not without considerable effort. Not only had she placed her guests in potential danger by allowing them to remain in her home, but she was tempting scandal by associating with this merry widow who ought to be in mourning.

Well, it would not be the first time, she thought. She had brought scandal on herself without anyone's help. The Herricks did not seem destined for ruination, or their reputation would have fallen by now.

Lady Nettleton and Rowena Herbert launched into a discussion of the social intrigues that had captivated their attention before they left London. Ivy sat upright, enthralled by their gossip, her eyes widening at the exploits of the *ton*.

"Delphinia has written our aunts who are to arrange a come-out for me," Ivy enthused. "I was a child when I left London. To think I will return a lady!"

Delphinia managed to hide her cynicism as she listened to her sister's wistful tone. Ivy was still a child. She would be a child until some man had his way with her, and then her virtue would be gone and her reputation ruined. Delphinia let out a tense breath, reminding herself her fears were assumptions. Allowing herself a shred of hope that

Ivy's experience would be more successful than her own, she sipped her brandy until a remark from Lord Nettleton drew her attention.

"I see where a shipment of tea was seized on the north coast," Harry said, his eyes focused on the newspaper. "Damned smugglers, stealing from the Crown."

"At least the cargo is safe now," Delphinia said absently, "for she sails under a full moon."

"You are certainly well acquainted with shipping schedules," Lady Nettleton said in surprise.

Four pairs of eyes filled with curiosity turned toward Delphinia. She felt her cheeks grow warm.

"As Lord Nettleton said," she improvised, "life would be tedious indeed without the newspaper. I read each and every word of it, as you can see. More brandy, Mrs. Herbert?"

Conversation progressed naturally from that point. Delphinia was relieved that Percy Wainwright had not been present to observe her lapse in attention. He arrived shortly thereafter, at the time he had specified in his note, punctual as always. As precise as the most delicate timepiece, she acknowledged, like myself. It pained her to realize she had developed the habit from long practice.

Clad in deepest gray, his hair unfashionably long, Percy looked more sinister than usual, disrupting the evening's pleasantries with his presence, as her husband had done when he was alive. The comparison dulled her joy in the evening.

"Delphinia, my dear," he greeted her, taking her hand in his and kissing it. She withdrew her fingers abruptly and made brief introductions before resuming her seat.

"So sorry to hear of your accident," Percy told her guests.

"Then you know of our troubles," Rowena exclaimed.

"News travels rapidly throughout the villages," Percy said with a smile, "especially when it involves lost horses. By now everyone knows of your misfortune."

"You're a local man, then," Lord Nettleton surmised.

"I live near Woody Bay, past Lynmouth, where my business interests lie. Shipping endeavors," Percy added smartly.

"Trade!" Lord Nettleton's eyebrows rose minutely. "I would have taken you for a man of breeding, Wainwright."

You would take him for a scoundrel if you looked closely, Delphinia reflected bitterly. She saw the derision in Percy's smile.

"Would you now?"

"Trade has a place in these parts, I suppose," the baron went on. "Here, I just read about the excise men seizing an illegal cargo in Ilfracombe. What do you make of that?"

Percy shook his head. "Now, there's a dangerous business."

"Don't you worry about the safety of your ships?"

"It comes with the territory, I fear." Percy smiled thinly. "It's a chance we must take if business is to stay afloat."

"Stay afloat. Right you are." Lord Nettleton puffed on his pipe and chuckled his appreciation of Percy's pun. Delphinia squirmed in her seat, uncomfortable with the turn the conversation had taken. She was glad Captain Hainsworth was incapacitated and could not join them. His presence would have made the evening even more unbearable. Sitting rigidly on the edge of her chair, she was relieved when Childers called them in to dinner.

"I'm afraid I cannot alternate men with women," she apologized to Lady Nettleton as they made their way into the dining room, "for our table is short two men."

"Nonsense, it's delightful," Marion assured her with a knowing smile. "We have Nicholas partially to blame for that, haven't we? And I find your friend quite charming."

Perhaps these Londoners are not so observant after all, Delphinia thought. They had failed to recognize the deception played out before them.

"He is really just an acquaintance," she objected.

"No need to explain, my dear," Lady Nettleton said serenely. "The wise woman takes advantage of every opportunity that comes her way. Mr. Wainwright seems most companionable."

Delphinia remained silent. Although perhaps ten years her elder, Marion had shown no recognition of the Herrick name when they were introduced, and Delphinia had offered no details about her past. The discretion of her guests, she reflected during dinner, was one of the factors that made their visit tolerable.

"I'll tell you a thing or two," the baron announced over the final course, raising his voice as the brandy began to take effect. "If Nick Hainsworth were still at sea there'd be no smuggling off these coasts, north or south."

"Is that so?" Percy challenged. "Is this the fellow upstairs whom I have not met?"

"A fine chap. Nick was first mate at Trafalgar, until his own captain was fired upon and he had to assume command. Turned out to be the youngest of the captains." Harry shook his head. "A man of integrity. Not a man to trifle with."

The guests fell momentarily silent. Picturing the man who remained bedridden upstairs, Delphinia was not inclined to trifle with a man whose character might prove a threat to questionable activities on the coast. She kept her gaze from meeting Percy's.

"It is truly a shame Nicholas cannot join us." Marion's brow furrowed in distress. "Not only did the accident affect our plans, but we have been an unexpected inconvenience here."

"Our injuries are nothing to prevent us from traveling shortly," Harry pointed out. "We can always hire a carriage."

"The bridge at Furzehill was washed out in the storm," Delphinia told them, "but a local carriage could take you on."

She glared warningly at Ivy, whose face puckered in protestation. With a furtive glance at her sister, Ivy lowered her eyes and remained silent, as she had promised she would. Delphinia sensed her deep disappointment and felt a surge of pity. Even if this resolve put her in the dismals, it was for her own good. One day she would understand.

"You could hire a conveyance in Combe Martin," Percy volunteered, "at the Pack of Cards Inn."

"There's a worthy idea," the baron exclaimed. "That was precisely our destination before we got lost on the moors."

"Here's your chance." Percy smiled. "Wouldn't want to miss that. I might even join you for a hand some night."

Delphinia felt a rush of relief as she dared to hope the guests would soon leave Briarcombe. Time was of the essence. From his artificial banter, she knew Percy was pleased by the possibility as well.

After dinner Ivy entertained the group with a serenade on the pianoforte. Having never been musical herself, Delphinia listened appreciatively to the plaintive trill of her sister's voice. Ivy's talents will take her a long way when she goes to London, she thought wistfully. She tried to clear her mind of the impending separation but found it difficult.

Percy was the first to leave, announcing he had business to attend to the following morning. Delphinia escorted him into the foyer.

"All the news from London," he said under his breath, his tone droll. "How exciting for you."

"They will depart for Cornwall shortly, if you don't delay them further by joining Lord Nettleton at cards," she said curtly. "They have been no trouble. I do not expect to see them again."

"Let's hope they do not have friends in the excise business who call on us next."

Alarm raced through Delphinia at the possibility. The excise men were not the only threat. Once Percy met Captain Hainsworth he would realize their guest was not one with whom to match wits.

Percy donned his greatcoat slowly and turned to her before he left, his eyes boring into hers with a menace that frightened her.

"I'm glad you have made new friends, Delphinia. But the drop is Wednesday night, and your chums had best be gone by then." He gave her a frigid smile. "I am quite sure you understand my meaning."

Chapter Three

By the next morning Nicholas felt his fever begin to break. The development improved his spirits tenfold. Two days of rest had renewed his strength considerably. He was tempted to try and move from the bed until a sharp pain in his ankle reminded him of the seriousness of the injuries that extended beyond the fever's lingering heat.

Hoping his recovery was at hand, he remembered his condition had caused him to miss dinner the previous night. This forced inactivity was bothersome indeed. Feeling out of sorts, he summoned the maid for his morning fire. After breakfast he lay in bed watching the flames reflected in the polished steel grate and wondering when Lady Delphinia would call. She had failed to visit him yesterday, and he had been irritated when the housekeeper came instead.

This morning he was not to be disappointed. His spirits soared when a firm knock and a familiar voice announced her arrival as she entered his room at his beckoning.

"Good day, Lady Delphinia," he greeted her. "I have no doubt it will please you to see your patient looking much better."

"Uninterrupted sleep has done you good, Captain," she returned shortly, inspecting the empty dishes on his tray.

He might have inferred from her averted face and terse tone that she wished he were still sleeping. There was a wariness in her demeanor that had not been there during their first encounter nor had the tension that failed now to detract from her beauty.

"Yesterday's visit from Harry and Marion was most agreeable," he said. "I think it aided my recuperation. Yet I believe I owe my life, Lady Delphinia, to your fine care."

"Your health perhaps." His remark earned a smile from her, transforming her face so completely he wished he could see her smile more often. "I did not save your life."

Nicholas attempted to win her favor through another channel. "My health then. Even though my initial incoherence has passed, I still find it impossible to express the depth of my appreciation to you. Because of your efforts, I imagine very soon the doctor will give us the heave-ho and send us on our way." He gazed wistfully toward a window filled only with clouds. "It is difficult for a man used to being on the sea to accustom himself merely to listening to a distant ocean through a closed window."

As she turned away from the breakfast tray her arm brushed against his. The cool flesh of her exposed forearm below the sleeve that was pushed up to her elbow made him feel shivery despite the slight fever that lingered still.

"If you would prefer some brisk air in the room I can open a window.

As for leaving, both you and your carriage have sustained too much damage to go anywhere." She stooped to retrieve the damp fever cloths that had tumbled from the bed. "Your valet has gone with the baron to view what remains of your carriage."

Damnation, could it be so bad? Considering the shape he was in, perhaps it was. He had been unable to assess the vehicle the night of the storm, being more concerned with the safety of its occupants. Blast it, he thought, sinking into the pillows. Leave it to Harry and Stebbins. They will review the damage, and we'll salvage what we can.

Lady Delphinia tidied the room perfunctorily, her motions characterized by a distraction that was at odds with her usual alertness. Nicholas hoped it was not the strain of entertaining house guests at his expense. While their presence was undeniably inconvenient, he found it difficult to imagine she did not enjoy the exuberant company the Nettletons and Rowena Herbert provided, isolated as she was on these moors.

"I know it is an imposition to put us up," he said as she approached the bed, his tone purposely contrite. "I apologize for the nuisance we have caused you and your staff."

She reminded him of his mother as she wordlessly removed the bandage from his temple. That stiff, efficient exterior surely must hide a kind heart and feminine nature, he mused, although he had not seen the briefest glimpse of either.

"Don't apologize for situations that are beyond your control, Captain," she said crisply. "I told you it is our pleasure to be of service."

Perhaps it was not such a soft nature after all. Had he imagined her to say she was the daughter of Adam Herrick? The earl was a powerful and respected speaker in the House of Lords. She certainly had not inherited his sense of diplomacy. Yet he saw in her a reflection of the stalwart determination that had earned her father his reputation.

He watched her as she busied herself at the nightstand. Her face held more character than classic beauty, yet there was a wild loveliness in the features he found startlingly appealing. If only he could find a wife with half her beauty and independent spirit how happy both he and his mother would be. Only a woman of sophistication, balanced with delicacy, would satisfy Callendra Hainsworth. And, as far as he was concerned, a woman with some tenderness, he decided as Delphinia bathed his cut vigorously.

"This wound must be kept clean from infection," she warned, applying a salve that stung his temple. "The doctor will be here this afternoon. He will judge how well you are doing."

He looked at her with admiration. "In his absence I consider myself privileged to be in the care of such an expert nurse. I could be in far worse places." He glanced at the elegantly moulded doorframes and delicate scrollwork of the ceiling, appreciating the room's aesthetics for the first time. "Though I have only seen but a bit of it I would be most interested in learning how you came to be in charge of so large a household."

"The house is my father's. He permitted me the use of it when I married. After I was widowed five years ago I chose to remain here."

"An intriguing choice. Not one many women would make, I should think. I'd wager most women would prefer the gaslight of London to the starlight of Exmoor."

She smiled as if his assumption had amused her. "We do not have gaslight here yet, but we have stars that shine brighter than they do in London."

"Yet it takes a certain strength of character to remain in so isolated a spot," he went on. "Tell me, what keeps you here?"

It took her a moment to respond, as if she were choosing her words carefully. Indeed, she seemed to take great care with most aspects of her behavior. "I prefer the countryside to London. There is great beauty here, and freedom, and room to run the horses I love so."

"Yet you are far from humanity."

"Not so far as you might think. We help those in need in our parish, whether they are from the chapel or the community. And we also help those such as yourself, Captain," she added with irony.

Nicholas lay back on the pillows, luxuriating in the sensation of the wet cloths she held to his forehead. Now that the intense heat had faded, the coolness was soothing on his brow.

"I imagine that's an effective way of atoning," he said casually.

"Atoning for what?"

Her sharp reply held an emotion deeper than indignation. Her voice rang with a defensiveness that did not seem justified to him. He had not accused her of criminal activity, after all.

"I assume that is why most people attend church," he clarified. "To atone for some act they regret. Am I mistaken?"

"It is the duty of the congregation to extend charity to all and to take an active role in helping the poor and sick in the villages. No more, but no less." She snatched the cloth from his forehead and tossed it into the basin. "Everyone plays a role."

The abrupt change in her tone had piqued his curiosity. "And what role do you play, Lady Delphinia?"

"Whatever role happens to be forced upon me at the time, Captain." Her flippant reply was hardly softened by the brittle smile that followed. "Did you find your breakfast adequate?"

"Truth to tell, I am quite famished after what I've endured." He ventured a smile. "I have never seen an appetite that did not improve once an injured man begins to get well."

"And you are greatly improved," she said dryly. "Very well, I shall see that a second tray is delivered to you."

In spite of the attention she bestowed upon him, Nicholas was beginning to feel she did not like him overmuch. Yet he found his own fascination with her growing despite her cold and contradictory behavior.

"Let me assure you, Lady Delphinia," he spoke up, "I intend to prove little trouble to you. I have surprisingly few wishes. I may be injured, but I am not sick enough to be an invalid."

When she did not respond he sensed he could more accurately read her silence. Not sick enough to be an invalid, but just enough to be a bother. He was certain she doubted the claim that he would prove no trouble.

He watched as she gathered up the empty tray. A large dog had joined her just inside his doorway, looking toward Nicholas tentatively and wagging his tail.

"Come, Brutus," she ordered, departing without so much as a glance. His ears twitching with disappointment at being called away from this new curiosity, the dog pattered after her.

There goes the only friend I might have had in this household, Nicholas reflected. Now that he could think more clearly he looked with dread upon his impending stay in this house and the idea of being bedridden, despite his interest in its elegant but enigmatic mistress.

Settling back among the sheets, he flexed his ankle gingerly and wondered if the doctor might offer hopeful prospects about his ability to travel. It might be the only news, he reflected, that would put a real smile on the face of the mistress of Briarcombe.

* * * *

Her feelings engulfed in confusion, Delphinia handed the breakfast tray to a maid in the hallway after she left Captain Hainsworth's room. The man is too observant for his own good, she thought shakily. She reflected how much easier caring for him would be if only he were a bit more of an invalid. The idea made her flush with guilt, yet she could not deny the realization.

He was far too interested in his surroundings for her to desire his presence at Briarcombe a day longer than necessary. A lengthier stay would require her constant vigilance. Even if his fever had lifted, his ankle required further rest and attention. The longer he was confined to bed, she feared, the more bored and restless he would become.

No wonder she felt distracted this morning. Despite her efforts to keep their conversations at an impersonal level Captain Hainsworth seemed to be striving for something more. And she had nothing more to give, she acknowledged, resolving to keep him at an emotional distance.

At least the other guests intended to leave for Cornwall once the doctor approved their journey. She had overheard Marion breaking the news to Ivy late last night. Ivy had protested to no avail. Suspecting the blame would be laid at her feet, Delphinia had locked herself in her room and pretended to be asleep when Ivy came calling earlier.

Given her tempestuous nature, there would be no avoiding her. The confrontation came just as Delphinia was walking toward her room. Ivy caught her in the hallway, her eyes dark with resentment.

"I need to speak with you at once," she said tersely.

"Shall we go in my room?" Delphinia suggested.

As Ivy walked rigidly past her she closed the bedroom door quietly behind them. Her sister turned on her instantly.

"Our guests are planning to leave!" she burst out.

"They were planning to leave even as they arrived," said Delphinia patiently. "You knew their stay was temporary."

"But it has only been a matter of days. You must have said something to make them feel they are intruding."

"I noticed how much better everyone appears and commented on it. All I said was that they must be anxious to reach St. Ives."

"But we posted a note to the captain's sister. She is not expecting them immediately."

"She still hopes to see them within a reasonable amount of time." In the face of such belligerence Delphinia did not know what else to say. "What is the problem, Ivy?"

"It's you, Delphinia. You have been inexcusably rude."

She stared at her sister, trying to understand her bold reaction. She had never seen Ivy so distraught. "After I have opened our home to these strangers you are criticizing my manners. You, who are barely out of the schoolroom."

"Is that why you treat me like a child, because you think I am still green?" A sob caught in Ivy's throat. "One minute you cordially invite them to stay, and the next you are cold and inhospitable. None of us knows what to think."

Crestfallen, Delphinia answered in a quiet tone, "I do not know what you mean."

Her dismay must have shown on her face, for Ivy softened her manner at once.

"How can I make you understand?" Ivy dropped onto the bed heavily. "I have grown to care for these people."

"Yes, and in a very short time," Delphinia said stiffly. "Mrs. Herbert takes plenty of liberties at your dressing table. And the baroness is practically a confidante, sharing the secrets of her closest friends. You have become friends with them rather quickly, when really you do not know them at all."

Ivy's green eyes blazed as she stood. "I know them as well as I know anyone here, where I have so few friends."

"You have many friends in the villages," Delphinia reminded her. "People who love you and depend on you."

"It is not the same. I mean people like us, people of our own class."

"Do you know where I found Childers yesterday? Sitting in the library with the captain's driver. They were smoking. In the library!" Delphinia's tone turned to one of outrage. "Hobbs is a terrible influence on our staff."

"And what if he is?" Ivy shot back. "Childers has been here forever, longer than you or I. He needs company, too. It's some excitement for a change. How bad an influence can Hobbs be on anyone at his age? I don't know how much you really do understand. Can't you see how lonely I am?"

Her lower lip quivering, Ivy collapsed into a chair and ran her hands through her dark curls, disheveling the artful design over which Rowena Herbert had labored so carefully. Tears streamed unabashedly down her cheeks.

"Why are you so reluctant to have these people here?"

Delphinia caught her breath at her sister's heartbroken expression. Vulnerable and delicate in her pain, Ivy looked for all the world like a crushed flower rather than the strong, steady vine for which their mother had named her.

"The captain is a decorated war hero, yet you seem reluctant to offer him shelter," Ivy continued. "Where is your sense of Christian charity? I see it in church, but I don't see it anywhere else in your life."

Delphinia was so taken aback she could not speak. Words were inadequate to express her deep regret at having failed her sister. What was it Captain Hainsworth had said about atonement? There was something so persistently annoying about him.

Repressing the desire to wrap her hands around his neck, she decided to wrap her arms around her sister instead. She took a step toward Ivy, but her sister stopped her with a look.

"I have never understood you, or why you are so short-tempered with me," Ivy said passionately.

"And I suppose Rowena Herbert does," Delphinia flashed, feeling suddenly bitter. "The worldly Mrs. Herbert, who has survived widowhood and still manages to enjoy life."

"You act as though you're jealous of her."

Yes, Delphinia realized, I am. I'm jealous she has the courage to do what I cannot. I'm jealous she has earned your trust so readily, when I have not been able to close the distance between us in more than a year together.

"I knew you were not happy in your marriage," Ivy rushed on, unable to stop the torrent of words. "But that was a long time ago. You cannot blame me for that, or the rest of the world either, for that matter. Why are you so curt with me, when these strangers have been so helpful and friendly?"

"I am not convinced a gay widow like Mrs. Herbert who should still be in mourning can help you to understand the *ton*, a woman who herself is barely on the fringe of society. Reputation is everything, Ivy. Please try to remember that." Delphinia held her breath, bringing herself under control. "I know you have enjoyed their tutelage in the ways of society, but our spell of inclement weather is lifting, and they will be leaving as soon as Doctor Goodwin permits them to travel. That is all there is to that."

Ivy's eyes flashed with indignation. "Soon I will be entering my Season, for which you have not prepared me a whit. My new friends have done more for me in this short time than you have. Don't you want me to make a good impression in London?" Ivy spread her hands in a gesture of frustration. "You seem anxious to be rid of me, yet you do not tell me what to expect."

Dear God, end this torment, Delphinia begged silently, closing her eyes. Ivy does not understand how much is at stake. There are things I cannot discuss with her, sacrifices I have made for her of which she must know nothing. To think her sister had misunderstood her well-intended behavior weighed heavily on her, but she had no choice but to maintain the charade.

"Why could you not return to London with me, Delphinia?" Ivy asked plaintively. "I can't imagine you really care for Percy. He is not worthy of you."

"These things are none of your concern, Ivy."

The statement was lifeless and impersonal even to her own ears. Delphinia saw defiance in her sister's eyes before resignation hardened her features.

"All right, Delphinia," she said coldly. "You have made your choice. But I don't know why you are so ill at ease here in your own home. I have never understood you and your mysterious ways."

Delphinia gazed at her in alarm, ignoring her last remark. "It is your home, too."

"This has never felt like home to me. At this point I am not even sure you want me here. Perhaps I should leave also."

Her words cut Delphinia to the quick and left her speechless. How had Ivy been able to conceal such resentment this long without her knowing? It was the influence of these people from London with their questionable reputations that had brought out this temperamental side.

What had exposed such temperament hardly seemed to matter. Delphinia was still pondering the matter as Ivy slammed the door behind her.

* * * *

Although the confrontation lingered in her thoughts throughout the day Delphinia refused to allow her emotions to get the better of her. It would take time to recover from the sting of Ivy's attack, but she managed to put the situation in perspective when she remembered that her younger sister would soon begin a happier life in London.

It was Ivy's obvious fondness for Rowena Herbert that troubled her, Delphinia realized as she helped Agnes prepare lunch. The unfettered widow had apparently accepted her marital situation, and clearly she possessed money enough to have secured her future. Prematurely out of mourning, she seemed quite capable of coping with the inevitable stares.

I envy you, Delphinia thought. If only it weren't for Father's reputation. If only one did not mind being ostracized. Divorce did not seem so disgraceful after what she had endured.

But Mrs. Herbert would soon be leaving. Delphinia would not feel safe until their guests had left for Cornwall and Captain Hainsworth had joined them. If Percy's concerns about them were valid, they could all be in jeopardy. Their days here were long, with little to occupy their time. The handsome captain was particularly attentive to his surroundings. Dangerously so.

And I am too suspicious, she told herself. It is the result of dealing with men. I have come to despise marriage and divorce. Perhaps, she thought as she washed her hands, there was simply no happiness to be had at the hands of men. Mrs. Herbert apparently did not miss her husband overmuch. We at least have that in common, Delphinia conceded, even if Ivy cannot see it.

* * * *

The best news Delphinia could hope to receive arrived with the doctor late that afternoon. She waited nervously while he examined the group of travelers individually, beginning with those who were mobile, rejoicing silently when he declared each in turn fit to continue their journey. The sprained shoulder, twisted knee, and assorted bruises they had suffered were healing in accord with his expectations. The exception, not surprisingly, was Hobbs, whose broken leg would require a longer recuperation.

The doctor's next words sent Delphinia's spirits plummeting.

"While most of the travelers are making a rapid recovery," Doctor Goodwin said as she escorted him upstairs, "Captain Hainsworth is another matter."

After inspecting the wounds she had so carefully cleaned, the physician turned his attention to Nicholas's ankle. Delphinia waited by the window, feeling no need to leave the room in her capacity as nurse. She saw the captain flinch as Doctor Goodwin applied pressure to the swollen ankle. He replaced the sheets slowly.

"You do not appear altogether pleased with what you have seen, Doctor." Sitting upright in bed, Captain Hainsworth looked to be in physical discomfort despite his placid expression.

"It is worse than I originally thought," the doctor admitted soberly, "or perhaps I should say it is what I feared."

With a twitch of his white mustache the physician adjusted his spectacles. Delphinia waited anxiously for him to continue.

"Your attendant nurse has done a fine job of bringing down your fever, and there is no sign of infection in that nasty cut on your temple, a fact for which you can also thank Lady Delphinia. That ankle, unfortunately, is of great concern to me."

Nicholas frowned. "You don't think it's broken?"

Doctor Goodwin shook his head. "I think not. It is a bad sprain, however, one severe enough to require extended bed rest before you will be able to walk on it again." He gazed grimly at Nicholas. "Traveling is out of the question for the time being."

A look of disappointment registered briefly on Nicholas's face before he nodded his acquiescence. "Precisely how long will it take for the ankle to heal in your estimation? How many days?"

"Days! Oh, no, Captain," the doctor said with an apologetic smile, "I would judge it to be a matter of weeks. Four at least. You should be glad you did not break the bone. If infection had set in and gangrene had resulted, we might have had to amputate."

Four weeks. The ewer Delphinia had taken to replenish slipped from her grasp and dropped to the floor, bouncing on the carpet with a thud. She sensed both pairs of eyes on her as she knelt quickly to retrieve it. Replacing the ceramic jug in its basin on the nightstand, she attempted to stop herself from shaking. Another month was simply out of the question.

"Four weeks, eh?" Nicholas's eyes clouded momentarily before he addressed the doctor. "What am I supposed to do in that time?"

"Anything you wish, as long as it does not involve moving that ankle."

Nicholas smiled thinly. "Then my activities will be severely limited. I am not used to being indoors for such a long spell, but I suppose I shall have to adjust," he acceded. "I will follow your orders, of course, if you feel it is absolutely necessary."

Delphinia could no longer hide her shock. "Surely you cannot be suggesting Captain Hainsworth remain here."

The doctor looked at her and replied with words of eminent sense. "Where else is he to go, Lady Delphinia? The delicate condition of that ankle makes travel most unwise. He would only do more damage." He turned to the patient, admiration in his voice. "I think the good captain knows that quite well. I imagine you have seen more than the average man's share of injuries in your experience as a naval commander, and even tended them as well. Your friend Nettleton told me of your many talents. You would have been a great success in the medical profession."

Captain Hainsworth gave him a lopsided grin. "Harry has been known to exaggerate on occasion."

"But another month!" Delphinia could not contain her distress. "I am sure the captain cannot sacrifice more time than he already has. He must have pressing matters that require his attention." She gulped, hoping for agreement. "One must be practical, Doctor."

The physician removed his spectacles and stared at her. "You seem more upset by this news than the patient. I would have expected such a reaction from him, not from you. There is nothing indiscreet about keeping a sick man under your roof, Lady Delphinia," he remonstrated sharply.

Embarrassed, she hastened to explain. "No, of course not. I just meant perhaps Captain Hainsworth would be more comfortable elsewhere."

The doctor turned to him questioningly. "Are these arrangements acceptable to you, Captain? Has not Lady Delphinia proven adequate as a nurse?"

Delphinia watched as a lock of burnished gold hair fell across Captain Hainsworth's forehead, flattering his rugged countenance. He shrugged resignedly.

"My nurse has been far more than adequate. She is a delightfully pretty woman, and quite charming as well." He looked directly at her with a gaze of complete sincerity in his clear eyes. In the waning afternoon light they were as green as the sea she wished he still sailed upon. He bestowed upon her a dazzling smile that momentarily disarmed her. "In truth, I can't think of a place I would rather be incapacitated."

"Well, then, it is settled," the doctor harrumphed. "Surely it is not a problem, Lady Delphinia."

Stunned by the captain's assessment of his situation, she could not think of a suitable reply. She was not in the least moved by the doctor's chastisement of her attitude. She knew that when the villagers looked at her they saw only wealth without complications. Most knew nothing of her life or her nocturnal activities.

"Now then, Captain," Doctor Goodwin continued, "you must stay off that ankle if you expect it to heal properly. I shall check on you again."

"Your opinion will be most welcome," said Captain Hainsworth.

The doctor chuckled. "It has been my experience that most people decide when they can get around without the opinion of their physician. I'd give it a month at least. You're a worldly man, Captain. You will be the best judge of how much weight that ankle can tolerate. I would not strain it if I were you."

Delphinia could find neither the words nor the courage to address the doctor. All she saw was a trace of humor in Captain Hainsworth's expression. Doctor Goodwin wiped his spectacles and replaced them on his nose.

"Stubborn, this injury. It seems the simplest kind, and yet it might prove the most difficult to cure. I've seen many sprains caused by these moors. Believe me, it will take time."

And time, Delphinia thought desperately, is the one thing I do not have to give.

Chapter Four

Delphinia tried to make polite conversation the next morning as Lord and Lady Nettleton and Mrs. Herbert helped themselves to their final breakfast at Briarcombe. Her gaze strayed to the dining room's tall windows that overlooked the moors. The day had dawned cloudy, and Delphinia feared they would lose their way and return as unexpectedly as they had come. Despite the persistent fog, the travelers would set off in conditions far more temperate than when they arrived. Delphinia was thankful Percy had hired a local carriage to convey them safely to St. Ives.

Knowing she ought to offer assistance rather than avoid her guests, she nonetheless occupied herself by reviewing the day's menu with Agnes while they spent most of the morning packing. Torn between etiquette and necessity, she suspected her stiff attitude had created the awkward undercurrent that led to their abrupt departure.

In their final conversation alone, Marion spared her the burden of responsibility by placing the blame on, of all people, Captain Hainsworth.

"Sylvia will be disappointed that she will not be able to see her brother for some time," she said as the servants carried her trunks to the foyer. "It is rather worse for him, I think, having us here. The visits to his bedchamber are exceedingly awkward. Not the entertainment he had planned for us." She smiled. "He needs his rest. His friends in the Prince Regent's circle will be so concerned when they hear of his accident."

A pang of fear seized Delphinia. Captain Hainsworth had acquaintances in the royal circle, just as Percy had feared. She was glad he was confined to bed. With luck his immobile state would prevent him from causing serious trouble, at least for the time being. It would not, however, stop him from thinking and observing, two skills he seemed to possess in abundance.

And that was what troubled Delphinia most.

* * * *

As the servants loaded them into the awaiting carriage, the cases and trunks that had been rescued from Captain Hainsworth's disabled vehicle made a formidable line by the door. Before setting off, the women hugged Ivy as if they were parting from a dear friend. As if they were sisters, Delphinia observed with resentment. Ivy responded with equal fondness, more than she normally showed her sister, bestowing upon the women small water-colours and dried nosegays as tokens of her affection. They gave her embroidered bookmarks in return and promised to treasure the handmade gifts, as Delphinia stood by awkwardly, nursing her injured pride and wishing she had skipped their departure.

Now our routine will return to normal, she told herself with satisfaction as the coach pulled away, feeling selfish as she noted how the gloomy weather matched Ivy's taciturn mood. Shortly afterward Delphinia discovered that her sister had buried herself in the library. Seemingly resigned to the parting, Ivy was absorbed in a questionable publication from the Minerva Press.

"Wherever did you get that?" Delphinia demanded.

"Mrs. Herbert left it with me," Ivy said airily, not troubling herself to lift her nose from the pages. "I shall return it to her when I see her, which will be soon, I hope."

"In London, you mean." Delphinia fought the uneasiness of impending loss. "Perhaps you would like to help me freshen the flowers before dinner. Most of the bouquets from the other evening are wilted and need tossing. I thought we might go for a walk and select some replacements."

"No, I think not." Ivy yawned, retreated into her novel, and proceeded to ignore her sister.

Very well, Delphinia conceded. She cannot say I did not offer. Ivy's displeasure was not her greatest difficulty. Now she could turn her attention to the real problem. There was still Captain Hainsworth to be reckoned with for the next four weeks. Whatever was she to do with him in that time?

She looked at her sister with new inspiration. Perhaps she could interest Ivy in their remaining guest. The two might prove a source of great entertainment to each other. Confident she had hit upon a satisfactory solution, Delphinia left the library with a lighter heart while her sister remained captivated by the Minerva Press.

* * * *

Delphinia was free to spend her afternoon in other pursuits now that all but one guest had gone. Percy's words of warning about visitors combined with Marion's casual remark about Captain Hainsworth's highly placed friends made her wonder about the patient who remained in her home. Was he intimate enough with the Prince Regent's circle to confide in friends there? Might they have sent him here intentionally, as an agent of the Crown?

No, that was foolish, she decided. The accident proved Captain Hainsworth was not as competent on land as he was at sea. If he were truly an agent of the Crown he would know the roads on the moors as well as she did. Considering how far afield his carriage had strayed, that was clearly not the case.

Still, as a former naval captain, he would more than likely be familiar with the local waterways. Someone who had started as an ensign at Cambridge and who had been the youngest captain at Trafalgar, according to Lord Nettleton, would certainly prove a formidable enemy. While the thought alarmed her, she had no intention of letting his maritime experience be her downfall.

She realized with dismay that Percy would probably call to make arrangements for Wednesday's drop and to see for himself that the guests were safely off. Hoping to avoid him, she sought refuge in Captain Hainsworth's room where she might be able to learn something useful. Confident he suspected nothing so far, she would have to see that he remained unaware of her activities.

Upon entering his room, she found him sleeping soundly. She paused to study him while he could not observe her. Such a handsome man, she mused. She hoped his injury would not leave a scar beneath those blond curls that fell over his temple. Sitting in a chair at the foot of the bed, she opened her copy of *Mansfield Park,* published two years earlier. She had read recently that Miss Austen had a new novel coming out, and here she had not yet read her last.

Delphinia immersed herself in the novel, as she frequently did when she wanted to forget her problems. She always found Miss Austen's writing skilled and insightful and, she thought smugly, far superior to the novel Rowena Herbert had given Ivy to read.

* * * *

Delphinia awoke with a start, momentarily forgetting where she was. The weight in her lap made her realize she must have nodded off over her book. She looked up with suspicion to see Captain Hainsworth scrutinizing her with a mild interest that made her uncomfortable. Her encounters with him made her suspect he had a deep intuitive awareness, an aspect she recognized, for it matched her own.

"Good evening, Captain," she began in a formal tone.

"Hello, Lady Delphinia. That must not be a very entertaining book if it put you to sleep so easily." He glanced at the darkening windowpane. "I see evening has come already."

"How are you feeling?"

"Better since my head has ceased throbbing, although the pain in the ankle is still excruciating. But I would rather talk of happier things. Where is that amiable dog of yours?"

"Brutus? He was downstairs when I last saw him."

"I wish he would join us here. He would be excellent company right now." With a wistful gaze he returned his gaze to the window. "So my friends are on their way at last. Sylvia will be happy to receive them. I regret having to stay behind."

"My sister and I will do what we can to see to your comfort. Agnes has made some stewed damsons, if you are interested."

"Thank you, but you have done quite enough for me." As if fearing he had offended her, he now attempted to reassure her. "I don't mean to complain. You have been most kind. I know you have had a difficult time of it with all of us. You must let me compensate you for your troubles."

"You will do nothing of the sort," she replied shortly. "It will not be long before you are on your way also."

"Tell me, did I miss much at the Pack of Cards Inn?"

"Hardly, unless you find a hundred-year-old inn built with a gambler's winnings a curiosity of sorts."

He raised an eyebrow. "Hence the name."

"Its four stories represent the four suits, and there are fifty-two windows for every card in the deck." She reflected on the inn with distaste. "Frankly, I consider it a waste of glass."

He smiled, amusement turning his face ruggedly handsome. "Well, I hope Harry enjoys himself immensely."

"Lady Nettleton convinced him to go directly to St. Ives. I am sure you will miss your friends, as they'll no doubt miss you—Mrs. Herbert especially." Her resentment returned as she thought of Ivy. She felt her pulse quicken as she looked into his eyes.

He looked at her with surprise. "Will she? She never let on that she noticed my presence one way or the other. My mother would be pleased to hear it. She has been trying to marry me off for years. She has, in fact, given me an ultimatum to find someone this Season, or she will choose someone for me. I doubt Rowena would be her first choice. She is certainly not mine. Anyway, your home here interests me far more than the inn."

Delphinia found his reaction to her mention of Mrs. Herbert oddly uplifting as he gave her a smile that seemed genuine, but she could not ignore her distrust of the man. She wanted to discourage any curiosity he might have about her home and its contents.

"I know I am fortunate to be here," he said with an ease that made her uncomfortable. "I meant exactly what I said to the doctor. You are so very attractive, even when you are angry."

He was baiting her, she was sure of it. Closing the covers of her book, she stood and retreated to the safety of the far window. Suspicion and caution stirred within her. If he was going to be so impossibly forthright she would have to be more careful.

"Our appearances are beyond our control," she said coolly, knowing it was more prudent to control her rising anger than to succumb to flattery. "It is hardly something one can help."

"That's right. You did tell me not to worry about situations beyond my control." His voice rose with resurging interest. "Yet you seem to have mastered the art quite nicely, Lady Delphinia. Is there anything over which you do not have control?"

"Over you, Captain, I have none." She smiled briefly.

"Perhaps you have more control over me than you know."

His suggestion was offered in a playful tone, but this time she did not rise to the bait, choosing to remain by the window.

"We all control very little, Captain." She kept her voice tight.

"I suspect you control a great deal. This house, for instance." He studied the room's graceful architectural lines and imaginative design of the fireplace. "That strength of character continually shows itself in you. I wonder what compels you to remain in so secluded a spot when London offers such amusements."

The comment surprised her, putting her on her guard. This man asked unsettling questions. Fielding them exasperated her, but perhaps it was better to satisfy his curiosity than allow him to wonder. "As I have told you, I prefer the countryside. There is great charm here and opportunities to ride."

"There is charm in London as well, don't you think? So much culture and activity. My mother assures me there are few brides who would bemoan their fate of having to spend their lives in town."

"I have no doubt she is correct about most," Delphinia conceded, "though I have found there is far less trouble to get into here than in London."

"Fewer temptations, perhaps. But what kind of trouble does London offer? And what is it that keeps you here?"

His provocative questions had begun to make her feel defensive. To cover her wariness she tidied his bureau.

"I enjoy the privacy here, although," she added, trying to keep her tone light while putting him in his place, "I sometimes find unexpected guests troublesome, if not downright tedious."

"As you do now. Yes, I see your point. Here you have fewer of them but for the occasional traveler stranded in a storm." Captain Hainsworth smiled uncertainly and changed his curious tone to one of earnestness. "I assure you, I shall prove little trouble to you. I shall make surprisingly few requests. As I have told you, I am not sick enough to be an invalid."

Delphinia reflected how much easier caring for him would be if only he were a bit more of an invalid. She flushed with guilt at the idea. He stared at her as if trying to read her mind and proved amazingly accurate when he spoke.

"Not quite an invalid, but helpless enough to be a nuisance. Is that what you think?" He gave a woebegone chuckle. "You needn't be so testy about it. I can leave anytime you like."

"If you really feel that way, I am sure arrangements can be made to move you elsewhere," she countered.

He was momentarily speechless, which was a relief. There, I have hastened his departure, she thought with triumph. His sea-green eyes locked with hers in a challenge.

"As long as Dr. Goodwin has forced me to stay on as your guest for the time being," he said, more patiently this time, "it might make the days pass more pleasantly if you would sit and talk with me for a spell. You needn't be afraid of me, you know."

He had come too close to the truth. She would not allow herself to be intimidated by a guest in her home, an unwelcome one at that. Smiling, she took a bold stride toward him.

"I have seen enough of life that there is very little you or anyone else can make me afraid of, Captain."

But she was afraid he would talk with the servants and trick them inadvertently into revealing information she did not want him to know. The fear sent tremors through her. To prevent it, she would have to tend him herself, the last thing she wanted.

Striding purposefully to a corner of the room, she withdrew a polished cherry wood cane from behind a trunk. Taking hold of it firmly, she moved to the bed and hooked it over a bedside chair so it was within his reach. Arms crossed, she stood before him. "As you said yourself, Captain, you are not an invalid. The doctor has left it up to you to decide when you are ready to test that ankle. I will leave you this cane to aid your mobility. It was our mother's." Her gaze wandered the length of his blanketed form doubtfully. "She was a good bit shorter than you, but any support is better than none."

"Are we to part with such an unceremonious farewell?" he gazed at her steadily, a glimmer of regret in his eyes at her pending departure. A look of deep speculation altered his features so he appeared older than his thirty-odd years.

"It is not a farewell, Captain. It is simply a reminder that you are a guest in my home and nothing more." She moved to the door, putting an effective distance between them. "Is there anything more I can do for you?"

Delphinia maintained a stiff posture, determined he would not draw her into any further personal conversation. He sighed as he dismissed her.

"Yes. You can send Stebbins to me so I may learn what we are to do with what remains of my carriage."

* * * *

The woman was an enigma, Nicholas thought after she had gone. So often her phrases seemed cloaked in double meaning, but he did not know her well enough to understand their significance. He hoped one day he would. Even stranger was that he felt drawn to her in spite of her contradictory behavior.

Why the deuce did she have such an odd effect on him? He had noted the state of calm that came over her in sleep in the few seconds before she sensed she was being watched and had awakened. She was amazingly sensitive to be able to sleep so lightly, he mused. While her eyes had been closed her face was warm and open, in contrast with her frank speech.

He pulled himself up in bed with some difficulty and tried to assess his condition. Most of his nausea and dizziness had passed, which was a fortunate thing, for her words had done little to make him feel better. He wished she were looking forward to his stay so they might get to know each other better. But nothing in her demeanor indicated even a remote interest on her part, beyond concern for his health. Quite the opposite.

He was hardly at his most dashing, yet he had never met a woman so completely indifferent to him. His attempts to win her fancy had failed miserably. Perhaps it is no wonder, he thought, wincing at the familiar pinch in his ankle, in the sorry state I am in.

He had been rather cavalier in volunteering to leave, if that was her wish. What surprised him more was his own hesitation in seizing the opportunity to be transferred to a local inn, where he might at least be entertained by the colorful stories of travelers and village gamesters. The sudden fierceness in her tone had made him wonder if he should be afraid of her rather than the reverse. But something in her reaction to his offer to leave rang true.

She was afraid of something, he realized, though he had no idea what. He was able to put his thoughts of her aside only when his valet arrived.

"Tell me, Stebbins, how is Hobbs managing?" he demanded.

Stebbins stood before him, his manner uneasy. It occurred to Nicholas that although his valet had seen him in a variety of unsavory conditions none had ever rivaled his present state.

"Feeling a bit better, sir, not as sore as he was. Leg's still useless, though."

"Yes, that will take some time. And the horses?"

"Up and running, as usual. Spitfire and Polish never looked better, sir, particularly Spit. Ready to go whenever you are."

Nicholas grunted. "That may take more time. Now tell me about the carriage. Yesterday you brought me news I hope will not worsen. Did you see the wheelwright today?"

The previous day his valet had reported back to Nicholas, after having gone to examine the carriage with Harry. Stebbins had delivered the news in a most apologetic tone. The wheels on the left were badly smashed, and one axle was broken. The door would need to be refitted, rehinged, and repainted.

"By George, is there anything on the left that remains intact?" Nicholas had exclaimed.

"Part of the window glass."

Nicholas had raised an eyebrow. "Only part."

"Yes, sir. The glass will need replacing, too."

Today's news proved not much more positive.

"Melcher—that's the wheelwright, sir—says he'll repair the carriage like you specified, but it can't be done any too quick. He's doing some repairs for local folks, and yours is special work. Said it'll cost you a pretty penny, sir."

Nicholas gritted his teeth. "How long and how much?"

The news was not as bad as it might have been. Cost was the least of his concerns. Even if his ankle healed more rapidly than expected, repairs to the carriage would delay his departure longer than he had planned. Damnation! He had already spent a week and a half in this woman's home. Three more would seem like eternity.

He felt quite desolate after Stebbins had gone. With his friends having departed, he was left alone at the hands of Lady Delphinia Marlowe. Was I ever, even on my worst days as a commander, he wondered, as belligerent as she? I sincerely doubt it. Well, he thought resignedly, I'll just have to make the best of it. He was no more thrilled to be here where he was not wanted than she was to have him. Annoyed with the state of his carriage, he had little left to think about besides his mysterious hostess.

He sensed an uneasiness about her every time she was near. Surely it was not maidenly modesty that kept her at bay. There was a specific reason she did not want him in her home. Her reluctance was clearly not a question of money or of manners, he mused, and certainly not of breeding.

He saw no sense in pondering further. Harry always said the same. Who could understand the hearts of women? With a deep sigh Nicholas nestled under the covers, closed his eyes and dismissed her from his mind. The weather was so gloomy and his ankle still so tender. He had nothing better to do than sleep.

* * * *

Nicholas slept fitfully, with flashes of the moors returning to him. In moments of partial consciousness he feared he had dreamed the presence of Lady Delphinia. But when he awakened, remembering the onyx-haired woman who had so carefully bathed his raw head wound following the accident, he knew she was real.

The rest felt refreshing to him until the middle of the night when he awoke and found himself unable to return to sleep. This illness has confounded my senses, he thought irritably. I managed to obtain more sleep during the final nights of the war than I have here this night.

Writhing in discomfort from being bedridden for so long, he propped himself up on the pillows, rested his palms squarely on the sheets, and raised himself up on his hands, stretching his back as he did so. He saw no point in remaining still if he could not sleep. Judging by the charcoal hue of the sky and the complete silence he decided it must be well after midnight. He had seen that sky often in battles at sea, when it seemed as if the morning light would never break. He felt that way now.

A flitting movement below his window captured his attention as he reached for the bedside candle. Through the dim glow of the lantern by the door, a shadowed figure moved rapidly. Nicholas had the briefest glimpse of a gentleman's hat, greatcoat, and boots and a flash of dark hair.

The image made a quick but lasting impression, yet he sensed something amiss in the vision. The masculine clothes did not suit the walk. The stride was naggingly familiar. He had an uncanny feeling the figure was not a man. Absurd, he thought, until he remembered how startled he was by the identity of a French spy he had discovered during the war.

Despite the throbbing in his ankle, he quickly raised himself up and squinted into the night. The figure had disappeared in the shadows of the moors and become one with the blackness. He eased himself back under the covers, so filled with curiosity about what he had seen he temporarily forgot the injury.

Closing his eyes for a second, he tried to visualize the figure again. The clothes were loose and ill-fitting, the way they might fit a woman. He realized suddenly what it meant. His initial impression was that he had seen a woman in men's clothing.

His pulse quickened. The determined stride. The black streak of hair. He knew one individual who did not appear to care a whit about how she dressed, and the clothes this person had worn were certainly not hers. Yet he had no doubt as to the identity of the figure he had just seen crossing the moors.

He was quite certain it was Lady Delphinia.

Chapter Five

An echo of a warning his friends had given him before he left London rang loudly in Nicholas's ears.

"You'll be in the very heart of smuggling territory, by Jove," the Duke of Roxley had said wryly. "Keep an eye open, my boy. You might be surprised. Never know what you'll hear."

At the time Nicholas had laughed at the idea. Entire communities took part in the illegal trade along England's western coast, where the treacherous, rock-laden shoreline made it one of the most difficult areas for the excise men to penetrate. With so many residents having a stake in the enterprise, few were willing to give evidence against those who relied on it for their livelihood. Since the war had ended there was too little industry for those who sought work.

When he went home to St. Ives, Nicholas often turned a deaf ear to the inhabitants of the rural village, feeling he had little right to interfere in the activities of those who kept to themselves and frequently chose to remain aloof. Perhaps it was time, he mused, for a change in attitude.

The very heart of smuggling territory. Could he believe what his eyes told him? Lady Delphinia's inexplicable wandering gave him an opportunity to speculate. At present he had nothing better to do with his time. But first he must give her the benefit of the doubt. He had seen firsthand what an efficient nurse she could be. Perhaps someone had been taken sick in the community and she had been summoned to assist in the patient's care. Yet if the situation were so urgent that she had been called out during the night, why had she not taken a carriage across the moors?

Could Delphinia actually be a smuggler? It was hardly an occupation for a well-bred lady, yet the pieces seemed to fit the puzzle. He noticed she had not taken Brutus on her nocturnal walk. Obviously she encouraged few visitors, a fact he found suspicious given her isolation in this wild countryside.

We each play a role, she had told him. And hers was undeniably unique. That much he had discovered on his own. What that role consisted of precisely he had yet to learn.

* * * *

Nicholas did not see Delphinia the following day until early evening when she came to his room to retrieve his dinner tray. Observing the empty plates, cup, and dishes, she expressed approval at his hearty appetite.

"And how are you feeling, Captain?" she asked softly.

It surprised him to find her mood far more amiable tonight, as if no unpleasantness had existed between them. A great weight seemed to have been lifted from her shoulders.

"Quite well, actually, thank you." He chose his words carefully. "I am most concerned about getting back on my feet. I think exercise might help this leg along. Unfortunately, I am not easily able to endure much activity at the moment."

"Worry not," she said cheerfully, picking up the tray and turning. "You will be up and about soon enough. Then you shall get plenty of exercise. Walking is good, and fresh air, too."

"Even the night air?"

She froze, gripping the tray.

"You evidently must think so," he continued casually, "for I saw you walking on the moors late last night."

She stood with her back to him. The room had grown still but for the voice of a groom speaking to the horses below the window from which he had watched her. Finally she turned back to him, her expression an odd mixture of indignation and scorn.

"When did you see me walking last night?" she asked, the pitch of her voice higher than usual.

"Quite late. Sometime after midnight, I should think. I am quite sure it was you."

"I have no idea what you are talking about," she said simply. "I never left the house last night. I was up late reading and have spent most of the day in my room resting."

"So you have not been ill then."

"Certainly not. It is you who are in need of rest, not I."

"It must be that fascinating book that held your interest so. The one you fell asleep over the other night."

She looked at him with such innocence Nicholas began to wonder if he had dreamed the vision outside his window. She was a cursed fine actress if she were lying.

"I saw someone leave this house late last night," he insisted. "Does that not concern you? Surely you want to know the comings and goings of your servants."

"You are mistaken, Captain. No one left this house." Speaking in a crisp tone, she gazed at him intently. "I will question the servants, however, if it will please you. I thank you for your concern for my staff's activities."

Her icy expression at odds with her polite words, she held the tray so tightly he feared it would snap in two before she marched to the door and left. Nicholas remained convinced she was lying. Her reaction confirmed it for him. She had covered her surprise well, but perhaps she was accustomed to deceitfulness. What legitimate business could she have on the moors so late at night? He had spent a week and a half in her home. With three more to go his days were just beginning to get exciting.

Lady Delphinia's nocturnal excursion might offer a clue as to why she displayed such restraint in her personal dealings. Trying to solve this mystery would give him the incentive he needed to get back on his feet and beyond the doors of this lonely room. He would make it his private assignment while he recuperated. This was a challenge he relished.

How much more he could accomplish once he was mobile! His mother was justified in criticizing him. He had grown lazy in retirement. Here was the opportunity to do some useful work while serving the Crown. Too bad he had not paid more attention when he was in St. Ives. He would have known the signs to watch for.

A rhythmic, playful knock on the door brought him to attention. He hoped Lady Delphinia had returned for another round of interrogation, but his hopes were dashed when it was only her sister who let herself in at his command. Ivy Herrick's shoulders sagged noticeably at his reaction.

"Do not look so disappointed, Captain." With a petulant pout Ivy paraded before the foot of his bed. "I had hoped my presence would elicit a happier response. Since you were unconscious when you arrived, I was uncertain whether you remembered meeting me or not. I am Lady Ivy Herrick, Delphinia's sister."

She flashed him a beguiling smile. Her dress, deep green with ivory detailing, was stylish but unusually formal for this hour of the morning. Nicholas had not remembered her being quite so coy on their previous meeting and hoped fervently she would not turn coquettish now. The isolation must be unbearable for a girl so full of vigor. If only her sister were so bold. *Her* attentions would be most welcome.

He looked at this younger sister closely. Her beauty and figure were more classically appealing than Delphinia's. When she matured in a few years she would be considered striking. There were few women upon whom Nicholas did not bestow a second glance, but Ivy Herrick was too young to be a serious prospect. And her sister fascinated him far too much for him to look elsewhere.

"I miss your friends dreadfully," she admitted bluntly. "They were so jolly and lively. We so rarely have interesting guests in this area, especially during the winter months when we are cut off from society."

"Yes, I miss them even more than you." Here was a chance to see what he might learn from this restless young woman with so little to occupy her days. He smiled congenially. "I apologize if I was not as responsive as you might have wished. I fear in this illness I have come to look forward to visits from your sister."

"Oh, yes. Delphinia." Her expression clouded. "Either you haven't wearied of her indifference yet, or you have more tolerance for it than I."

"Is she indifferent?" Nicholas asked in surprise.

"I find her so. Her behavior as a hostess leaves much to be desired."

Ivy shrugged, but her tone hardened perceptibly.

"I think circumstance placed her in an indelicate position and showed her at her worst." He chuckled. "I agree a congenial hostess might visit her guests more frequently, particularly those who are injured, but I confess I am a bit prejudiced. Her visits seem to have become fewer and fewer. I suppose it is difficult when one keeps nocturnal hours as she does."

Ivy stared, amazement animating her face. "You've noticed! I don't know what fascinates her so about the moors, but she spends a great deal of time there." She shuddered. "I would not want to be outdoors after dark."

"Then this is a common practice of hers?"

"She has done so regularly in the year and a half I have been here. I have not watched carefully enough to know how often. On occasion I will wake in the night or be unable to sleep, and I will visit her room to find her gone. Perhaps once a month or so she takes these night walks."

Night walks. It did sound like smuggling. "And you have no idea why or where she goes?"

"She will not talk about it. She says she becomes restless sometimes, but I find that hard to understand."

"When I saw her she was dressed in the disguise of a man, which makes even less sense." Nicholas described the clothing to her.

Ivy frowned, looking bewildered. "Maybe I should sneak into her wardrobe and confront her with the outfit, if I can find it."

"I have a better idea." A plan forming in his mind, he studied her face with great deliberation. "Perhaps we should join forces and find out why she behaves as she does. At the moment you can go places where I cannot. We could be conspirators."

Ivy's green eyes brightened. "What a marvelous idea! Two heads are better than one. Perhaps I shall finally find out what Delphinia is up to."

And that, Nicholas thought, will be the most interesting revelation of my stay here.

* * * *

Later that day, as Nicholas was attempting to regain his strength by sitting upright in bed for longer periods of time, another knock at his door brought relief from the isolation of his sick bed.

"Enter," he commanded mechanically, struggling to arrange the sheets about his knees.

Lady Delphinia entered the room wordlessly, her expression serious, accompanied by a man Nicholas had never seen. Something in his appearance made Nicholas dislike him instantly. Perhaps it was the contempt in the man's face or his air of surly arrogance that made Nicholas want to call the fellow out even at a glance.

"Captain Nicholas Hainsworth, may I present Mr. Percy

Wainwright." Delphinia's tone was stiff and detached. "Mr. Wainwright is an old family friend."

If this was an old family friend, Nicholas thought cynically, he would wager his Cornwall estate at the Pack of Cards any day.

"I was disappointed I was unable to meet you at dinner last week," Wainwright said with a smile. "You were not feeling up to snuff."

"Still not, but making progress." Nicholas shook his hand firmly. It was a callused hand and hard, used to outdoor labor.

"I hear you will not be able to walk for some time."

Nicholas spread his hands. "Confined to bed, according to the learned Doctor Goodwin."

"Nuisance, that. Three more weeks in bed he's given you, eh?" Wainwright stepped to the window and stood looking out for what seemed an unusually long time. Despite the condolences he offered, Nicholas sensed no genuine sympathy in his words.

"I doubt very much I will need all of that time to recover," Nicholas assured him. "We shall see how the wind blows. It is merely a twisted ankle."

"Spoken like a true naval man. But healing requires time," Wainwright said smugly, "especially for a Londoner not accustomed to our treacherous moors."

The disdain in Wainwright's tone made Nicholas want to get well twice as quickly simply to prove him wrong. Harry had mentioned meeting Wainwright over dinner and found him an acceptable sort— for someone in trade, he had added quickly. But Nettleton was not always an astute judge of character and was often prone to take people at appearances, something Nicholas had learned never to do. As a captain whose skills had been sharpened in battle, he knew spies were everywhere, sometimes in quarters where they were least expected.

"I wanted to see for myself who Delphinia was hiding under her roof." With a cold smile Wainwright eyed Nicholas in a calculating fashion.

Nicholas indulged him with a smile no warmer than his own. "And now you've seen me. Our hostess has been most gracious in permitting my party to recuperate under her roof, but she has hardly hidden me. The only reason I have not made an appearance downstairs is because I have not been physically able."

"Delphinia can be very gracious when she chooses to be."

Nicholas saw Delphinia's eyes flash though she said nothing.

He sensed Wainwright was baiting her somehow. In the time they had been in the room she seemed unable to relax, instead standing stiffly by the door, as if ready to flee.

"I won't keep you longer. I know how important it is for you to rest, so I'll be going." Wainwright gave Nicholas a parting look that was cold enough to freeze blood before he turned away. "You needn't see me out, Delphinia, my dear. I am, after all, so well acquainted with the upstairs rooms."

Nicholas resented the suggestion in Wainwright's tone and knew his vulgar implication must have offended Delphinia, though her only reaction was a sharp intake of breath. Rather than argue she turned to Nicholas, promising to visit him after dinner.

As Wainwright turned to leave, Nicholas heard a low growl from the corridor. Lady Delphinia silenced her dog with a single sharp command. The mastiff lay down immediately, emitting a disgruntled sound as he did so.

"Brutus does not seem to like you, Mr. Wainwright," Nicholas observed dryly, relishing the chance to comment. "Funny, I have found him to be quite a friendly fellow."

"It's unfortunate you'll not be around long enough to get to know him better," Percy said, an edge to his voice. He turned and chided Delphinia. "I've told you before, this beast should not be allowed upstairs. He isn't devilish fond of me."

"I have always found dogs to be excellent judges of character," Nicholas said lightly.

"Have you now?" Percy narrowed his eyes, giving Nicholas a cold stare. "Perhaps you're the one who is not such a good judge of character, Captain. Good day to you."

His mind reeled. Delphinia's reserved manner in Wainwright's presence, Nicholas thought, made his own exchanges with her seem almost intimate. Whoever Wainwright was, he was certainly no family friend. He watched as she followed Wainwright from the room and listened as their footsteps trailed off down the hall. He strained to catch their words, but he could not detect a sound.

Surely a woman of such efficiency and beauty could not be the paramour of this gauche country squire, if that was what he was. She had not identified him as such. What was Wainwright to her? His presence made Nicholas want to get well quickly, if only to present him with a challenge. He strongly suspected Lady Delphinia was a prize well worth pursuing. Strange emotions stirred within him, uncomfortable and confusing. What did it matter what her relationship was to this Wainwright character? Nicholas knew he could not remain under her roof much longer. His sprain would heal. The carriage would be repaired. No longer would he be able to look into those magnificent eyes and wonder what secrets they concealed.

Those eyes, so wild and beautiful, held the colors of the moors in their depths. In so many ways she was a product of the landscape she considered home. But there was a reserve in her eyes, a fear he had seen many times before in the men he had commanded. What was it she feared in the security of home? He did not know her well enough to hazard even a guess. Here in this bed he would remain, limited as to what he could accomplish in getting to know more about her, until his physical condition and the carriage repairs would force him to depart.

And here, in the heart of smuggling territory, Nicholas was beginning to wonder about the fate of his own heart.

* * * *

"I hope you are satisfied, Percy. You saw the view from the window. Captain Hainsworth has been confined to bed. He could not possibly have witnessed anything."

Delphinia closed the library doors behind them, trying to hide her tension. Percy made his way to the sideboard, as she had expected, where he poured himself a generous amount of brandy from the decanter she left there expressly for him. She stood and watched him cautiously. She had not been entirely truthful, for she had not been able to bring herself to tell him of the captain's questions.

It would be safer, she knew, for her to handle it in her own way, with discretion and firmness. Captain Hainsworth could not contradict her in her own home without appearing to be at best inquisitive and, at worst, rude. She did not think he would pursue any matter she did not seem inclined to discuss.

"Still, we can't take any chances. At least Lee Bay is a safe distance from here." Percy downed the brandy in a gulp and, with a raised eyebrow, lifted the empty glass to her. "Quality merchandise, I would say."

"I rarely touch it." Although I did serve some to our guests, she thought with a slight touch of guilt.

"You merely store it. For that we are most grateful."

Percy gave her a suggestive smile. Delphinia turned away to hide her revulsion. Percy's appreciation was not something she wanted to encourage.

"At least most of your guests are safely off," he continued lightly. "I'm sorry they had to leave so soon."

"Save your sarcasm, Percy. I prefer honesty from you."

"I'm simply saying I'm glad they did not interfere with your interests." He inclined his head meaningfully. "Interference can be a deadly thing."

"Those people were innocent wayfarers," she retorted. "They stumbled upon our home quite by accident."

"We have no idea who their friends are. We wouldn't want them to alert the authorities." His voice was filled with a quiet menace. "That Nettleton fellow, so pompous with his dislike of trade. Who does he think he is?"

"It's not his fault you blackened your own name and were forced into trade." She looked at him with scorn.

"That sister of yours has become quite attractive. Lively little thing, isn't she?" He poured another glass of brandy. "She has a spirit much

like yours. Perhaps we should show her more of the night life Exmoor
has to offer before she leaves for London believing life here is boring."

"Do not even think it." Incensed at his veiled threat, Delphinia
gave no thought to her own safety. There was nothing she would not
put past Percy.

"Before I forget I have a letter for you."

Her heart lurched as she took the envelope he extended to her.
She attempted to hide her eagerness.

"It's from Mr. Warren," she said casually. "Do you have an address
where I can write him? I'd like to send a reply."

"I can take it for you." Percy watched her intently. "Anyway, you've
not read the letter."

"I prefer to read my correspondence in private."

"Delphinia, my dear!" he exclaimed with mock dismay. "I didn't
think you kept any secrets from me."

"And I suppose it's fair for you to keep yours," she returned. "You
must know his address."

"I believe Mr. Warren lives in town. But I don't think it's wise for
you to contact him. I suggest you leave him alone."

His tone was gentle, but she sensed a warning in his words that
held more of a threat than concern. She realized abruptly that he must
know of her attempt to contact Warren. She leaped to her feet from
her position on the sofa, throwing caution aside.

"Who is Warren, Percy? That is not his real name, is it? You must
tell me. I have a right to know." When her demands failed, she assumed
a new approach. "I don't think he is a real person at all. I know everyone
in these parts." Pausing, she attempted to repress her frustration. "Is
he a local squire? A magistrate? He must be someone I know, a local
man using a pseudonym."

He smiled indulgently, as if he found her attempts to learn the truth
somehow gratifying. "I assure you, he is very real."

"He initiated this correspondence. Why won't he meet me face-
to-face? He knows my identity. It is only fair I know his. Tell him I
demand to meet him." She tossed the note down. "He has a peculiar
attitude of entitlement, to think he can use my home for storage of his
goods without having made my acquaintance."

"You're hardly in a position to demand anything, Delphinia, and
you know it." Percy replaced his goblet with a thud on the sideboard.
"Now, do you want me to take a letter to him or not?"

Borrowing an attitude from Ivy, she responded in the tone of
petulance her sister had perfected. "I think not, Percy. I'll write it at
my leisure and give it to you when I'm ready. If you have nothing
further to tell me, I have work to do."

"You have until next Thursday to write a reply. That's when I'll
meet with Warren again."

As soon as she had seen Percy to the door, Delphinia returned to the library and opened the letter with a combination of excitement and trepidation.

"Dearest Lady Delphinia,
Wednesday night's drop was a resounding success. I thank you again for your cooperation. I understand you wish us to meet and have been searching for me. I would advise you not to try, for your own safety. I suspect it is far too dangerous.
    Yours,
    Warren."

He had underlined his surname with a flourish, as he always did. She crumpled the note in frustration, recalling in vivid detail the visit she had paid to his cottage two weeks ago. She learned his address from a fisherman who directed her to a small cottage near the Valley of Rocks, a mere three miles from her home. In the cottage she had found only a Frenchwoman who spoke no English and who grew increasingly agitated during the brief visit. With her limited French, Delphinia could make out little the woman said except the repeated claim that she knew nothing.

On returning the next day, Delphinia had been disappointed to find the cottage abandoned with no trace of recent habitation. That Frenchwoman must have told Mr. Warren I called, she surmised. He was so anxious to avoid her he left immediately.

If only she could know who else would be exposed once she was finally able to turn the tables on Percy. She wanted to learn who Warren was before she made the business public. Ultimately it did not matter, for she would do what she knew was right. Now she would have time to return to the project that had held her interest before the visitors had interrupted her.

She could hardly wait to put her plan into action. While she had no choice but to wait, it would not be much longer. Once Ivy was safely launched into London society, she would be free to act independently without fear of reprisal. The day would not come soon enough for Percy, she thought with fervent abandon.

If only there were someone she could turn to, someone she could confide in. Someone, she acknowledged with a start, like Captain Hainsworth. Beneath her roof he had consistently displayed the behavior of a gentleman. Of course she could not tell him or anyone else. Life on the moors had made her resourceful and independent, but circumstances had taught her the folly of believing she could confide in an outsider. Nicholas Hainsworth was in no physical condition to offer protection against Percy. Worse, if Percy discovered her betrayal Ivy might truly be in danger of becoming trapped, as Delphinia had.

If she were to defeat Percy, she must continue to work privately to turn the tide against him.

Somewhere proof must exist of his involvement with the illegal business in which they were engaged. Percy had taken charge of the business after her husband's ship had gone down. She would continue to look through James's papers in the trunks in the cellar. Perhaps she would find some incriminating paperwork that she could use as evidence against him. *If there is a way to prove it*, she vowed, *I will find it.*

Delphinia returned to the matter at hand. Warren could not have disappeared into thin air, as much as he might have wished to. Perhaps the cottage was a rendezvous point for the operation. Percy was correct in stating it was a dangerous business. It held danger not only for himself but for her as well.

She tapped the envelope impatiently against the arm of her chair. *Never you mind, Percy*, she thought with sudden inspiration. *Next Thursday, when I am prepared, I shall follow you and deliver the letter myself. Then I shall find out who Mr. Warren is once and for all.*

* * * *

After breakfast several days later, on a morning in late March that dawned clear and fair, Delphinia announced to Sophy her intention to ride into town.

"I shall be taking the trap out for awhile and Rosie with it," she informed the housekeeper, thinking fondly of the mare in her stable. "She'll be glad of the chance to have a real ride after our long winter. If you should need me for any reason, do not hesitate to send for me. I plan to call at the local inns regarding a matter that requires my attention. I will begin in Lynmouth at the Rising Sun Inn and work my way to the Stag Hunters' Inn at Brendon."

"We'll find you if need be," Sophy promised, "but it's a quiet morning, miss. Every morning's quiet now that our visitors have gone."

Delphinia sighed. "Try not to place undue emphasis on their absence else Ivy becomes overwrought again. And please tell no one where I've gone."

She waited in the foyer while her groom brought the trap around to the entrance. Sticking her head out-of-doors tentatively, she decided to wear a cloak suitable for the milder weather that seemed to be returning to the countryside. Hoping the seasonal storms had passed, she was happy to leave behind her heaviest wool, choosing a lightweight cape she had not worn in nearly a year.

Even her spirits felt lighter. Something about the coming of spring, she mused, brightened her whole outlook. She was adjusting the satin ribbons of her bonnet when Ivy appeared in the drawing room doorway, smiling broadly.

"Good morning, Delphinia," she said. "You've chosen a most pleasant day for a ride. The weather has cleared so nicely."

Her sweet tone prompted Delphinia to give her a second look. The remark seemed innocent enough. Ivy continued to watch, alert and full of interest, as Delphinia fastened the frogs that decorated the front of her cloak.

"Your mood is rather improved over the dismals in which I have seen you in recent days," Delphinia said cautiously. "May I ask what brought about the change?"

"I guess I've had a change of heart."

The lightness in Ivy's tone surprised Delphinia and made her suspicious simultaneously. It was not like her sister to recover so quickly from great disappointment. If she did not know better she would have thought Ivy seemed almost happy. She did not know what to make of it.

The more she considered the change in her sister, the more she decided it might have been wise to assign Ivy to caring for Captain Hainsworth. If it made her sister content it was worth the aggravation of enduring the captain's presence at Briarcombe. Attributing Ivy's good mood to her newfound patient and companion, Delphinia reached down to pet the head of her mastiff who had been beside her all the while.

"Not this time, Brutus," she apologized regretfully.

"You're not taking Brutus with you?" Ivy asked in surprise.

"No, he had best stay here. Well," she announced with a smile, "I'm off. I shall see you in a few hours, when I've completed my errands."

"I shall finish my book. Do see that Rosie gets lots of exercise."

With a yawn Ivy started slowly up the stairs, her demeanor so serene Delphinia wondered what she was up to.

* * * *

In the uncomfortable narrow bed that seemed more suited to a prison than a manor house, Nicholas continued to stretch his legs, reflecting on the warnings his friends in London had given him when he last saw them. The very heart of smuggling territory was how they had referred to this area. In the context of their words, the figure he had seen crossing the dark moors seemed suspicious indeed.

But what did he really see? He pondered the bewildering question. He saw a woman in gentlemen's clothing. Not the current fashion either. If he knew one person who was not concerned with being *au courant,* it was the mistress of the house herself. Most likely she had chosen the outmoded clothing as an appropriate disguise. But a disguise for what? What cause had she or anyone to wander the moors after midnight? Only highwaymen were about at that hour. And how was that Wainwright fellow connected? The idea that she might be meeting the man in secret disturbed Nicholas deeply. His thoughts darkened at the memory of his encounter with Wainwright.

An urgent knock at the door put an end to his ruminations. Almost before he could bid the caller entry, the door was flung open and Ivy Herrick rushed inside, her cloak catching on the door latch in her haste.

"Oh, Captain!" she said in a voice of anticipation.

Nicholas was startled by her shortness of breath. "What's happened?"

"You'll never guess! A most fortunate happenstance. My sister is riding into town, a thing she rarely does except to go to chapel. I just overheard her telling our housekeeper."

In her excitement she perched indiscreetly on the edge of his bed, a seating choice that was highly improper. It was a good thing for Ivy her sister was not here to correct her, Nicholas thought with amusement, for she would be horror-stricken at Ivy's behavior. The news that Delphinia had left the house surprised him, for it seemed not in keeping with her habits.

"Do you know where is she going?"

"I heard her say she plans to go to the local inns. I can't imagine the nature of her errand." Ivy shook her head, deep in thought. "For the first year I was here she rarely left the house. Within the last six months she rides on the moors more than she used to, but I have never known her to go into town for any errand she could send a servant to do."

"Perhaps it is some business on which she cannot send a servant," he suggested. "Could she be looking for someone?"

"Who?" Her eyes were very bright. "I intend to follow her. I wish you could come. What fun it will be!"

Concern rose within Nicholas. "I am not sure that is the wisest idea."

"Surely it is the best way to find out what she does with her time. Isn't that what we want to do?"

"It is, but it is your safety I'm thinking of. Your sister obviously has a secret mission she does not want you to know about." A sudden flash of inspiration made him more confident about her intention. "Take Stebbins with you. Should anyone ask, you can say I need provisions, that I had not planned on such a long stay. You'll need an excuse to spend time away so Delphinia won't suspect anything. That way we can make a real errand out of this adventure. I feel more at ease with that arrangement." He eyed her with admiration. "You are a most enthusiastic fellow conspirator, Lady Ivy."

Ivy could hardly contain that enthusiasm. "To town we shall go then. I ought to fix my hair, but there isn't time."

How unlike her sister she was, with her effervescent and impulsive nature. Or was she? Nicholas did not know either of them well enough to judge, although this sister's behavior seemed far easier to interpret. He wondered what Delphinia would think if she knew she were about to be followed.

"You don't think she's meeting that fellow Wainwright?" he asked, his tension rising at the prospect.

"I doubt it. There's something about him I don't trust. I don't understand why Delphinia does."

"Does she, or does she merely tolerate him?" Nicholas smiled, clinging to a weak hope within.

"Why else would she let him call?"

"I would certainly like to find out," he said determinedly.

"You're awfully curious about her," Ivy observed.

"There isn't much you miss, is there?" Her candid nature made him grin. He saw no point in being evasive with Ivy. "I admit I find your sister a most attractive woman. Anyway, I have nothing better to do, have I? Are you sure you will have no trouble following her?"

"Even from a distance it will be easy. She has a strawberry mare we cannot miss. Our father gave Rosie to her as a wedding present." She wrinkled her nose impishly. "Rosie remained with her longer than her husband."

"Perhaps Rosie was more loyal."

"It isn't hard to understand how that could happen," Ivy said emphatically, getting to her feet. "Delphinia can be so difficult. But enough of my sister." Her eyes twinkled. "Tell me where I can find Stebbins at this hour."

Nicholas gave her instructions on how to locate his valet, wishing fervently he might go with her rather than remain in this wretched bed. He watched as she set off with high hopes. If the plan backfired, Lady Delphinia would undoubtedly be furious with both of them. Perhaps, he thought ironically, it is better for us all if I take responsibility for this adventure.

He wondered how Lady Delphinia could be angrier with him than she already was, and hoped he would not have to find out.

Chapter Six

Delphinia's beloved mare Rosie cantered contentedly in the crisp air that hinted of April. Perched behind her on the seat of the trap, Delphinia directed her across the moors the short two and a half miles to Lynton. Where the road divided she took the sharp gradient that led into the twin village of Lynmouth below the cliffs. The drop to the bay was so alarmingly steep it took her breath away, but she managed to guide her horse safely to the bottom of the slope without either of them pitching forward.

The Rising Sun Inn rested near the convergence of the East and West Lyn Rivers. Delphinia alighted from her carriage and tethered Rosie securely before approaching the little inn. She paused nervously in the doorway, letting her eyes adjust to the darkness within, unsure who would be about this time of day. Five men by the hearth glanced up furtively at her arrival, then turned their backs to her. Respectable travelers passing through on legitimate business rarely lodged in this disreputable place. She was surprised to see the innkeeper making an effort to sweep the floor. Although his motions were careless, she realized, his full face was flushed from the effort.

"Good morning, Mr. Teasdale," she began.

"Morning, my lady," he greeted her perfunctorily.

"I have a question for you," she continued. "You know everyone in these parts. I'm looking for a Mr. Warren. Can you tell me where I might find him?"

The great fireplace had not been lit today, and she shivered in the inn's dark interior. The men by the fire who had been conversing in an undertone ceased their discussion, as if waiting to learn more about her business. Their interest struck her as sinister, but the cavernous, dimly lit room was just as likely to set her on edge. She wondered how many travelers, if any, were lodging upstairs.

The innkeeper looked at her for a long moment before he resumed his sweeping.

"I know the name. Used to have his mail delivered here. He'd stop in now and then and have a drink. Good customer."

The revelation excited Delphinia. Here was a promise of hope. There might still be a chance Warren was not a local dignitary after all. "Then you know him. What does he look like?"

He shrugged noncommittally. "Typical fellow, I'd say."

"Does he have a beard? A mustache? Is he tall?"

"Can't rightly recall if he had a beard."

"Did he lodge here? Did he receive much by way of the post?"

The innkeeper kicked at a patch of dried mud with the toe of his boot. "Don't really remember. He didn't lodge here."

Sensing reluctance on his part to say more, Delphinia tried to hide her frustration. Had Warren paid Teasdale to keep quiet? Because the innkeeper had a share in their business, she had to be careful questioning him so he would not suspect any ulterior motive on her part.

The innkeeper paused in his sweeping and leaned on his broom, as if dismissing her. "Don't know much more. Sorry."

"What do you know about him, Mr. Teasdale?" she asked in exasperation.

"I know Mr. Warren is a man who likes his privacy, my lady." His bluntness stopped her short as he gazed steadily at her. "As all men do. If you wish, I can tell him you were asking for him next time he comes by."

Delphinia took a deep breath. "Thank you, Mr. Teasdale, that will not be necessary," she answered evenly. "As it happens, I have a letter that needs to be delivered to him immediately. I will continue my search for him elsewhere."

She returned to her carriage and took the reins in hand, prepared to visit other inns in the region. If nothing else she had established Warren had received mail at the inn, though he had not lodged there. Why did he not get his mail through the regular post? Did he not want his whereabouts officially known? With such a significant role in their operation he must room nearby.

She decided to try the fisherman she had spoken with last week. Intent on her goal, she barely noticed the beauty of the Watersmeet Valley as she continued past its sylvan woods and glens. She jogged along in the cart until she came to a tiny cottage by the roadside where she recognized the fisherman's wife. The woman was walking alongside the fence in her small yard, a basket over her arm. Pulling Rosie up short, Delphinia inquired after her health and chatted for a few minutes before mentioning her desire to take a letter to the man who had once lived on the moors.

"Dearie me, I'd no idea he no longer keeps house there," the fisherman's wife said in surprise. "It's tough times now, it is. P'r'aps he's gone lookin' for work elsewhere."

Trying to hide her disappointment, Delphinia wished her and her husband well and proceeded on her way, refusing to be discouraged by the fact that Mr. Warren had been so close but had managed to slip away. She turned the trap northwest, away from a sharp descent in the valley where the land sloped to a treacherous marsh. On a mild day like this, Moorcombe Marsh seemed far less dangerous than it truly was.

Taking Rosie along the coast road, Delphinia passed the Valley of Rocks, its enormous prehistoric shapes towering over the scrub and heather. From her perch she could see wild goats grazing leisurely in the crags. She would have to be especially careful if she were to follow

Percy when he kept his assignation with Warren next Thursday. If they came by way of the marsh and the valley, the rocks and shadows that were so pastoral by day could be dangerously deceptive at night. She had no doubt Percy would not attempt a meeting of such significance in daylight.

The moorland that lay before her had turned to mud from the spring rains. Perhaps she would go as far as Parracombe, she thought, at the western edge of Exmoor, to the inn next to the River Heddon, since it was an ideal day for a ride.

Someone else must have the same idea, she mused, hearing the distant rumble of carriage wheels on the road behind her. Glancing back, she saw nothing but empty moors except for an occasional farmer and the wild ponies and red deer that grazed on Exmoor. The other carriage must be just below the crest of the hill her vehicle had just climbed. Perhaps one of the local squires had taken his family out for a day of enjoyment. Villages were so sparse on Exmoor that neighbors were few and far between. If it were not for the business at hand she might have waited to greet whoever rode behind her.

But the matter was too pressing to waste time this morning. Delphinia continued along the coast road, stopping in Kemacott and Martinhoe to inquire among the local residents for Mr. Warren. She was only mildly discouraged when the name was unfamiliar to them. If he were an outsider, she reasoned, he would probably stay at an inn rather than a private home.

Her search led her to Parracombe, where she asked, without success, about Warren and the Frenchwoman. Not only were they not registered at any of the local inns, but no one in any of Exmoor's tiny hamlets admitted to knowing any newcomers.

Feeling disheartened, she climbed back into the trap and turned Rosie homeward. She rode only a few minutes before realizing she had forgotten to leave her name with the innkeeper in case Mr. Warren should appear. Heading back along the muddy road, she reached the inn in time to catch a glimpse of the back of a young woman in the doorway talking with the innkeeper. The black curls beneath the stylish bonnet, the smart blue pelisse, and the ladylike stance jarred Delphinia with their familiarity.

She drew a sharp breath. Whatever was Ivy doing so far from home? Delphinia had not passed her on the road, nor did she see any familiar conveyance outside the inn. Her curiosity piqued, she decided to investigate. Since Ivy had not noticed her, Delphinia pulled the trap further up the road, stopping beyond a larger carriage where it would not be seen. She stepped down and slipped into the shadow of the inn. From this vantage point she could spy on her sister without being seen.

A minute later, a chaise from Briarcombe's own stable pulled around front from the innyard on the side. Her eyes widening with shock,

Delphinia watched as Ivy was assisted into the conveyance. Was that Stebbins riding with her sister? What were they doing here in Parracombe?

Emerging from the shadows, Delphinia returned to her carriage and watched in indignation as they headed out on the solitary road that led back across the moors. She was so certain she had not been detected, yet she was now equally as certain she had been followed. What was Ivy up to?

Delphinia waited until the chaise had pulled past the medieval church of St. Petrock before turning Rosie back toward Briarcombe, pulling at the reins with unreasonable anger. She had wanted to call at the Stag Hunters' Inn in Brendon on the way back, even though she doubted Warren would have crossed the border into Somerset. But her mood had changed so upon discovering she had been spied upon she could no longer think clearly.

That task would have to wait for another day. She would have a little surprise of her own waiting for Ivy at home.

* * * *

In the library at Briarcombe, Delphinia attempted to focus on settling household accounts at her desk, but her heart pounded with apprehension about the confrontation she knew was to come. Barely able to control her anger as she reconciled payment for local merchants, she hardly cared if the figures were correct or not in the face of her sister's deception. She had left the door open a fraction so she could hear Ivy upon her return. She wanted to question her while the knowledge of her treachery was fresh.

It was nearly three-quarters of an hour later when she heard the front door close quietly. She wondered how long it had taken Ivy to realize she had managed to return home before her sister.

"Hello, Sophy." She heard her sister greet the housekeeper in a subdued voice. "Is it one o'clock already? I was busy doing errands for Captain Hainsworth and lost track of the time. Has Delphinia returned?"

Planting herself firmly in the doorway, Delphinia hoped she would appear and sound as imposing as she felt.

"Yes, Ivy, Delphinia returned some time ago," she answered her sister directly, "and she is most anxious to speak with you."

Ivy whirled at the sound of her sister's voice, her bonnet dangling rakishly from the left side of her head, her cheeks flushed with what must be guilt.

Delphinia waited for Sophy to return to the servants' quarters before she continued. "When did you realize you had made a mistake?"

"Mistake?" Ivy said faintly. "I don't know what you mean."

Ivy's eyes widened in a pretense of innocence. Delphinia made a mental note to remind herself in future encounters how convincingly her sister assumed that beatific expression. "Why don't you come into the library so I can tell you?"

Once her sister had followed her into the room Delphinia slammed the door in a fury, making Ivy jump. "Your first mistake was coming after me this morning."

Ivy reddened. "I didn't—"

"And your second mistake is lying. I returned to the Parracombe Inn just in time to see you leave. The next time you play Bow Street Runner you might be a bit more subtle."

"I was running an errand for Captain Hainsworth," Ivy replied smartly, tossing her bonnet on a tabletop. "I resent the implication that I was sneaking about behind your back."

"Then what, precisely, were you doing? It was Father's chaise I saw at the inn."

"The captain asked me to get some provisions for him."

"And you had to go all the way to Parracombe for them? What did he need that we do not have here?" Ivy hesitated just long enough for Delphinia to pounce. "You were behind me the entire time, weren't you?"

This time Ivy had the grace to look just the slightest bit uncomfortable. "I came after you because I was concerned about you," she said distinctly. "What business could you have at the Rising Sun Inn? Everyone in the village knows it as Smugglers Inn. Who is this Mr. Warren you asked about?"

Delphinia was shaken. She had not expected Ivy to be so direct or to have learned so much. She had believed her sister to be so absorbed in her own amusements that she took no notice of her older sister's activities. Delphinia would have to be far more careful in the future.

"That is my business," she said, her tone deliberately cold. "I have no intention of discussing it with you."

She was relieved to see Ivy took her seriously, for disappointment clouded her face. Delphinia noted the tangled arrangement of curls left in the wake of the discarded bonnet.

"And just look at you with your hair all amuss," she said in a haughty tone. "It looks to me as if you were playing the coquette with the captain's valet."

"If I were playing a coquette with a valet, I wouldn't do so in an open carriage for all the world to see," Ivy said boldly. "Does it make you feel better to know that?"

"What does not make me feel better is the captain's atrocious influence on you." Delphinia assumed what she hoped was an air of great pomposity. "All this time I thought it was the captain in whom you were interested when it was really his valet for whom you had developed a *tendre.*"

To her astonishment Ivy let out a laugh so raucous it resounded throughout the library. The sound was most unladylike.

"Oh, come, you don't believe that anymore than I do," she challenged. "How could you? It's ludicrous."

Ivy wiped a tear of mirth from the corner of her eye in a gesture Delphinia did not find the least bit funny. Really, she thought, this generation was impossible. It was a blessing their mother had not lived to see how her younger daughter had turned out—or had not, as the case might be.

"We both know you are trying to force my attention elsewhere so you can change the subject," Ivy said patiently, once she had sufficiently tamed her giggling. "Why don't you just tell me what you were doing this morning?"

Now it was Delphinia's turn to blush. Her sister was trying to make her feel as if she had committed an act for which she must be called to account. With an effort she brought her anger under control and attempted to conquer her fear of discovery.

"There are many responsibilities in running an estate of which you know nothing," she sputtered. "There are also trivial things that must be done, things I took care of this morning."

"Then teach me those things so I may help you."

There was that plaintive tone again, behind the earnest emerald eyes. Ivy was an expert at coaxing the truth from people. For the briefest moment Delphinia wished she could share her burden with her sister. Then she thought better of it and collected herself, as she was used to doing.

"No, Ivy," she finished decisively. "There are many things that need not concern you right now. Your thoughts should be on London and your upcoming visit with Father and Aunt Rose and Aunt Tilly. I am still waiting for word as to when they will be ready to receive you. And," she added meaningfully, "I'll thank you not to follow me in secret again. If you want to ride with me, you need only to ask."

As usual, when she knew she had lost, Ivy's shoulders drooped with resignation, and her face assumed a look of lost interest. She sighed and fetched her bonnet from the table where it had landed.

"Isn't it about time you studied your French?" Delphinia suggested gently.

"Isn't it about time you changed the captain's dressings?" Ivy quipped. "I don't mind entertaining him, but I won't change his bandages. Such a practical skill will hardly increase my worth in London in a few weeks."

Never fear, Ivy, Delphinia thought, snapping the account book closed as her sister fluttered out the door. You will undoubtedly go far in society, for you have already learned to dissemble exceptionally well.

And now for you, Captain Hainsworth. She set off for his chamber, determined to get to the bottom of this charade.

* * * *

In the privacy of his room, Nicholas attempted valiantly to put pressure on his injured limb. Two weeks of immobility had left him restless. He was now determined to stand, whether his calf was ready or not. Although the ankle was still very tender, the lack of exercise was doing more harm than good. If ever he was to recover he might as well start now.

To his surprise, his feet supported him. He felt only a mild twinge in the lower leg. His balance, as he had expected, was somewhat clumsy, but it would return with time and practice. With one hand clutching the cane Delphinia had left for him and the other holding onto the bureau for support he managed to walk a few feet across the carpeted floor.

Hearing the now familiar footsteps ascending the stairs outside his door, although they seemed a bit more rapid than usual, he thought how much fun it would be to surprise Delphinia after he had made significant progress. He was not yet ready to give her the satisfaction of any sign that he was recovering. Moving as quickly as he could, he hooked the cane over the headboard and stumbled into bed, pulling his leg back under the sheets as the formidable footsteps grew closer.

A moment later she arrived, eyes flashing. She stood beside the bed rigidly, her hands balled into fists. "You have some answering to do, Captain."

He looked at her with wide-eyed pretense. "Have I?"

"Please explain to me the idea of sending your valet after me, in my father's carriage, with my sister at that. Exactly what was your intention?"

So she had figured it out. Nicholas wondered how she knew she had been followed, and what the consequences had been for her sister. Not knowing what else to do or how much Ivy had told her, he came instantly to the defense of his valet.

"Stebbins knows his place. Surely he could not have performed any outrage against your sister," he said, adding as an afterthought, "lovely as she is."

That idea seemed to anger her further. She glared at him with a malevolence he found almost appealing. He was pleased to see she possessed very human emotions after all. He actually relished the idea that he had upset her. He had sparked a trace of fire within her. Was it anger or envy?

"You know perfectly well that isn't what I'm implying."

"I had Stebbins check on the progress of the carriage repairs. They seem to be taking a long time. I know you find it difficult to believe, but I will not always be a bother to you, as I am now. One day soon I will be leaving."

He smiled as he spoke the words. There was a look of doubt in her expression, making him think that either she did not believe he would ever leave or that she did not consider him a burden. He hoped it was the latter.

"So you sent Ivy to investigate the situation," she went on.

"She seemed eager to be out-of-doors," he countered, "as I would be if I could. It's such a lovely day. I thought she might check to see that the job was being done properly."

"And what would my sister know of carriage repairs? It was not the focus of her study in the schoolroom. Your valet could have investigated Melcher's capability as a wheelwright without her help. The truth is, you sent them to follow me."

He tried to pretend amazement as he looked at her. There was no expression he could assume that would erase the suspicion from those delphinium-blue eyes that seemed to be all-knowing.

"Why would I have done such a thing?" he inquired.

"I've no idea, but I would certainly like to find out."

The asperity in her tone made Nicholas regret his part in the deception. He could no longer toy with Delphinia Marlowe's trust, as he had on her previous visits to his bedside. Her deep resentment made him wish he had not encouraged her sister to embark on such an excursion. Lying, he reflected, was the most effective chance he had of saving the situation, however.

"I suggested your sister accompany Stebbins because I did not want him to get lost," he said in apology. "It seemed harmless at the time. Please forgive me."

"No, Captain, I will not," she said severely. "There is no storm today. Stebbins could not possibly get lost unless he were a complete idiot. And as he has already been to see Melcher once, I doubt he is such a fool."

"I would hardly know about the weather," he confessed, grasping at straws and feeling guiltier by the moment, "confined as I am to this dismal room."

"You just told me what a lovely day you were missing." Making no attempt to hide her sarcasm, she snatched back the draperies, letting the thin sunlight filter into the room. "You said your ankle feels better, Captain. If that is truly how you feel, then it is time you made the effort to get back on your feet. I would be happy to assist you. I am reluctant to rush you, for I do not wish to cause further injury, but you must build up your strength. The sooner you are back on your feet, the sooner you will be on your way."

And that, he thought, sobering, would be a great relief to her. He knew he ought to feel the same, but after weeks of wishing to leave Briarcombe, he now felt unwilling to go.

"Now ease your legs carefully onto the floor," she ordered.

Delphinia stepped back modestly, standing as far from the bed as was proper and possible under the circumstances, while she waited for him to obey. It aggravated him that her anger had dissipated in her desire to accommodate his need to walk so she might hasten his departure.

"I am used to giving commands, Lady Delphinia, not taking them," he answered tersely, his patience finally wearing thin. "It was I who gave the command to follow Nelson, you may or may not be aware. It was I who chose the moment to enter the battle, even though I knew full well that by doing so I was jeopardizing the lives of everyone, including the powder monkeys."

She stared. "What have powder monkeys to do with this?"

"The young boys assigned to fetch the black powder and deliver it to the cannons have the speed and size needed to do the job. No one can take their place, you see. Kill a powder monkey, and you have crippled another ship's cannon. The enemy takes aim at the children—they at ours and we at theirs. It is one of the cruelest strategies of war, my lady. It was not a decision I relished, yet I made it nonetheless, and I live with the guilt every day of my life." He smiled bitterly. "Your charity work of taking care of me does not restore lives, does it? War is not something you reform, nor is health. If my ankle takes four weeks to heal, it takes four weeks. Some things are beyond your control, I am sorry to say."

She stood before him, pale and silent, her hands folded tightly together. Her emotions were unreadable, but judging by how tightly her lips were pressed together he guessed he had not only stunned and enraged her but touched something deep within her. He suspected her rage was not a thing he wanted to discover.

If she wanted him to walk again, he would make every effort to do so. Being mobile would at least enable him to follow her directly without placing the burden on Ivy. Yet he would have to excel at acting to make her believe he had not been practicing his walking skills.

He glanced in mock confusion around the room. "Now, as for exercising this ankle. Where did you leave that cane?"

"It's at the head of the bed," she murmured, barely raising her eyes from the floor but pointing it out with a gesture instead. "Do you think the cane will support you?"

"I doubt it will support me fully. It's a bit low. I may need to lean on your arm."

He smiled at her gently, expecting to win back her trust. The hardness in her expression told him it was not about to happen.

Her eyes were dark as she delivered her next challenge.

"So you are accustomed to living with guilt, are you?"

"I understand guilt, yes." He stared at her, unsure what she would say next.

"Surely you are not so vain as to believe guilt has selected you as its solitary beneficiary. Whether you choose to commit heartless acts has nothing to do with anyone but you, Captain. It is within your control and yours only."

She glanced down again, her mind apparently made up.

"You are not quite yourself today, Captain," she said in clipped tones as she turned to the door. "I shall return when you are feeling better."

"Lady Delphinia," he commanded. "Wait."

"No, I will not wait, Captain. Here in my home I am not accustomed to taking orders from anyone but myself."

It was too late to apologize, he realized with a sinking heart. She had already left the room.

Chapter Seven

Delphinia had finished Miss Austen's book and was looking in her library for another literary work to engage her mind when Sophy delivered a letter to her the following morning. She recognized the pale mauve vellum as Aunt Rose's stationery. The note had come from her father's London household in Park Lane.

"I believe this is just what I've been waiting for," she said expectantly, taking the envelope from her housekeeper.

"Yes, miss," Sophy said in a sad tone as she turned to depart. "But what will it mean for our young Miss Ivy?"

Delphinia knew that for months the talk among the servants had been Ivy's impending visit to London. With it coming so soon after the departure of their unexpected guests, the staff probably wondered how they would fill their days without Ivy to look after.

The missive, as she had hoped, was a warm invitation to Ivy to come as soon as possible to London where their aunts would be delighted to see her into Society. Delphinia was certain that as soon as her father and aunts had received the request they would have begun making plans for Ivy's arrival. Yet she was startled to find the contents somewhat contrary to what she had expected. The note temporarily diverted her from her seething anger toward Captain Hainsworth.

The great surprise was they had invited her as well.

She let the letter slip from her fingertips, flustered, barely noticing as it fluttered down and landed on the back of Brutus, who lay at her feet. Her spirits sagged at the idea of leaving Briarcombe.

It was true she had not seen Aunt Rose and Aunt Matilda in several years, as the note pointed out, but to her credit she had written them regularly. Surely that counted for something. While her marriage to a man far beneath her station had scandalized London, her aunts had continually expressed their affection for her throughout the most arduous of times. Delphinia had always appreciated their loyalty.

The thought of leaving her home filled her with a mixture of emotions that included fear and, conversely, hope. How would she be received? She had been to London only once following her marriage, having lived at Briarcombe since her father had granted her the use of the country estate. After her mother's death he hated to return to London even to visit. It had seemed a fitting place to consign a difficult daughter and son-in-law of whom he strongly disapproved.

With dismay, Delphinia realized she did not want to go to London. She was so opposed to the idea she felt briefly inclined to destroy the note before Ivy could see it and decide she liked the idea of a chaperone nearer her own age, even if, Delphinia thought darkly, it is the company of an older sister she ordinarily did not want to be with. The prospect of

Ivy alone with her aunts, as kind and entertaining as they were, and with her father, who was not necessarily either, made her reconsider the urge to toss the note on the fire.

Their father could be overbearing at times, even smothering. It was his intrusion into her own life that had made Delphinia marry as spontaneously as she had. Heaven forbid Ivy should make the same mistake, she thought with alarm. And Ivy was even more impulsive than Delphinia had been at eighteen.

She could not let Ivy face their family on her own. Who knew what might happen if she chose the wrong man but could not find a sympathetic, objective ear? Leaving Briarcombe meant Delphinia would also be leaving Captain Hainsworth, whether or not he was well enough to travel by then. Her aunts had indicated they would be ready to receive Ivy in a fortnight. Delphinia could think of no reason his ankle would not be mended by then.

I will be well rid of him, she told herself. After leaving his room yesterday she had slipped away to the sanctuary of her own, hurt and embarrassed, torn between a sadness that cut into her soul and a shame that plunged her into misery. She had shown undeniable rudeness to the Nettletons and to Mrs. Herbert. Now she had been thoughtless and unkind to Captain Hainsworth when his opinion of her genuinely mattered.

Ivy had been absolutely right. He was a decorated war hero, deservedly so. Were it not for her private venture and Percy's hold on her, she would never have treated him so. Why did she consider him such a threat? It was more than the risk of exposure. Soon, she told herself, he would be gone and his opinion of her would no longer matter. Prior to his arrival her days at Briarcombe had been predictable and orderly. Now not only her emotions but her life was in turmoil and disorder. She could not bring herself to study her emotions more closely than that.

She had learned the hard way that men were not to be trusted. In her experience men treated women the way that best served their own ends, with flattery often masking ulterior motives. Captain Hainsworth had given her no reason to believe he was any different. She owed him an excuse for her rude behavior. Yet she was not ready to submit to her better instincts and give him the apology he deserved.

Her meditative mood offering no solutions, she reached down to cradle the heavy face of the mastiff at her feet who responded by looking up and nuzzling her with his cold nose. She wondered why she had ever named him Brutus, until she remembered the first time she read Shakespeare's great play. She had thought Brutus as loyal as Caesar had, and coming on the heels of James's departure, the naming of her dog was a testament to the disillusionment she had felt at the time.

"No one is more misnamed than you, Brutus," she murmured, "for you are the only male who has never betrayed me."

* * * *

While Delphinia pondered her missive from London, Nicholas sat in his chamber perusing a letter Stebbins had brought. Nicholas's correspondence, also from London, gave him reason to think more seriously about the activities of his hostess.

The letter, written by a friend who had contributed his share of teasing when he learned Nicholas was paying a call in smugglers' country, advised him to take particular care during the long Devonshire evenings at the time of the new moon. Concern filled Nicholas as he read the account of a smuggling run unintentionally thwarted by a passing traveler who was killed when he stumbled upon it. The incident occurred in Ilfracombe, a few miles up the coast. His friend closed by saying he hoped the note would find Nicholas alive and not the unfortunate bypasser.

Struggling from his bed, Nicholas lumbered to the wardrobe and tucked the note inside his luggage so Delphinia would not see it. Ignoring the smugglers in St. Ives was one thing. Turning his back on a woman for whom he cared, a woman who might be endangering her life by the practice, was another matter altogether.

He tried to clear his conscience by justifying the unkind words he had hurled at her, but his guilt only increased as the day wore on. By late afternoon he fully regretted his words and hoped she would bring his dinner so he could apologize. But the tray was delivered by a servant who came and went without expressing the slightest concern for his health. He feared Delphinia would never want to return to his room, a prospect that left him feeling dismal.

He had never been so short-tempered with her. Yet she had provoked the rebuke with her desire to control everything within reach of her voice. While she was not an unreasonable woman, she would not listen to reason. Whatever secret she kept from the world influenced her behavior to the point where she no longer cared how people perceived her. She could be charming and conscientious in caring for the sick one moment while utterly rude and callous the next. It was the only explanation for her contradictory behavior. He did not believe Lady Delphinia Marlowe was hard-hearted. Hardheaded, perhaps, but very soft inside.

An annoying sense of duty nagged at him. The secret she protected might place her in real danger. If she were a smuggler he owed it to his country to expose her. Could he threaten to report her to the Crown, even if he did not intend to, or would such deception push her further away? He needed time to win her trust, but time was the one thing he did not have. People without trust were often victims of their past. Was it so with Delphinia? He detected no sadness due to her widowhood, as he might have expected. She had only mentioned her husband once.

That she once had a husband ignited a fierce jealousy within him. He could not deny his instant attraction to her. If he let his mother assume the task of selecting a wife, he would never find anyone like Delphinia. In thirty-seven years he had not felt as he did now. He had bedded other women purely for pleasure, but none had been suitable candidates to meet his mother while living up to her standards. Delphinia Marlowe, he suspected, was both.

How could he leave her? The answer was simple. He would stay until he learned whether or not she was guilty of smuggling. If she were the matter would be settled, for it would preclude any approval from his mother. How much easier his stay would be if Percy Wainwright were not in the picture. He was a cad indeed to suggest he possessed a thorough knowledge of Delphinia's upstairs chambers, implying a more intimate knowledge of the lady herself.

What did she see in such a man? For that matter, what did Wainwright see in this unfriendly, oddly beautiful woman? She was tall and strikingly attractive, with ravishing eyes that Nicholas would never grow tired of gazing upon. Yet most of the time she was unfashionably dressed, her hair unkempt. How much more magnificent she would be if she dressed to fashion as his sister did. He pictured the hands that had so carefully bandaged his wounds clad in elbow-length ivory gloves. An odd image, he thought, to pop into his mind at this particular moment.

What was he to do if she were in league with bootleggers? He wished he might get his hands on a copy of the *Times* to check the shipping schedules, departure times, and cargo listings. It might carry a mention of the Ilfracombe incident. He was familiar enough with the Bristol Channel and its waterways to estimate the regularity of ships and coves that might serve for smuggling. His knowledge of naval strategies would serve him well during this time when he had so little else to do.

Since Ivy had not visited, he supposed Delphinia had instilled a fear in the girl that would put a stop to any further spying. Captive as he was, he was no threat to her either. He would have to get back on his feet to make any headway in this investigation.

And he would have to do it on his own now, without any cooperation from Delphinia, since she refused to see him.

* * * *

Twilight passed into a gloomy night, and still she did not come. Raising himself onto the floor with the aid of the cane she had left him, Nicholas found walking difficult but not impossible. What else was there to do? Practice makes perfect, he told himself, struggling with his weak ankle. Lying on the rug at his bedside, Brutus thumped his tail at Nicholas's movement. At least he had one friend in this house. Apparently Brutus perceived him as less of a threat than his mistress did.

Nicholas persevered until after midnight, making tedious but steady progress. Abandoning hope that he would see Delphinia tonight, he blew out the lonely candle on his bureau. Pausing to rest, he heard the unfamiliar clopping of horses' hooves beneath his window, muffled but recognizable. His stride slow and clumsy, he made his way to the window with a sense of expectation. In two weeks at Briarcombe he had seen no cart approach the door.

But now, as he hid behind the draperies and peered at the courtyard below, he saw a wagon, drawn by a pair of horses, waiting outside the back door. His heart pounded. Was this the clue he needed to confirm his suspicions? The scene remained unchanged for perhaps ten minutes, until the door opened and the lantern light revealed two shadowy figures emerging from the house. A pair of men carried a barrel-shaped object covered by a blanket.

Unless my eyesight is going that is most definitely a keg, he thought. Most likely a tub of brandy. He shrank back into the darkness, his eye trained on a procession of men who came and went. There appeared to be five men altogether who loaded the barrels into the wagon before draping a blanket securely over their load.

What Nicholas saw next chilled him. The man who had been directing the operation stepped toward the door. The lantern glow revealed a guarded expression on the face of Percy Wainwright. In words too quiet for Nicholas to hear, Wainwright spoke to someone in the doorway. As the figure emerged into the light he saw it was none other than Delphinia herself.

Nicholas felt torn between triumph and regret. His heart tightened as he waited for a sign of affection on Wainwright's part. But the exchange was brief and businesslike, and after a moment the five men settled themselves in the cart and drove off, with Percy holding the reins. Nicholas remained by the window, watching Delphinia who waited until the men had cleared the hill before she withdrew into the house.

As he slid between the bedcovers Nicholas struggled with the confusion rushing through him. Tonight did not prove conclusively that she was a smuggler, he conceded. She might share some legitimate business interest with Wainwright. But why conduct a transaction like the scene he had just witnessed so late at night, unless the act required cover of darkness? Her actions were consistent with what he knew of smuggling. Wainwright's men would most likely help distribute the goods. And the smuggled items must be hidden in the cellar, no more than two floors below him.

Filled with grave doubts about Delphinia's integrity, Nicholas did not sleep that night. First thing tomorrow, he vowed, I shall work on improving my strength so I can escape this place.

When sleep finally came he thought no more about illegal trafficking.

Instead his head swam with fitful fancies about the dangers Delphinia faced. He awakened the next day to the depressing thought that her activities should not matter to him, for his mother would never find her suitable anyway.

* * * *

It was late that night when Delphinia mounted the silent stairway to her chamber, realizing the entire day had passed without her paying a visit to Nicholas. In the privacy of her room a heaviness pressed on her heart as the need to apologize to him gnawed at her conscience.

What would she be left with when this episode of her life was over? Would there be anything worth remembering other than the few years with Ivy? With only Brutus for company she changed into her nightgown and took her hairbrush in hand as she prepared for bed. At least her dog had remembered the source of his bed and board and had finally left Captain Hainsworth's side to return to her.

Gazing out the window toward the dark moors, she could see nothing. Her seven years in Exmoor, she reflected, had been bizarre by anyone's calculations. A life dictated by the timing of the tides and by the phases of the moon. A life spent in darkness.

Her walking must have disturbed Brutus, for the mastiff rose and scratched at the door, looking to her for confirmation. With a murmured acknowledgment she opened the door and watched him make his way eagerly out her door and down the hall to Nicholas's door where he paused to scratch.

"Even you have switched loyalties, Brutus," she whispered as if it were an accusation. "You've turned out like all the rest."

Feeling miserable, she closed her bedroom door to shut them both out, unwilling to assist Brutus in his betrayal. Before Nicholas had come Brutus tolerated her nocturnal activity without such restlessness.

Returning to the window, Delphinia brushed her hair with slow strokes. Until now she had assumed remaining at Briarcombe was what she wanted. Bitterness had sustained her for so long she had never allowed herself the chance for a life beyond this one.

Yet these days had been among the most significant of her life. This single fortnight, in which she had been forced to entertain unwanted visitors before the first drop of the season. When she had feared the local operation might be exposed. When she had to keep up the pretense of indifference before the guest down the hall, whose presence made her feel as she had not felt in years. Like Brutus, her own feelings were changing.

She could not blame Brutus for preferring Nicholas. She blushed as she recognized the same desire in herself. Nicholas Hainsworth fascinated her with his masculine physique, his naval prowess, and his easygoing acceptance of his physical plight.

Having been on her own so long, she considered herself too self-sufficient to need a man, yet she did not think she would mind being his wife. She smiled involuntarily as she thought how much her father would have liked Nicholas. But she could not deny the reality that once his condition improved he would move on and out of her life. Then the tides would again rule her existence.

Was she ready to say good-bye to Nicholas? He was the first man to have looked upon her with kindness since she had parted from James. He made her yearn for a happiness she did not know she missed. Events were following their proper course, she convinced herself, as she pinched out the candle beside the bed and crawled beneath the counterpane. Soon he would be gone and life would return to normal, and it would all be for the best.

Delphinia was stunned by the overwhelming resistance she felt at the thought of her life returning to what it had been. She stared up at the suggestion of a moon behind the dense clouds. The next drop was less than two weeks away. Then she and Ivy would be off to London.

She whirled away from the window, startled when she heard a thud outside her bedroom door followed by a groan. The sound seemed to come from the depths of someone's soul, and it made her jump to her feet. She snatched her robe from the armoire and pulled it on hastily.

Throwing open the door, she was horrified to see the prone form of Captain Hainsworth on the hall carpet, his legs stretched out awkwardly beneath him. He lay still, her mother's cane to one side.

"Nicholas!" she cried, dropping down beside him, forgetting all pretense of formality. "Are you all right?"

He did not respond immediately. Dear God, she thought in desperation, I have been so anxious to be rid of him, and now he has fallen and done who knows how much damage? She could not imagine what notion had prompted him to try to walk as far as the hallway. He must be far more anxious to leave her care than she had realized. She slipped her arms about his shoulders and turned him over with great care.

He managed to rise unsteadily on one elbow. "Lady Delphinia," he said in a low voice, "might I ask your assistance in helping me to stand?"

"Of course, don't be silly."

"Silliness is something I am not often accused of." His words came with great effort, and she realized with some guilt that his ankle must pain him severely. "Thank you for your assistance. My mother will be most obliged to you for your efforts."

Carefully slipping her arm about him, Delphinia tried to avoid the areas where he had been most seriously bruised. She held him to her as she struggled into a standing position while balancing his weight. He gripped a side table for support and pulled himself to his feet in a motion that was less than graceful, but it succeeded in getting him upright. Once he was on his feet she was reluctant to let go for fear he might fall again. She gazed up into his face, not far above hers.

That lock of burnished gold hair tumbled rakishly across his forehead, just as it had when she had first seen him lying on the foyer floor. He was studying her intently, as if trying to make out her reasoning. Did he truly think she would not help him? Surely he could not think her so heartless. His eyes locked with hers in a lengthy gaze she thought must be deliberate.

"You called me by my name," he said softly.

Even enemies have Christian names, she reminded herself, drawing her gaze away. And he was certainly the enemy. Perhaps one day he would be able to help her, but tonight was not the time.

"Your room is this way, Captain." She felt her cheeks flame and felt foolish at her feeble method of assistance. Obviously he knew the way to his room, but she needed to respond to get past the intensity of the moment.

Lowering her arm slightly to his waist, she attempted to turn him discreetly about and support him as she helped him to his room. His weight was heavier than she had expected, probably from muscle earned in his years at sea. His arm, heavy yet gentle, reached around her shoulders, his fingers smoothing the hair that flowed unrestrained about her neck. The sensation filled her with a longing she had not felt in years, a feeling she tried to deny but had to endure as they moved slowly and silently down the corridor to his chamber.

Keeping him steady, Delphinia assisted him with great caution to his bed where she released her hold as he dropped onto the blankets. He looked at her directly. In his eyes she saw an expectancy that frightened her. She took a step backward.

"Goodnight, Captain," she said softly, flashing him a brief smile. "I would suggest from now on you limit your walking attempts to daylight hours."

Chapter Eight

With careful precision, Stebbins set another pebble on the flat part of the stone wall and stepped aside swiftly. Within seconds, a bullet whizzed by him, shattering the tiny rock.

Nicholas lowered his pistol to his side.

"Not bad," he said with satisfaction, "for a man who hasn't spent more than two hours at a time out of bed in the last two and a half weeks."

"Good show indeed, sir," Stebbins agreed. "Shall I set up another?"

Nicholas considered. "No, that's enough target practice for today. Let's leave it at that."

Taking a deep breath to help him regain his balance, Nicholas lowered himself onto the low stone wall surrounding the little garden. With a wagging tail, Brutus came to lay by his side. Beneath the weak afternoon sun, Nicholas gazed through the low-hanging branches of the apple tree overhead at the rolling moorland that stretched for miles. He wondered if Delphinia came here often during the summer when it would be in full bloom. It hardly mattered, for he would not be here to see her if she did.

As he set down his pistol, he thought how much stronger his ankle was a mere three days after his fall in the corridor outside Delphinia's room. Involuntarily, his thoughts strayed to the gentle pressure of her arms about him. Despite his physical pain he had been moved by a more powerful emotion. The pain of knowing he would soon be forced to leave her behind filled him with an anguish he did not fully understand.

He had been tempted to pretend the following morning that his ankle had been more severely injured in his ungainly fall than it really was. Doing so would give him an excuse to linger. Although she had deceived him, he could not lower himself to lie to her. She had an excuse. His safety did not depend on deception as hers did. It was better, he reflected, that he leave as soon as possible. If indeed she were a smuggler, he would feel obligated to expose her. He was not convinced that he could.

Hearing a rustling in the leaves behind him, he turned in time to see Ivy Herrick approach the stone wall and take a seat on the other side. She faced him curiously, her deep green cloak spreading out behind her.

"The shots drew me to my window," she said with a smile. "I've been watching you at target practice."

"Then you must have noticed that I took several early shots from this wall where we are sitting," he admitted. "My strength seems to be returning gradually, if not in leaps and bounds. Give us a moment, Stebbins, will you?"

On command his manservant moved discreetly to the far side of the garden.

"Delphinia was so incensed that I followed her I did not dare to come to your room for a time," Ivy admitted. "I followed her to various local inns and discovered she was inquiring for a Mr. Warren."

"Warren," Nicholas said meditatively. "Does the name mean anything to you?"

Ivy shook her head. "No, and I know all the local families."

"Perhaps that explains why she was looking for him at an inn," Nicholas suggested. "Maybe he is not a local man."

"Anyway, it can hardly matter who he is, for I shall not be here much longer." She smiled wanly. "We have received word from our aunts and our father that I am to journey to London with Delphinia in another couple of weeks."

"With Delphinia?" he repeated in surprise.

"Yes, it was a shock to her as well," Ivy said wryly. "She had not planned on going, but Father has requested her presence at our home, and so that is that."

"I will be seeing London before long as well, I suppose. Perhaps neither of us shall get to see how it all turns out here."

Absently he petted the head of the mastiff at his side. He had no doubt Delphinia was a smuggler, but he was reluctant to tell her sister for fear she might cancel plans for her come-out. While Ivy had done her part and paid for her courage with Delphinia's wrath, smuggling was far too dangerous an operation for an eighteen-year-old who could not keep a secret.

"There was a time I couldn't wait to return to London," Ivy continued with a sad smile. "Now life has become far too exciting to want to leave Briarcombe."

Brutus leaned heavily against Nicholas, his tail wagging lazily in the presence of someone he had come to consider a friend. It would be hard enough to leave the dog. It would be far more painful to leave the woman herself.

"I understand how you feel," Nicholas said. "But I would not be surprised if you forget all of it once you immerse yourself in London society and meet someone special."

She brightened visibly at his words. "How different London will be from Exmoor. My neighbors here have been my lifeline to the world for so long." She breathed a sigh of anticipation. "I cannot wait to visit the Opera House at Covent Garden and the Lyceum Theatre. I am so anxious to meet and marry someone wonderful. I hope to meet a man with flair. Father expects me to marry someone stuffy like himself."

"Stuffy perhaps, but respectable," he reminded her, amused. "With talk like that it is no wonder your sister worries about you."

"I appreciate the fact that Delphinia does not want me to choose a partner in haste, as she did, and marry the wrong man."

Nicholas absorbed this bit of information with interest. Did Delphinia feel she had chosen the wrong man? Perhaps it was only Ivy who felt that way. He would have to pursue this later.

"Choosing a spouse takes a great deal of forethought and consideration," Ivy continued. "It is not a decision one should take lightly."

Nicholas winked at her. "Why do you think I have waited so long?"

"I have no idea," she replied bluntly, "but I do not intend to wait as long as you. If I am fortunate I shall be married before the Season is out. Oh, I almost forgot." Ivy pulled an envelope from the pocket of her skirt and handed it to him. "This came for you. It provided me with a perfect excuse to visit you here. It is the only way I dare go anywhere without a chaperone these days. Delphinia is so concerned for my reputation."

Ivy finished with a dramatic flourish of her arm, her expression a mixture of pity and disgust.

Nicholas, noting the envelope was not franked nor was his name written on the outside, tore open the crude missive. The crabbed handwriting was that of Melcher, the wheelwright in Lynton to whom his carriage had been taken for repairs. The message within said his carriage would be ready by the end of the week.

He crumpled the note savagely. Damnation! Melcher had originally predicted the repairs would require great time and money. Glumly, Nicholas realized he had paid the man too well. The carriage was almost ready to travel, and his ankle was nearly healed. The two factors together might defeat his desire to remain at Briarcombe. To get away as soon as possible, oddly enough, was what he had wanted in the beginning. That was no longer the case.

"Is it bad news?" Ivy asked, watching his expression.

"Nothing serious." He folded the note and slipped it into his pocket as a thought occurred to him. Smiling, he proceeded to lie. "Melcher says carriage repairs will take longer than expected. I might be required to stay here after all."

"How unfortunate for you," she sympathized. "You have made London sound ever so much more interesting than Exmoor, no matter what my sister is up to. At any rate, it is time I return to my packing."

As Nicholas watched Ivy make her way back to the house on stone steps set into the hillside, he savored his plan. Melcher obviously responded when money beckoned. He would bribe the wheelwright to delay the restoration of the axle. He would send Stebbins today with a note and a tidy sum.

Now he could add bribery to his questionable allegiance to the Crown. His disloyalty paled next to Delphinia's treachery, if she were indeed guilty of smuggling. He had not the heart to expose her to the law even if he ought to. He had come to realize how much he needed her just when he feared he could not win her.

He had to learn the truth about Lady Delphinia Marlowe. He looked back at the stone and timber-framed manor house on the hill, the waning sunlight reflecting off its mullioned windows. He still suspected the house harbored a smuggler, yet he no longer had any need to suspect his own feelings, for he knew precisely how he felt. He had fallen deeply in love with her.

* * * *

With assistance from Stebbins, Nicholas painstakingly climbed the hillside steps to the house. By the time he reached the foyer, he found his strength had not waned as he had expected. Dismissing his valet with instructions to deliver the note and funds to the wheelwright in Lynton, he found himself alone in the foyer, surprised how quiet it was.

He rested a moment across from an oil painting of a spaniel on the far wall, wondering if the dog had belonged to Delphinia. Not a soul had passed through the foyer in the few minutes he had spent wandering about. All busy with dinner preparations, he guessed. Perhaps this moment offered a good opportunity to do a bit of investigating on his own.

With the cane supporting him, he inspected the family portraits that lined the foyer walls and the graceful porcelain vases on the tables. The accessories exemplified wealth and taste. It seemed odd that not a single portrait appeared in any public area of the house of a man young enough to be Delphinia's late husband. He wondered how serious a mistake Delphinia had made in marrying that there was no apparent portrait of her deceased husband in her home.

He glanced about the empty room swiftly, possibilities racing through his mind. In a home the size of Briarcombe a smuggler would be likely to conceal stolen goods in the cellar. He doubted Delphinia would have broken tradition. This was the perfect opportunity to investigate.

He followed a corridor off the entry hall that presumably led to below ground offices and storage areas. He imagined the cellar here would be a rambling combination of odd-sized rooms like that of his own estate, Tregaryan, since the two houses had been built in neighboring counties albeit probably decades apart. He managed his way awkwardly down a rustic flight of steps, their construction appearing to be among the oldest of the house.

In the dim light at the bottom of the stairs he could make out a shelf with a supply of candles, kitchen crockery, and other household goods. If his suspicions were correct, this was the area where he was most likely to find what he was looking for. Somewhere among these rooms he would find a collection of casks filled with brandy.

Quickly and silently he made his way through the maze of rooms off the main pathway of the large downstairs area. While most doors were open, the doors that were closed were unlocked, and the rooms beyond contained nothing more suspicious than preserving jars and children's playthings from an earlier age. He looked about with frustration. The clutter was remarkably dull and similar to what he saw in his own home.

He froze when he heard a rustling sound. A distant dull thud from some wooden object followed the brief silence. The closing of a lid perhaps? The rustling resumed. Assuming he had not been heard, he deemed it safe to proceed.

Holding his breath, Nicholas stepped lightly across the ancient gravel floor. He lifted the cane so its telltale tap would not betray his presence and slipped around a corner toward a lone open door. Peering inside cautiously, he spotted a slight movement beside a large old trunk that proved to be the blue muslin of a woman's dress.

Delphinia paused just beyond the doorway with her back to him. She held up a folded and wrinkled document to the faint candlelight, as if trying to make out the writing. Before he could withdraw in silence she sensed his presence and whirled about with a gasp. A cry of relief escaped her as she sank onto the lid of the closed trunk.

"You startled me," she said breathlessly. "I did not know who was there."

Nicholas gave her a tentative smile. Her reaction eased his tension while confirming his suspicions. She had reacted with guilt at being discovered in the cellar rather than with anger at the fact that he had trespassed. Her behavior made him wonder what sort of wrongdoing could make her react so oddly.

"No wonder you wear old clothes if you spend your time down here," he said. "It's rather dusty, isn't it?"

He had expected her anger to surface the first moment she realized he had strayed where he did not belong. Strangely, she seemed more preoccupied than outraged as she stood and then bent to collect the papers that had scattered about the floor when she sat on the trunk so suddenly. He noticed a brass plate attached to the trunk that bore the initials J.W.M. Marlowe, he guessed. Were these her husband's belongings?

"Cellars can be inconvenient when one is searching for something," he said awkwardly.

"Yes," she agreed, "especially since I have still not found what I was searching for."

Her discouraged tone raised his curiosity about what she had been seeking.

"Was J.W.M. your husband?" he asked gently.

The reference to the trunk seemed to bring her to her senses. "Yes, the trunk belonged to James."

She resumed her seat in a protective gesture. Over her shoulder

Nicholas was startled to see a familiar object lying on a side table. He recognized the hat with its broad dark brim as the one he had seen her wearing on the moors.

"There must be many objects here that are familiar to you." Casually he approached the table, taking the soft hat in his hand. "This, for instance. It's the hat you wore on the moors."

She colored slightly as she glanced at the headgear. "Don't be absurd. It's Percy's hat. He left it here."

"Does he visit your cellar often?" Giving her a look of mock surprise, Nicholas could not repress a laugh. "He might well have left it, but it certainly looked more flattering on you."

Trapped in an obvious lie, she glared at him in silence and turned away, her lips pressed tightly together. Being forthright, he realized, would get him nowhere. How could he break down her defenses? How did one open a closed heart? He was painfully aware of her proximity and of the fact that no one in the house knew they were together in the cellar, unchaperoned.

"I only want to help you, Delphinia."

Nicholas debated how to convince her of his sincerity and decided on what was perhaps a risky but effective method. Certainly he must move with care in order not to injure himself further. If he did, he mused, it would give him more time to remain at Briarcombe to investigate his suspicions regarding its lovely mistress.

Lowering himself to one knee beside her, he reached out and ran his forefinger lightly along her cheek, ignoring the twinge in his ankle. The gesture was just unexpected enough to remind her of his presence. She drew back sharply and stood again, her cheeks flaming, her fingers pressed to her face as if his touch had burned her.

"Your sister told me you will be leaving for London shortly," he said softly. "Were you looking for something you needed for your journey?"

When she turned back to him he saw she was pale. "Yes, I-I had come downstairs to retrieve some clothes."

Nicholas did not believe her for an instant, but he allowed her a graceful escape from an awkward situation.

"Do you look forward to leaving?" he asked.

"No." A look of misery flooded across her delicate features. "No, I would rather remain here. It appears I have no choice but to go."

"What is it you fear?" Nicholas spoke quietly, not wishing to frighten her.

Her lower lip quivered. She averted her face, but not before he was sure he had seen tears welling in her eyes.

"It has been so long since I was in London," she confessed, her voice breaking. She quickly steadied herself. "I do not know what I will find, whether I still have friends or not. And Ivy's future is a concern.

She is so impetuous. She must be careful to find someone who measures up to her own high standards."

"As you did not," he suggested gently.

She looked at him, her eyes misty. "That's just it. She is so like I was at her age. All she knows of men is the false side Percy presents to her."

"I think she is well aware of Percy's failings," he reassured her, amazed by her candor and relieved to hear from her that she did not pine for her deceased husband. "She watches you quite carefully. She may have sharper instincts than you think."

"I hope she is more intelligent than I was," Delphinia said defiantly. "She has not seen much of life out here."

"That is why she is anxious to spread her wings and sample life. With you as her example I doubt she will make the same mistakes. She seems mature for her age and has the ability to be a charming hostess, which will make her an asset as a wife. Are you sure you know what she wants?"

"I am her sister." Her tone was defensive. "But she is leaving so soon. There is never time enough. I wish our lives were not so controlled by factors we cannot change."

There it was again, that fear of factors beyond her control. Her plaintive speech, combined with the soft candlelight reflected in her eyes and on her lips, revealed a vulnerability Nicholas had not seen in her before. He wanted to reach out to her again, but knew he could not. Only his concern for her reputation and the alarm she would most certainly feel at his advances kept him from drawing her into his arms.

"Those who live with unhappiness learn to find pleasure in small things," he countered softly. "I believe your sister will make a genuine love match when she goes to London. Not everyone is a victim of life's vagaries, Lady Delphinia."

His words apparently flustered her, for she collected her faculties and retrieved the papers she had set aside. "It is rather presumptuous of you, Captain, to suggest Ivy has been unhappy. I have tried to protect her from the kind of unhappiness I have known." She turned toward the staircase. "It is high time we return upstairs."

Clearly the spell was broken. And just when they were getting to know each other, he thought regretfully. Perhaps he had gotten to know her too well.

"Aren't you forgetting something?" Unable to resist, he indicated the table behind her. "Won't you be needing your hat?"

Taking up her candle, she looked him squarely in the eyes, giving him the inevitable answer he knew he deserved.

"Captain Hainsworth," she said flatly, "while you are a guest in my house, perhaps you will be so kind as to refrain from trespassing where you do not belong."

* * * *

In the privacy of her room Delphinia tried not to think of her encounter with Nicholas as she prepared for her night's excursion. Tonight was the opportunity she had waited for, the night Percy was to meet Mr. Warren. She waited until about eight, when darkness had settled over the moors, before preparing to leave home. At last I shall meet him for myself, she thought with satisfaction.

Her visit to the cellar had turned up nothing further that would help her expose Percy for the blackguard he was. But she had discovered numerous garments that had belonged to James, clothing as black as the night that loomed before her. With them she would assemble a disguise for her jaunt across Exmoor.

She topped the black trousers and jumper with a matching greatcoat she hoped Percy would not recognize. The bound hair and baggy clothes covered all traces of femininity, giving her a look of anonymity. She would have to be careful to avoid Nicholas now that he was on his feet and able to get about.

The reminder threw her off her guard momentarily. Nicholas Hainsworth presented a new challenge to her emotions. The fact that he had come to matter deeply to her was a realization she had been unwilling to face. She invariably looked for faults in men, but she could not forget how pleasurable it had felt to put her arms about him when he had fallen and needed her aid. She had not wanted to let go. She had confided in him about Ivy. And she had considered telling him her darkest secret, something she had vowed she would never do.

What would he think of her position with the operation? The idea of revealing her role to him shamed her deeply. He would undoubtedly turn her over to the authorities. To think she had gone to such lengths to protect her father and sister, only to risk the possibility of ending up in Australia for her efforts with the worst of her countrymen, perhaps with Percy as her closest acquaintance.

If Nicholas was an agent of the Crown, would he help her at this point? Would he even believe her? She did not consider answers to her questions. She could not allow her life to become complicated by her heart. Nothing must upset the case she was building against Percy. She would not share her knowledge with anyone until Ivy was safely launched in Society. Once her sister's ship had sailed, she reasoned, it would be smooth sailing for her as well.

The last time she had looked, Nicholas was in his room writing letters and Ivy in hers preparing for her trip. Delphinia set off for Percy Wainwright's cottage in Martinhoe, confident no one would follow her tonight.

* * * *

The night was colder than normal as she slipped silently along the coast road from Lynton to Woody Bay. She tightened the oversized greatcoat about her neck against the rising wind, hoping the raised collar would help to disguise her appearance further. A sinister feeling in the quiet darkness pervaded her senses and kept her on edge.

It is the nature of my mission, she told herself. So much depended upon her learning the identity of the mysterious Mr. Warren. Because Percy had expressly forbidden her to search out their business partner, she felt an urgency to meet the man whose decisions controlled her life.

To her right the relentless sea reclaimed the shoreline, the pounding of the waves muted in the distance and the stillness of the night. Although nearly half the moon was visible, so often the ghostly orb slipped behind clouds that it offered no light at all, which was the way she preferred it. Her habits had made her accustomed to getting around in complete darkness.

Once she reached Martinhoe it was easy enough to hide in the bushes in the lane below the cottage. She watched as a light was extinguished and Percy emerged from the house, her acute night vision revealing his every movement. Her well concealed position in the shadows of hedgerows made it possible for her to follow him without being spotted as he began the walk back along the path she had just trodden.

With her skill at maneuvering her way in the dark, she managed to maintain a comfortable distance without losing him. Convinced she had not been detected, she watched from a stand of oaks on a far hill as Percy opened the door to the Rising Sun Inn. Light flooded the doorway before he stepped inside and plunged the innyard into darkness again. Delphinia fancied that even from a distance she could hear the laughter and shouting of the men within.

And now I shall wait, she thought. I will keep my eye on the smugglers' tavern while I decide what to do next. The wind rose sharply, prompting her to pull her coat collar still higher about her throat. Would Percy and Warren meet at the inn, or would they go elsewhere? No doubt Percy would have a few drinks to quench his thirst before he would be seen again. The door opened once to admit another pair of men before closing into shadow. She crouched in the scrub of the hillside, watching for some sign of activity.

To her surprise she only waited perhaps fifteen minutes before the door opened again. She sat up alertly. She was sure it was Percy leaving the inn. Another man she did not recognize walked beside him. Delphinia tensed, rising from the painfully hard ground.

She heard the men laughing in coarse, low tones. Can this be our Mr. Warren? she thought skeptically. Somehow she doubted it. He was the drunker of the two, judging by his weaving gait. Perhaps he was one of Warren's henchmen who might lead her to her destination. Keeping the pair in sight as they headed through the wooded hillsides toward the moors, she followed as closely as she dared.

Sobered by the night air, the men dropped their voices as they continued west through Lynton. Delphinia found she needed to hurry to keep pace and not lose sight of them. The wind lashed her with the sting of a whip as she tracked Percy and his companion into the hollow vale behind the cliffs known as the Valley of Rocks. There, amidst the crags and brambles, they disappeared into the shadows.

Delphinia was filled with sudden apprehension. The breeze was playing tricks on her. Her senses were ordinarily so acute, but now she could hear nothing but the insistent wind on the moors, making her lose her bearings. Menacing shapes, dark and grotesque, loomed above the heather and scrub of the valley like giants, all overpowered by the massive Castle Rock. Often on fair days she had scaled the rock and gazed out over the Bristol Channel. Exposed as she was on this rocky crest, she did not have the advantage of clear vision. She kept low as she retreated into the gloom, grabbing onto lichened rock to maintain her balance.

The clouds shifted, casting a pale light across the valley before darkness enshrouded the land again. She was relieved to see a slight movement ahead, but she could only make out one shadow where there should have been two. She tensed, snagging her hand on a thorny evergreen.

Why had Percy decided to go through the Valley of Rocks? Where was his companion? There were so many hiding places among the shadows, yet so few would protect her while she was moving. She would have to run from one to the next, hoping Percy would not glance over his shoulder the moment she did so.

The bleak mist of the sheltered hillside offered no protection as she stumbled through the bracken, wondering how to proceed. She ran with uncertain steps, feeling an unnatural terror even in familiar territory. She had traveled this vale many times after dark, but now it was different. Brambles rustled with a ghostly life, and stunted trees cast hideous shadows.

Why had she been so foolish as to venture out here alone? There was not even a single goat in the crags, as there was in daylight, to hear her if she were to scream. Tonight the valley was haunted and still, deserted but for the two figures she was trying to avoid who moved through this hollow somewhere. And to think Nicholas and Ivy were busy at home where they were safe, not even wondering about her whereabouts. She hesitated, briefly disoriented.

What was it Nicholas had told her? Some things were beyond her control whether she liked it or not. This was one of those things, she thought with an involuntary shiver.

The shadowy figure up ahead moved quickly behind a rock and vanished. Panic swept over her. Where had he gone? Should she wait until she caught sight of him again, or make her move now? This was a foolhardy plan, she thought with growing dismay. But it was too late to turn back.

She pressed perhaps twelve yards further into the valley before she stopped again. In the shadow of the great rock known as the Devil's Cheese Knife she sought cover.

Without warning she felt herself grabbed from behind. A hand closed around her throat, pinning her against the hardness of the boulder. She could feel the Devil's Cheese Knife at her back, sharp and unyielding, as her cheek scraped a jagged edge of rock. Fingers grasped her jaw, and Percy's face came slowly into view.

She quivered beneath his grasp. "Percy," she whispered. "Please—"

He emitted a low laugh that sounded more like a growl in her ears. His voice was cold and threatening.

"Now listen, my dear, Jack and I are going to visit Mr. Warren, and we are going alone. I warned you once already." His hand, still at her throat, had not released its grip. She swallowed hard, unable to catch her breath as he said, "This is not a place for women, Delphinia. There are too many misfortunes that could befall you out here."

While one hand pressed her throat against the rock at the back of her head the other moved suggestively to her waist, his fingers starting to work their way up her torso. Furiously, she thrust his hand from her. She would die here on the moors before she would allow him to touch her in such a way.

"I thought so," he said in a low tone. "You'd rather be with the good Captain. I suggest you run along home where you belong before you end up in serious trouble. You wouldn't want to end up like James's last girlfriend, would you?"

He released Delphinia roughly, shoving her to one side. She stumbled against the monolith and fell to her knees with a moan. Regaining her balance, she struggled to her feet and staggered away frantically, seeking safety in the shadows.

Chapter Nine

The next morning Delphinia was almost afraid to look in the mirror. Her reflection, when she found the courage to face it, was just as she had expected. Her cheekbone shone brightly with the swollen imprint of her harsh encounter with nature, the bruise a mottled black and blue seamed with a slash of red where the rock had cut her face. She looked as though she had been fighting, she thought. Whatever would she tell her sister and her staff?

She thought of Percy's words. You wouldn't want to end up like James's last girlfriend, would you? Her husband had thought nothing of having dalliances with other women even after they were wed. Most were women she had been able to forget easily. His last paramour had been the exception. She thought of Annie, buried in an unmarked grave on the edge of the property, and shuddered.

She skipped breakfast and spent part of her morning in the stable, where the grooms were so busy she hoped they would not notice her injury. If she took Rosie out riding she would not have to offer any explanations until her return. The bruise would hardly heal itself within a matter of hours, but the ride would give her time to concoct a believable excuse.

She had just had Rosie saddled and was leading her into the stable yard when she caught sight of Captain Hainsworth lumbering toward her with the help of her mother's cane. While she was not prepared to answer his questions regarding her bruises, she could not help noticing how handsome he looked in his fawn breeches, clean shirt, and tailored waistcoat.

A familiar longing tugged within her as he acknowledged her with a wave. She smiled awkwardly at him. From a distance he might not be able to see her clearly enough to distinguish the nasty discoloration. Turning her injured cheek away, she proceeded to stroke her mare.

"Good morning, Captain," she said lightly as he drew nearer, keeping her attention on Rosie's soft mane. "April is here at last. I would ask you to ride with me this lovely day, but I fear your ankle would complain at being put into action so soon."

"My ankle has serviced me well within the past few days," he rejoined, "better than I might have expected after nearly four weeks. But you are probably right. Riding the moors might prove too much of a setback at this point."

"I have no doubt Doctor Goodwin will be surprised and pleased with your progress," she replied easily, turning away and walking into the shadows of the stable.

A few blades of straw and a bit of dust from the remainder of the bale were stirred up unexpectedly from a mound of hay her groom was setting in place a few feet away. The motion caused Delphinia to sneeze, turning into the light as she did so. Her eyes, when she opened them, fell squarely upon Nicholas's face. It held the most serious expression she had seen yet.

"What has happened to you?" he demanded, reaching out to cup her face. "Here, come into the light where I can see."

His firm fingers grasped her chin with exquisite care so as not to inflict further pain on her wounded cheek. She allowed herself to be led by his touch, turning her face into the sunlight. He frowned as he studied her.

"What is this? Tell me," he ordered.

"Oh," she stammered, "I bumped my face on the bedpost when I was preparing for bed last evening. It was silly of me. I look like someone has given me a leveller, don't I?"

She tried to laugh, but the sound came out tinged with fear that he would discover her foolishness and criticize her for it. She averted her eyes so she would not have to see his suspicion directly.

"It looks worse than it is," she murmured, pulling away.

"Someone did this to you," he said in a tone too low for the servants to hear. "Delphinia, what's happened?"

"Please, let's talk about this somewhere else," she begged. "I don't want the staff to know."

"Very well." Nicholas took hold of Rosie's idle reins and walked with Delphinia and her horse toward the moors. The walk gave her time to sort out the turmoil she felt. For the first time she saw that daffodils had broken through the ground in sheltered spots, and touches of purple and green flecked the landscape. The leaves that had turned in upon themselves for protection against the winter had now unfurled and stretched their greenery skyward.

The bright colors were at odds with her mood over the dilemma she faced. Nicholas waited for an explanation. She could not tell him she had tried to learn Warren's identity without admitting her involvement in their operation. She was not ready to reveal her secret until Ivy was safely settled in London. Swiftly, she decided upon a course of action.

"Do not tell me you fell," Nicholas warned. "That does not look like the kind of injury anyone receives from a fall. Has it anything to do with this Mr. Warren you are seeking?"

She stared at him, realizing he could only have learned of her search from Ivy, and answered in a small voice, "No, it was Percy."

Before he could assume Percy had struck her deliberately she related selected details of her night's adventure, telling a half-truth without revealing the nature of their business. She recognized with every turn of events the risks she had taken.

"You see," she concluded, "if Percy is involved in something potentially dangerous, it is my right to know as his business partner. He did not mean to give me this bruise. He was unduly rough with me, that is all."

"It is far more than enough. Thunder and damnation!" He swore with a vehemence that startled her. "And here all along I've thought he cared for you." He turned and looked deeply into her eyes. "And you for him."

"No, Nicholas," she said with determination. "Please know that I have never cared for Percy. Not in that way." The very idea made her blush. "We share a business interest because I am obligated to him for something that happened in the past. I really cannot say more than that."

She hoped the strain of her speech did not make Nicholas suspect it was more likely blackmail that tied her to Percy. She wondered if he could fathom such a connection.

"That is all I need to know," he said softly. "Still, I could thrash him to within an inch of his life for having done this to you."

"I deserved it," she said automatically.

He stopped her with a swift glance. "Delphinia, do not try to defend him. What he has done to you is indefensible. It was heinous to threaten you this way. I would guess you have not deserved half of what you have gotten in this life, but do not answer me now, because I know you will not tell the whole truth."

She opened her mouth to respond, then closed it. She could not tell him more than she had. As it was, she had confided more than was prudent. She did not know whether to feel grateful to him or to cry at his obvious concern for her welfare. She had never known such concern from a man.

"By the way," he reminded her pointedly, "you never did tell me what type of partnership you share with Percy."

"It is business, that is all. Local concerns."

"It seems an unusual arrangement to me." Nicholas continued to walk casually beside her, pausing once or twice to allow Rosie to graze. "Often when there is such an arrangement between two people, there is a betrothal or impending marriage that follows."

"That I will never do," she said savagely.

"I am hardly surprised. Still, I cannot imagine what you and he have in common."

She paused cagily. His last remark had given her a solution. "We have these moors in common. Percy and I are involved in a tin mining operation that is quite lucrative."

From the shrewd expression on Nicholas's ruggedly handsome features she knew her confidence had gotten the better of her. Once again she had overestimated her ability to lie.

"Tin mining," he echoed. "What exactly do you know of tin mining?"

"Percy is more active in the mining aspect of the business than I am," she hedged. "I keep the books. I am quite good with figures."

"I have noticed."

His playful tone made her look him straight in the eye. His gaze swept the length of her cloaked form before his eyes locked with hers again. She tightened the ribbons at her chin primly and turned away, hoping he would understand her reluctance to speak on the subject of mining and talk of something else. Perhaps it was better that he continue to admire her figure, for even if he could read her mind he never did as she wished anyway.

"Please tell me what is going on here," he urged her, a look of profound earnestness in the depths of his dark eyes. "This is not a normal existence for a lady as fine as yourself. You deserve so much more than this. What is the nature of your business, Delphinia?"

The warmth in his tone made her stiffen. She tried to conceal her defensiveness and failed. Flustered by emotions that were unclear to her, she took a step back from him. The slight distance could not keep her feelings at bay.

"I live a very private life here, Nicholas," she said in a quiet tone. "I would like to tell you more, but I cannot. I hope one day that I will be at liberty to do so. Perhaps you do not know that I am a reserved person by nature."

A laugh escaped him, spontaneous and pleasing in its sincerity, even to her own ears, although she knew she had not fooled him for a moment.

"There is nothing naturally reserved about you." The gentle merriment in his eyes almost made her smile in spite of herself. "You are outspoken and painfully honest in all you do and say. If you are a private person, I believe it is because you have been forced into isolation against your will."

"No one forces me to do anything," she argued as he reached for her hand to prevent the words of denial he must know were forthcoming, "except you. You force me into foolish conversation when I merely wish to go riding."

Nicholas squeezed her small hands in his large muscular ones, refusing to let them go. "Even though you have made it clear that you are anxious for me to leave, I had always hoped we might come to know each other better." His sea-green eyes bored into hers with an intensity she tried to avoid but could not. "I want to know you without the incredibly well constructed wall of privacy you have built around you."

She froze at the force of his words. This was the first she had heard of any of this. What was she to make of it?

She laughed shortly. "That can never be."

"Why?" he persisted, his lips close to her ear. "Why can there be nothing between us? Give me a reason."

"Your ankle is better," she observed quietly. "Soon there will no longer be a reason for you to remain here. Your carriage will be repaired, and you will be on your way."

"Yes," he admitted frankly, in a tone of exasperation. "And I won't be coming through these parts again, if I can help it. I'd sooner be back at the helm facing the Spanish, even Admiral Gravina himself, than to be lost on those moors again." His gaze becoming more serious, he paused, as if giving her time to absorb the words she preferred to ignore. "Is that what you want, Delphinia?"

There was a lump in her throat that prevented her from answering. She kept her eyes on the ground and on the little daffodil that had worked its way through the soil at his feet, even though the image swam before her tear-filled eyes.

"Cornishmen ask strange questions," she said irreverently when she could bring herself to speak.

Nicholas took her solidly by the arm. The sheer strength of his grip took her by surprise. The injuries that had weakened him were clearly well on their way to being healed.

"It is a long and very lonely life when one does not have a husband or a wife. Take my mother's word for it, if you do not believe me."

His tone was soft and patient, but Delphinia detected a desperation that she could do nothing to pacify.

"Do you think I don't know that?" She pulled away from him abruptly. "Fulfilling your mother's desires will not necessarily make you happy, nor will it make me happy."

"Fulfilling my mother's desires," he repeated slowly. "Is that what you think I am doing? I assure you, I have desires of my own which have nothing to do with what my mother wishes. You must come away from here with me."

"With you," she retorted. "Captain, I cannot. And I do not take orders from anyone, as I told you."

"You need not remind me. Nothing prevents you from leaving, Delphinia. You could come to London with me. You would experience again the joys you have forgotten."

She looked at him in amazement. "My home here offers everything I could wish for," she protested.

"Except culture and a firsthand enjoyment of life," he returned. "Would you remain a recluse forever? A prisoner of the past? Is that what you want?"

His words took her breath away. It had been years since she had considered, and since dismissed, such possibilities. After allowing herself to feel very little but fear in that time, these emotions surpassed anything she had ever known.

She turned and looked up into his face. His expression was filled with a hopefulness that broke her heart. How could he ask her this now? It was simply not a time in which she could consider abandoning her own plans.

"London is a world away from here, Captain," she faltered. "I can never leave Briarcombe Manor."

She felt torn apart by the pain of rejecting him and called upon the strength that had sustained her these past seven years to bring her safely through this exchange. Her life on the moors had allowed her to create a role she had perfected over time, a role so comfortable and safe she never intended to leave it. What would become of Ivy without her efforts? What of her father's reputation and her case against Percy?

"I am very content with my home here," she continued. "A woman in my situation, who is older and alone, is fortunate to have such a life. It is not an existence I am willing to sacrifice on a whim."

Without another word, Nicholas took command of Rosie's bridle and turned her about, limping back toward the stable with the horse behind him, the cane in one hand, the reins in the other. Delphinia found such abrupt insolence alarming at first, then annoying. Nicholas might be a retired naval captain, but on her property she was in charge.

"You have interrupted my plans, Captain," she announced loudly. "I was planning a morning ride. Will you not return my mare to me? Captain!"

When he did not stop, she had no choice but to follow. At the stable he handed off the mare to one of the grooms and asked for one of his own horses to be saddled. He walked slowly around to the back of the stable, leaning heavily on his cane. Uncertain of his intention, she pursued him.

"Captain," she began, "I have made my wishes clear to you. Why did you return my horse to her stall?"

"You have made your needs clear to me, Lady Delphinia, but not your wishes," he said coldly, an air of finality in his voice. "Perhaps the reason Cornishmen ask strange questions is that Devonshire women drive them to it. Being even a whole county away from you, Delphinia, will never work. I shall never be far enough away from you, trust me." His anger subsiding as she stared at him, he sighed. "You would be too close for comfort."

Did he really care for her as he seemed to imply? Delphinia spread her hands in bewilderment.

"I do not understand you, Captain," she said.

He stared at her with great intensity. "Perhaps you will understand this, Lady Delphinia."

Leaning his cane against the wall of the stable, Nicholas stepped slowly toward her, grasping her upper arms with a pressure she could feel through her cloak. Inclining his face above hers, he folded his arms about her tenderly and lowered his lips to hers in a smooth motion.

The gesture came so unexpectedly and naturally that Delphinia forgot to resist. Instead she responded with an urgency she did not know she possessed. She had not thought herself capable of such forceful emotions, but somehow she could not pull away. His lips were full and warm against hers, and she drank in their desire as if hers were parched. She laid her arms against his chest playfully, her fingers curling around the folds of his cloak and easing themselves onto his warm waistcoat. With his hands pressed against her back, his arms cradled her as comfortably as if she had found the place she belonged at last.

She was about to reach for his hair, the soft hair she had pushed from his heated forehead so often in tending him while he was unwell, when a muffled voice from around the corner within the stable returned her to her senses.

"Your chestnut, Captain."

His lips releasing hers, Nicholas stared at her for a moment with a look she could not interpret before he thrust her from him and retreated toward the front of the stable.

"Thank you for your trouble," he said gruffly to the groom as he mounted his horse.

Turning away from the groom, Delphinia put her hand to her lips. It took her a long moment to quell the desire that raged within her. She had never known such deep emotion. It was terrifying and exhilarating, a soul knowledge so strong she was sure the servants could read the feeling in her face. Remembering her place, she conquered her physical yearnings and pulled her cloak protectively about her.

Before she could say anything more, Nicholas was in the saddle and headed off across the moors that had imprisoned her for so long.

* * * *

Riding is the perfect release, Nicholas thought, easing up on Spitfire's reins as they came to a muddy bog. He should have realized the ankle would give him such extraordinary pain, but the physical pain was easier to endure than being with Delphinia. Riding at least provided a distraction from the pain in his heart. He could not remain in her presence another minute. If he did, he might do her more harm than Percy Wainwright, with her stubborn refusal to open her damned eyes. Those beautiful eyes.

The further he rode the more he realized how much he longed to linger at Briarcombe. He could not leave without Delphinia. To allow her to remain would only endanger her life.

She said she had not been forced to do anything against her will, yet she retained a partnership of some sort with Wainwright. A more ruthless, untrustworthy type Nicholas had never met. He wondered if she had assumed a guise of independence for his benefit, but that made less sense. Exactly what kind of arrangement did she have with Percy? What would tie a woman to such a man? Nicholas had known her less than a month. How much did he really know about her?

Her capacity for caring was great, as evidenced by her feelings for Ivy. Her sister's come-out mattered more to her than the cut of her own dress, of her own life, for that matter. She worried so about Ivy's future. But what of her own? Surely she couldn't plan to spend it here alone.

She was a capable, independent, strong woman, perhaps too strong for her own good. She put her concern for Ivy before her own needs, but what were her needs? Wainwright could not fulfill them, of that Nicholas was sure. He also realized there were many rooms he had not been able to examine in his brief time in the cellar. There were many other areas where smuggled goods could be concealed.

He had not decided what his next strategy would be, but of one thing he was certain. Until he had cleared her name he could not even think of leaving her, much less loving her.

* * * *

Delphinia returned to the house, hoping for solitude in which to examine her thoughts. Instead, she learned Percy was waiting to see her in the drawing room where Childers had consigned him. Her defenses rose. She wanted to avoid him altogether, but with the next drop so close she wondered if something had gone amiss with their plan.

By the time she reached the drawing room Percy was already starting on his second brandy.

"Upstairs, were you?" he asked languidly. "I'd be surprised if you'd gone out this morning with that shiner."

She glared at him with growing hatred. "After what you did to me I cannot believe you dare to show your face here."

He gazed at her through eyes that widened slightly, trying to look repentant. "It was an accident. I didn't intend to mar your face. I think I made my point, however. At any rate, I am here on a more serious matter regarding Captain Hainsworth."

Her heart skipped a beat. Whatever could Percy want with Nicholas? His jeering tone did not bode well.

"It seems that the good Captain is playing games with both of us." Percy swirled his brandy thoughtfully, his eyes boring into Delphinia's.

"What are you talking about?"

"He was in touch with Melcher recently."

"Yes, I know. Melcher had orders to repair his carriage. What of it?"

Percy smiled. "Precisely where the problem lies."

She stared at him uncomprehendingly. "Have the repairs taken longer than expected? Is that what you came to tell me? You're upset that Nicholas must remain here longer?"

"So it is Nicholas now, is it? I'd be very careful if I were you." Percy gave her a sarcastic smile. "It's just the reverse, my dear. You see, Hainsworth paid Melcher for the repairs, and dearly, too. Melcher did just as he was asked. But when he sent word that the carriage would be ready shortly, our friend the Captain asked him to delay fixing it. Paid him to do so." He paused meaningfully. "It appears we have a spy on our hands."

Delphinia stared at him, pain filling her heart slowly. She dared not respond immediately. Of course Melcher would have gone directly to Percy. Melcher was a trusted member of the operation. If he had any reason to suspect Nicholas of being an informer, he would report his suspicions at once. She closed her eyes, trying to blot out the ugly picture that was forming in her mind.

"That can't be, Percy." She attempted to put some scorn in her tone, but she knew she could not influence Percy's opinion. "The Captain was a traveler on these moors like the others. He is not an agent of the Crown."

"Then why delay his leaving?" Percy seized her wrist in a painful grasp. "What is going on here that would make him want to stay, Delphinia? What have you been doing with him? What have you told him?"

She shook him away angrily and darted behind a chair defensively. "Nothing. And if you ever touch me like that again I shall have you thrown out of here permanently. I mean it." Her breath coming in spurts, she waited to make sure he had taken her seriously before continuing. "I have more to lose than you do. I told him nothing. I have done everything within my power to make this seem like a normal household, one without any secrets."

She walked away from him, feeling his gaze on her. She did not want him to read further into her emotions. Could she believe what Percy had said? Had she again been betrayed? Worse, had she allowed herself to fall in love with another man like her first husband? The thought made her feel sick.

"I don't know, Delphinia. There is a look in your face these days when you speak of him. Something has changed. Perhaps it is that you have been too long without a man."

She turned to him scathingly. "Don't be ridiculous."

"I do hope you are not falling in love. A former naval captain is not the kind of partner who would serve our operation well." His tone became cutting. "I want you to spend time with him. Find out what's going on, why he wants to remain here. Why would he, unless he suspects something?"

She gazed at him steadily. "I don't know, but I will find out. Are arrangements still as we planned for Friday night?"

"Off Foreland Point. The usual time." He dropped his voice confidentially. "I expect to see you there. Alone."

Her heart lurched, but she maintained her composure except for her impatience. "Of course I shall be alone. And when we are done I shall go to London, as I told you I would. Don't look for me during that time, for I shall not be here. Once Ivy is settled, as we discussed, I will return in plenty of time for next month's drop."

He stared at her for a long time, studying her with a penetrating scrutiny that chilled her. "So you're going to London," he said, his casual tone underscored with bitterness. "It's been years since you've left Briarcombe, hasn't it?"

"Yes," she replied with a brittle smile, loath to admit her nervousness to him. "I find it unsettling. I shall be glad to return home."

"I do hope so." He did not sound as if he believed her. "In London you'll have a chance to see your father, that prominent member of Parliament. Don't let on, Delphinia."

She turned on him instantly. "In all the time I have corresponded with him I have not once given him an inkling of what you have forced me to do here in his home."

"We have appreciated your help," he said placatingly.

"You and Mr. Warren," she retorted.

"I truly hope you are looking forward to coming home, Delphinia. Once you return we can begin to make plans."

"Plans?" she replied blankly.

"For our engagement." His face retained its foolish intoxicated smile as her stomach lurched. "I thought you might be ready to share the comforts of your home with me."

"Why would I want to do that?" She gave him a look of loathing. "If you stopped wasting your hard-earned money on wine and women and gaming you would have more than you knew what to do with. What a fool you are, Percy."

"Not as much of a fool as you might think, my dear." As he idly approached her chair, she prepared to move away if necessary. Sensing her revulsion, he kept his distance. "Perhaps not so much a fool as you. There is already talk in town, you know."

"About us?" She felt uneasy.

"About you and your guest, the good captain. People are wondering why he has remained under your roof so long when he is now up and about. I am very sure you do not want a scandal, Delphinia. Not another one."

His suggestive words made her want to strike him. She restrained herself, moving to the window.

"Now that the captain has stayed so long the only respectable thing is for you to marry," Percy suggested.

Her heart somersaulted. "Marry?" she echoed faintly.

"Yes. Marry me."

He spoke with such hopeful enthusiasm that she wanted to laugh at the preposterous idea. But the truth behind it troubled her, and she hesitated before responding. She had always feared scandal and had done everything within her power to protect her family's home and reputation. She could not afford a second scandal at the hands of a man. It was undeniable, she acknowledged with dismay, that Nicholas Hainsworth had tarried well beyond the point of prudence.

"Gossip is the favorite pastime here, after all." Percy sighed with mock regret. "It's a sad thing when one is at the mercy of gossip. Which of your servants will be the first to talk, Delphinia?"

* * * *

Nicholas returned to the house a short time later, for once hoping to avoid Delphinia. He was not disappointed. As he entered the foyer it was her sister who met him at the bottom of the stairs. More subdued than usual, Ivy did not run to him as she had previously, but instead smiled demurely and retained a polite distance. She seemed older already even though she would not depart for London for another week.

"It is almost that time again," she whispered. "The time of the new moon."

"It means your sister will be going abroad into the night again," he said with a sigh.

"Perhaps we should follow her this time," Ivy suggested.

"I will try to follow her, now that I am back on my feet," Nicholas offered. "There are dangers on the moors at night to which you need not expose yourself."

"But I know these moors far better than you," she protested. "I know every foothold. It can be no more dangerous for me than it is for Delphinia to be out there."

"I do not approve of her being out there either," he said firmly. "Can you imagine how angry she would be with me if she knew I allowed you to follow her? She will be angry enough with me as it is for pursuing her."

Ivy considered his words and laughed. "You're quite right. I shall let you take the brunt of her anger."

Nicholas smiled at her appreciatively, looking into the eyes of this younger sister. Unlike the soulful, smoldering blue-violet eyes of her older sister, Ivy's were a bright green that in his judgment suited her perfectly. He wondered how the walls of this ancient home could be strong enough to contain this impetuous young woman.

"You like Delphinia a great deal, don't you?" she asked.

He was surprised by her perception. "Ever since I first laid eyes upon her."

Ivy rolled her eyes heavenward. "Poor you!" she exclaimed with a trace of humor. "It's a grave mistake, you know. She has such a disappointing history with men."

As if to underscore her statement, the library door opened behind them and Percy emerged. Delphinia remained shadowed in the doorway.

Hatred coiled within Nicholas at the sight of Wainwright. The man was no better than a scoundrel. After what he had done to Delphinia he had no business being in this house.

He paused upon seeing Nicholas, apparently startled by his presence. Nicholas was sure Wainwright had spoken against him staying. After a moment Wainwright drew himself up and stepped forward.

"Hello, Captain Hainsworth."

The greeting was cool, with no attempt at civility.

Wainwright took a step toward the door, but Nicholas blocked his path, refusing to give way. He controlled his deep desire to strike Percy only for Delphinia's sake, remembering it would cause a scene within her house, an occurrence she dreaded.

"Where do think you're going, Wainwright?"

"I was just leaving, if you don't mind."

"Actually, I do. I'd like a word with you, if I may."

Delphinia's voice came from behind him, quiet but alarmed. "Nicholas—"

"I don't want to hear ever again that you've laid a finger on Lady Delphinia," Nicholas cut in. "Is that quite clear?"

Percy's mouth snapped shut. "See here, I didn't touch—"

"You came close enough. You came too damn close."

For a second Nicholas forgot everything but the blackguard who confronted him. He hardly noticed the shock on Ivy's face, having forgotten she had not yet seen her sister's bruises. He hardly even noticed Delphinia who waited to one side, speechless with fear.

"If it were up to me," Nicholas warned in a low tone, "you'd be in Dartmoor with the French prisoners. It's a grim place, I assure you. You'd be better off there. This house simply isn't big enough for the three of us, Wainwright. Someone has to go."

Wainwright's face flamed. "And I suppose that means me."

"That's exactly right. If I hear that you have touched so much as a hair on her head," Nicholas threatened, "you will live to regret it."

It was not until Lady Delphinia herself stepped forward and intervened that Nicholas remembered his place.

He was reminded in a most painful way, although he could hardly believe what he was hearing as she said breathlessly, her voice quavering, "Yes, Captain, you are right. Someone has to leave. And I am afraid it must be you."

Chapter Ten

Caution did not always make for an effective strategy in war, Nicholas reminded himself, when he was alone in the quiet of his room the next day. Delphinia's rejection only reinforced his determination to learn her secret. He doubted her sincerity not only because of Wainwright's presence during her outburst, but because he suspected his own warning had antagonized her into action. She was the one who always sought control and was not about to mend her ways now. He reached down to pat Brutus, who lay beside him on the rug.

"It seems folly to linger in a place such as this," he muttered to the dog, who cocked his head and wagged his tail in response. "An idle inclination on my part, that is all. If I do not leave she will be the ruination of me. Why do I not remove myself at once?"

It must be love, he decided, that kept him here, where his efforts to honor the laws of his country were not appreciated. He wanted more than the acceptable bride his mother wanted for him. He had been attracted to Delphinia from the beginning. But what to do with his feelings presented a greater problem.

If his suspicions about the new moon were correct tonight was the night she would take to the moors again. It seemed like a year since he had first seen her crossing the dark landscape in a man's hat and greatcoat and wondered about her destination.

Nicholas opened the door to his wardrobe. He had access to a hat and greatcoat as well. Tonight he would follow her and settle the question once and for all.

* * * *

He ate dinner in the main dining room as he had grown accustomed to doing since he had been able to walk again. Tonight, not surprisingly, only Ivy joined him at the table.

"Delphinia is resting at the moment," she said in a troubled voice. "I had no idea Percy had treated her so cruelly. If only I had known, I might have helped her."

Since she had first glimpsed Delphinia's bruises Ivy appeared to have aged considerably. Nicholas sensed they were both too tense over the incident with Wainwright as well as over Delphinia's expected excursion for any kind of lively interchange during the meal. Instead he decided to reassure her as best he could.

"There is nothing you could have done to help her even if you had known," he said in a voice too soft for the attending footman to hear. "I am not surprised she is resting. I imagine she will need to rest to prepare for her trip tonight. We shall watch and wait until well after dark, and then see what happens."

"You remember the directions I gave you for locating the back staircase?" Ivy asked, anxiety in her face.

"I already found the spot from the second floor." Smiling, he reached for a glass of brandy and tried to focus on lighter matters. "You will be pleased to know that the *Times* says the Prince Regent is expected in London within a week, coinciding with your own arrival. And then who knows what adventures may befall you?"

"Who knows what adventures may befall any of us?" She smiled at him meaningfully. "At least we do not have long to wait to find out."

* * * *

Shortly after midnight, as Nicholas waited in his room, he heard a door close softly beneath his window. Drawing back the draperies with a gesture too slight to be noticeable from below, he glanced down carefully toward the lantern's glow. The figure, familiar now in the oversized greatcoat and wide-brimmed hat, was setting off into a windy night, the ill-fitting coat flapping at the ankles. Long strands of black hair had escaped from under the hat and tumbled over one shoulder.

You will not fool me any longer, Lady Delphinia, he thought with triumph. I know those tresses only too well.

Confident he would not be recognized in dark trousers borrowed from Stebbins, Nicholas was prepared to give chase. Hearing only silence beyond his door, he slipped into the corridor with careful stealth and made off into the night.

* * * *

Setting a greater distance between herself and Briarcombe with every step, Delphinia crossed the moors rapidly, brushing wisps of hair from her eyes impatiently. Walking allowed her mind to wander, but she could not afford a lack of concentration tonight of all nights. Despite her efforts to push Nicholas from her mind he continued to return to her thoughts. Too soon he would be gone, and only Percy would be left to her.

With little else to think of until she reached her destination, she indulged her fears. Her stomach tensed at the idea that Percy might make good on his threat of marriage. Could he make it happen? Unless her proof against him was solid, he could make her do anything he wished. Why can I not die tonight, if that is to be my fate? she mourned, her spirit sinking.

She would not, she vowed, give in to worry. She had to find a way to destroy Percy's hold on her before he could destroy her. The only way was to bring her feelings under control. She dared not tell Nicholas of the dilemma she faced for fear it would compromise her family's honor, a temptation that was complicated by her attachment to him. Feeling as she did, he was more trouble than help. Until his departure she would have to guard her heart.

James had been false, and now Nicholas had found it just as easy to betray her. The blow had devastated her when she learned he had lied about his purpose in wanting to stay at Briarcombe. Why did she not hate him as she did Percy? She ought to find it easy. In her heart she had hoped he wanted to stay because of her, but she had suspected all along she was too optimistic. Yet she was glad he would remain a bit longer. For the time being she would say nothing about his treachery. What did it matter? If he did indeed suspect her and was waiting for proof she would make sure he never had the opportunity to find any.

There was no danger of her falling in love, for he was her enemy. Having permitted him to kiss her so thoroughly only strengthened her deception. She had enjoyed the feeling of his lips on hers and had not minded succumbing to him. Doing so might make him confident enough to trust her with his real motives.

Yet it was the intensity of the exchange that had surprised her. She shook off the memory. She could not afford to be so inattentive to her purpose. If only she could persuade him to wait, she thought, a sudden desperation weakening her resolve and clouding the mind she needed to keep clear. If only she could win his pledge of secrecy for another week. Freedom was simply a matter of time.

Something in the wind caught her attention. A calm southwesterly breeze brought with it the hint of an unfamiliar presence. She had become an expert at being elusive, having developed a sixth sense about walking at night. Now her skin prickled with the certain knowledge that she was not alone.

She had been walking for more than twenty-five minutes. The stretch of moorland she had followed offered little opportunity for concealment. Had someone been following her all this time? She was so distracted by her thoughts she had paid little heed to her own movements, much less those of anyone else. Percy would be furious if he knew she had been so indiscreet.

She hoped he would not have to find out. She looked into the darkness behind her and heard only silence except for the distant murmur of the sea. A local man would have identified himself by now. If the excise men had tailed her here, she decided swiftly, tonight's drop would be off. She would light a furze beacon if she had further reason to suspect intruders were present.

A brief spurt of hope somehow managed to penetrate her fear. London was only a matter of hours away at this point. The thought lingered as bright as a beacon in the darkness of the realization of what she must do before then.

Summoning her courage, Delphinia turned and proceeded toward the coast, listening intently, her senses alert. Not a leaf stirred behind her. Had she been mistaken? Her nerves had never been more on edge. That, she surmised, must account for her misjudgment.

* * * *

Hindered by his stiff ankle, Nicholas cursed the physical limitations that slowed his progress as he attempted to follow Delphinia. The unexpected descents in the vales threw him off balance, just as they had the night he was lost on the moors. His knowledge of smuggling, combined with his own hunch about her activities, convinced him she was bound for the sea. If he found an empty coastline when he reached the Channel, his return to Briarcombe would be a fitting test of his endurance. He grimaced at the thought.

The undulations in the landscape gradually turned in his favor by lessening, allowing him to keep Delphinia in view while he followed at a safe distance. Once his eyes had adjusted to the dark he was able to make out familiar objects that assumed a fearful look at night. With no light to illuminate his way, the path disappeared into patches of black, the hollows distinguished from one another only by degrees of darkness.

Nicholas had forgotten the fears unknown terrain could bring. He had not felt such stirrings over harmless elements of nature since he had been frightened as a young boy by the fierce storms along the Cornwall coast. This was another kind of storm, he reflected, with the potential for more violent consequences.

He watched Delphinia move swiftly and deliberately across the landscape, following a route known only to herself and her band of smugglers. He managed to track her until his eardrums rang with the muffled roar of the waves beneath the cliffs.

He was taken by surprise when she stopped abruptly and crouched low, the masculine hat silhouetted against the pale sky. In the darkness before him a spurt of light and the gradual brightness that followed revealed the concentration on Delphinia's face. She had kindled a bough of furze that crackled and flared into a blaze, fanned by the night wind.

The sudden brilliance obscured the scene from Nicholas's view. Muted voices from below told him he was almost at the cliff's edge. He heard the scattered pounding footsteps of men running on the shore and the frantic splash of oars dipping into water as her comrades attempted to escape by boat.

Nicholas realized Delphinia had delivered the signal to the men on shore as well as in the water, canceling the drop. She must have realized he'd followed her. He cursed himself for being the cause of the panic. Damnation! What happens now? Nicholas thought wildly. He remained on the path, watching as she darted back toward him, drawing herself up short a foot in front of him. She stared in recognition.

"You!" she exclaimed, lowering her voice. He thought he heard her curse in the darkness. Nothing about her would have surprised him at that point. "I thought you were . . ."

"An agent from the Preventive Service?" he guessed.

She ignored his words and asked instead, "Why did you follow me here?"

He needed no light to recognize the anger in her voice. In the dimness he could barely make out her features, but as she stared up at him, a hint of light from the clouds touched her bright eyes and glazed the tip of her nose with a soft sheen under the brim of her hat. He thought she had never looked lovelier.

"I had to know," he said simply. "I wanted the truth. I doubted I would hear it from you."

A sigh escaped her. In the darkness he had no idea how angry she truly was, but he did not need to gaze into her amethyst eyes to sense her aggravation.

"Go back to the house," she ordered in an undertone. "I will join you soon, but first I have business to attend to."

"I can guess your business," he said dryly.

"Please, not now." She cut him short. "We are not alone. Go at once before you are discovered. I shall meet you in the drawing room. I must speak with someone privately first."

"Is it Wainwright?" he demanded.

"I am in no danger," she said tersely. "It is you who are in danger. It will be worse for us all if you stay."

"I want to help," he insisted. For once he had no desire to control his stubbornness.

"You are a hindrance to me here. Go, or I will not be responsible for what happens to you."

With that curt dismissal she brushed past him and vanished into the darkness. His ankle throbbing, Nicholas knew if he wanted to learn the truth he had best leave the situation in her capable hands. Hoping she would follow in time, he took her advice and turned back.

* * * *

Delphinia made her way back to the house three-quarters of an hour later, anticipating the upcoming encounter with Nicholas while simultaneously dreading it. She had delayed returning to give herself time to decide how best to answer the many questions she knew were awaiting her. How would he receive the truth even if she could bring herself to reveal it?

She found him waiting for her behind the closed doors of the drawing room, as she had instructed. He was seated on the sofa, but he looked less comfortable than she had felt on the moors tonight. She entered the room quietly, locking the doors behind her. She knew he was watching her as she slowly removed the greatcoat and tossed the hat aside, shaking her hair loose. She did not fail to notice his smile as her long locks fell in great masses about her shoulders.

"Surprised, are you?" she challenged. "Disappointed in me?"

"I was thinking your disguise gives you an enchanting look. Daring and innocent at the same time." He continued to smile tenderly as he gazed upon the unflattering masculine breeches and black jumper that she knew must emphasize her pallor. "The outfit doesn't do you justice.

Is it your father's?"

"My father's might be recognized, so I wear my late husband's."
She glanced down at her cumbersome attire. "I would not do anything
to disgrace my family, although not everyone hereabouts views
smuggling as disgraceful."

It was the first time she had used the word in his presence. In
doing so she had admitted her role in the illegal operation. She glanced
toward him to see him watching her with wary eyes.

"I know this moment must be excruciatingly difficult for you," he
confessed, never taking his eyes from her. "I waited here instead of
following you so you might have a chance to collect your thoughts. I
admit I find this conversation altogether strange and fascinating, just as
I find you. I waited a long while for you. Were you delayed?"

"I wasn't at the coast the whole time," she replied. "And it is I who
should be asking the questions, Captain. It seems to me it is you who
owes me an explanation, not the other way around."

"Since when did you resume calling me Captain rather than by my
Christian name?" Nicholas stood so quickly she stepped back in alarm.
He spoke in a low tone. "I risked my life for you tonight because I was
trying to save yours. I was worried about you."

Delphinia felt mollified by his concern, but she was not prepared to
let down her guard. She turned and walked swiftly away, the tension
leaving her as she heard him return to his seat.

"Worry about yourself," she retorted. "You took a foolish chance
following me. Do you expect me to feel anything but anger toward
you? You confused me and made me ruin tonight's drop."

Yet she could not express the inexplicable relief she felt, for she
did not entirely understand it. She could not tell him his actions had left
her with mixed feelings. His decision to follow her had forced her
hand, making her readdress the issue of whether or not to solicit his
help.

She decided to try another approach. Perhaps she could barter
information for help.

"Perhaps it is time we talked," she countered with a smile. "May I
pour you a brandy, Captain? Nicholas, rather?"

"That would be delightful. I thank you kindly."

He accepted the glass she extended to him as she sat beside him
on the sofa.

"I was delayed because I was walking in the garden," she resumed,
"thinking of how I could explain this tangle to you."

"You might start with honesty," he said pointedly. "That would be
most pleasant for a change."

She chose to ignore his sarcasm. Instead she held her breath as
she broached the next question. "If I tell you," she asked quietly, "will
you promise to help?"

Her heart stirred as he gazed at her steadily, his sea-green eyes boring into hers. Oh, how she wanted to believe what she saw there.

"You have my solemn vow," he replied just as quietly. "Now tell me, what is it you smuggle?"

"You're drinking it." She felt her amusement bubble to the surface.

"Am I?" Glancing with concern at the glass in his hand, he took another sip. "Very fine quality, I'd say."

"As is the tea you drank at breakfast this morning."

He raised an eyebrow. "Also illegal?"

"I'm afraid so," she said rather apologetically. "It comes from the West Indies. They say nearly four-fifths of all the tea drunk in Britain has not had any duty paid on it."

"That much?"

His momentary silence before he spoke revealed the depth of his surprise. She wondered if he were as startled by her participation as by her knowledge of smuggling. The thought made her throat tighten, but she forced herself to answer.

"The brandy, of course, is from Cherbourg. The French ships don't always come into the Bristol Channel. The brandy is temporarily stored in Lundy before it is sent here."

Nicholas considered. "Such a small island, with such a large role. Its proximity is ideal as a drop-off point, lying just beyond the Channel as it does. Thousands of pounds worth of smuggled goods must lay in wait there unbeknownst to the excise men. Does this enterprise account for the Herrick fortune?"

She regarded him with utter scorn. How could he think such a thing of her? Surely he knew her better than that by now.

"Of course not. My father derives none of his fortune from this occupation. At least I need not go far to perform my duties. If I were to be seen and discovered I would risk bringing shame upon my father. That is a risk I would never take."

Delphinia swallowed hard. She fought back tears as she reflected how scandal would affect her father, especially if she were the cause. Too late she realized she had admitted more than she should have. Somehow Captain Hainsworth's presence encouraged an openness from her of which she had not thought herself capable.

"You needn't go far at all," he mused aloud. "The local terrain is ideal for such a venture."

His nonchalant acceptance of her revelation filled her with relief. "The north coast is lonely and untraveled and perfect for such an endeavor, with the highest sea cliffs in England. Kipscombe Hill and Foreland Point are ideal lookouts with the inlets serving as landing points. We've used other locations. You can probably guess them."

"Lee Bay and Woody Bay," he surmised.

"And Heddon's Mouth, once," she confirmed, impressed with the accuracy of his instincts. "We do not go past Trentishoe. Brandy Cove is too difficult with its rock pools and jagged cliffs."

"And your cellar offers plenty of storage space. You do not fear the excise men?" The concern in his voice sounded genuine.

"I have no choice in the matter." She felt her calm waver momentarily as her conviction to remain silent began to crumble. Perhaps relying on her sense of humor would keep her past impenetrable from Nicholas until she could bring her fears under control. "The wars were an ideal time for smuggling, with most of the excise men called away. I try to be careful. The shipment is stored here to be transported across the moors later."

After a quick gulp, he set his brandy aside, his eyes averted as if he were ruminating on a troublesome issue. "Surely it is not just you and Wainwright."

"I am certain you know better than that, Captain. This is Devonshire. Forgive me if I regard you in your official capacity while we discuss my questionable pastime." Delphinia gave him a wintry smile, trying to keep the sarcasm from her voice. "The smugglers are laborers from the villages and the hamlets, some of whom you have probably met."

"The wheelwright," he guessed.

"I will not betray them by giving you names. They come from Kentisbury and Parracombe and Furzehill. It is their livelihood, their main source of income. Those who don't go down to the cliffs as tub men help in other ways. A woman from Blackmoor Gate helps to distribute the tea. Even our local parson buys brandy more cheaply from us than he would from the Crown."

Nicholas flashed her a dry smile, its hint of humor filling her with relief. "One must support the local economy."

Nicholas spoke so frankly she wondered how much he had already guessed about the extent of the smuggling operation, the depth of its roots, and the local code of secrecy. The fact that his family had a home in St. Ives made her uneasy. She felt a twinge of panic as she thought of her father and prayed silently she would not bring another scandal upon him by agreeing to this conversation.

"I sincerely pray my father will never discover any of this—and that you will respect my wishes. I don't do it because I enjoy it." Shaking her head, she began to tremble and heard her own voice quaver, tremulous as thunder. "Do you think I would deliberately deceive the Crown and endanger my father's reputation? I participate very much against my will. You must believe me."

Instead of waiting for his response, she jumped to her feet, unable to sit still in her anguish. She feared suddenly that her trust was misplaced, but it was too late to take back her words. Before she could think, Nicholas rose and took her by the shoulders, easing her gently onto the sofa beside him.

"Of course I believe you. I give you my word I will never tell your father any of this," he said softly, gazing into her eyes with more patience than she felt she deserved. "I have nothing to gain by informing your father. Even if I did, I would find it impossible to betray you or jeopardize your faith in me. Please tell me how it all came to be."

A shuddering sigh escaped her as she began mentally to relive her past. "It is hard to know where to begin. Years ago I did something very foolish. I am still paying for my mistake."

"Tell me about this hold Wainwright has over you," Nicholas urged when she didn't continue. "Whatever it is, it cannot be so bad you would allow it to ruin your life this way."

While his kindness had earned her trust, she did not feel she had earned his full respect as she wished to. She averted her eyes to help her speech come more readily. "I ruined my life long before I met Percy. I am ashamed of it now, but at the time it seemed so important, so right. You see, I married James Marlowe against my father's wishes."

She focused on the far wall absently, lost in memory. She felt Nicholas take her hands tightly in his own, grateful for his attempt to steady her, yet reluctant to see his reaction once he knew the truth.

"I was in my first Season, and I had great promise—at least that is what my aunts told me. I was very young, or so it seems to me now, and impressionable. Being in London was an experience for which country living had not prepared me. The only guidance I had came from my governess, a rather cold woman. My mother had died six years earlier, and Father was occupied with Parliamentary matters. I do not blame him. What do men know of matters of the heart?"

Abruptly, she remembered where she was and returned her gaze to Nicholas. She was relieved to see his eyes were warm, his smile tender.

"Forgive me," she breathed. "I know how dreadful that sounds. Not all men are as James was, I'm sure."

"You're right about that. I know something of matters of the heart, and all of it I have learned from you." He lifted her hand to his lips and kissed it. "But I did not mean to interrupt."

She resumed with a feeling of dread. "I was courted by many young men who were handsome and prosperous. They all seemed nice, and I did not know which to choose. Then I met James." She released a troubled little sigh, wishing it were as easy to change the past as it had been to attract eligible young men of whom had father would have approved. "He was rough around the edges, more like country people, and he put me at ease at once. My father did not like him and set about arranging more suitable young men for me to meet. But no one compared with James. We married before the Season was out. Father was furious and sent us here to live. After our mother's death, he did not return here often, so it was an ideal place to put a rebellious daughter who was too headstrong for her own good but could not see it."

She fought back the tears that filled her eyes before she was able to continue. "It was a mistake from the start. I learned too late what kind of person James was. He did not tell me until after we were married that he had gambled away his fortune." She laughed, its ring harsh even to her. "He expected to live off mine."

"Why did you not have the marriage annulled?"

"Father was angry and humiliated, and I had too much pride to admit my mistake. It was easier to try to make a go of the marriage to prove him wrong," she said in a small voice. "Of course he had not been mistaken. There were occasions when James went to London on business while I remained here. It did not take me long to realize the truth."

She smiled at Nicholas, but she could feel the sadness in her expression. She wondered if Nicholas's hands hurt under the pressure with which she clung to them. If so, he did not seem to mind.

"How many others were there?" he inquired delicately.

"How many women are there in London?" She laughed mirthlessly, as if making light of her faulty judgment could lessen her pain. "For a time I could not bring myself to speak to him of it. Finally I could deny it no longer, even to myself, for he brought them here."

Nicholas squeezed her hands silently. "Here to your home?"

She blinked back tears and nodded. "At least he spared me the indignity of having to face the same woman more than once. It was always someone different. Percy brought women here also. As James's closest friend he knew he was welcome to do so despite my disapproval."

"The old family friend," Nicholas murmured, his tone bitter.

She didn't bother to respond to his comment but forged ahead. "The phrase 'mistress of the house' took on an entirely new meaning for me. Early in our marriage I would sometimes accompany James to London, but as time went by, I could no longer face my friends and family. I had tried so hard to make my marriage appear perfect that I had trapped myself. Who would believe I wasn't happy? So I remained here, isolated and very lonely."

"My poor Delphinia." Nicholas spoke softly, stroking her wrist with his fingertips. Hear me out, she thought desperately, before you offer comfort. "The burden must have been unimaginable. How did you cope?"

Delphinia took a deep breath, finding strength in his gentle tone that was devoid of judgment. "The marriage failed miserably in our two years together. It became intolerable when a young woman with whom he was involved, a farm girl named Annie, followed him here.

She seemed sweet, very much like myself before I met him. I don't know what he told her about our relationship—certainly not the truth, for she would have run from him had she known. She told him she was with child. He had given another woman the one thing I had wanted most from our marriage."

"Annie demanded he take charge of the situation, but what could he do? He already had a wife, not that he cared about me. It was an awful time for it to happen. It was during a week of storms that knocked out the bridges all around. There were five of us stranded here, James and Annie and me, and Percy and a woman he had brought with him. And then it happened. The worst I could imagine."

She sighed tremulously, twisting her hands together, the physical act pulling her away from her emotions and back to the present. She was grateful Nicholas had not interrupted her, for she was not convinced she would have been able to reveal as much as she had without his supportive silence.

She turned to him now, relieved to see he listened intently while refraining from expressing any emotion. His eyes held a sympathy and encouragement that gave her the courage to proceed. "When Annie saw he was not about to help her, she grew desperate. James and Percy had spent the day drinking. I had gone to my room early that night, but I could hear Annie arguing with him. She did not want a child out of wedlock and threatened to make trouble. James said he did not need her by-blow. I heard awful sounds—crying and screaming and James shouting, and then all was quiet. So quiet I knew something was dreadfully wrong."

She felt herself turn pale and sensed Nicholas's tension, but she couldn't look at him. She had to get this out before she faced the horror she was sure was in his expression. "I finally emerged from my room. James stood at the top of the landing. He was no longer in the drunken rage I had seen him in earlier. His face had lost all its color, and Annie was at the bottom of the stairs. I could tell by the way she lay that she was dead. Her position was so unnatural, her body twisted so . . ." The lump in her throat prevented her from going on.

At last she broke down, quietly at first, and then huge sobs and gasps broke from her, emotions that had been pent-up for years. Nicholas drew her into his arms, laying her head on his shoulder while he caressed her back. She felt like a child in his arms, loved and protected for the first time in years, as the secret she had told no one fell away, a secret that had warped and distorted her happiness.

Lightly, he brushed his lips against her hair. Accepting the handkerchief he offered her, she called up the strength to go on with her story.

"I never knew if he pushed her or if she fell accidentally." She gulped down a sob. "He buried her and marked the spot with a cairn of rocks. I could see it from my window. I had to avoid looking at it. It was a constant reminder of his deceit. Later, I wanted the stones removed, but I was that would expose the crime. Finally I planted vines to cover it."

"I can think of nothing more horrible," Nicholas said, comforting her. "The devil himself could behave no worse than that blackhearted rogue."

She nodded. "Nothing was the same after that. I knew James would never change but for the worse. I was absolutely desperate." As the vivid memory returned, she trembled and closed her eyes. She felt Nicholas's arms around her. "I warned him I could bear no more and asked him to leave. He refused and laughed, of course. He always laughed. He was laughing when I shot him."

She started as Nicholas withdrew from her a fraction of an inch. It was a subtle distance that frightened her as much as the horror she expected to see on his face did. Instead of horror, however, his features held a puzzled expression that sought clarification rather than one prepared to deliver judgment.

"You aren't saying that's how he . . . died," he stammered.

"No," she assured him hurriedly, reassured at the relief she saw in his eyes, "please don't misunderstand. It was only a rib injury."

"But you shot him?" Nicholas said.

Again, she nodded. "I was still his wife, and he expected me to perform my wifely duty." The memory made her flush with humiliation. "How could I subject myself to that after he killed a woman who carried his child?"

"Delphinia, my love, no woman should be subjected to such treatment," he whispered abruptly.

Tears of grateful relief threatened to fall, but before she could give in to them, Nicholas drew her tightly against him, laying his head against her hair.

She felt her strength return at his touch, and she resumed her story.

"It was fortunate my father had not taken all his pistols to London. I slept with one under my pillow because I knew I might be next to fall down the stairs, having been a witness of sorts to Annie's death." She found herself able to ease into the topic as the past ebbed away with her confession. "After I shot him, I didn't know whether to hope he would live or die, even if he deserved death. For three days I tended him night and day, hardly ever sleeping."

"A costly way to develop one's nursing skills," he murmured against her neck. "I understand now how you learned your craft."

The irony in his words made her smile slightly before she proceeded. "After I knew he'd live, I had the gun trained on him when he awoke. I can still see his eyes. I knew one of us would kill the other at the first opportunity. I told him I would tell the sheriff about Annie if he did not leave. I watched from the edge of the property, still holding my gun, as he rode away, heading for Bristol and then on to America. He threatened me, saying if I notified the authorities he would tell them I had committed the murder out of jealousy."

"What a lying thief and scoundrel," Nicholas muttered.

"I couldn't have said it better myself," she replied grimly. "You once told me you understood what guilt was. Until then, I did not think anyone could experience guilt as I had."

"I do not believe they could."

He gave her a gentle smile, tinged with sadness. Dear, dear Nicholas, so patient despite her failings. Somehow he had not yet rejected her. Unwilling to question her miraculous good fortune, she rushed on to tell him what remained of her story.

"I was too sickened by what had happened to return to London. Ivy was only thirteen, too young to understand, and thankfully, she was still in the schoolroom. It was months later when I received a letter saying there had been a storm at sea, and a shipwreck had claimed the lives of all aboard. James was traveling with Percy's cousin Georgina who also drowned. I remember Percy, of all people, handing me the letter." A smile played about her lips. "I felt I'd been freed and that Annie had been vindicated somehow. I thought it was over. And then three years ago Percy came back."

Nicholas closed his eyes heavily before opening them again and studying her, watching her expression with a care that warmed her heart and filled her with the confidence to continue.

"Just like James, he threatened to tell the authorities I had killed Annie if I did not cooperate with his new venture. He had decided to try his hand at smuggling in cooperation with a man named Warren." She smiled, feeling weary. "Not surprisingly, he found it was the one thing he was quite good at."

"You did not go to the local constable with the truth?"

"Who could vouch for my character?" She chuckled bitterly. "An ill-behaved young woman who disobeyed her highly respected father and ran off with a rake, and I had not seen my friends in years. My friends would have been more likely to believe Percy, so besotted with James was I." She chuckled bitterly. "I thought the arrangement would be temporary. Ivy was coming to Exmoor in another few years. I was not about to create another scandal and jeopardize her chances at marriage because of my own past foolishness."

"So for the past three years you have been at Wainwright's mercy," Nicholas concluded.

"Yes." She gave him what she hoped was a mysterious smile. "But I do not plan to remain that way much longer."

Chapter Eleven

Nicholas watched as Delphinia's face flushed with triumph. For the first time that night her smile seemed genuine. He remained rooted to his seat, moved by her agony and the ordeal she had endured as well as by her poignant bravery.

"For some time now," she confided, leaning toward him on the sofa, "I have been collecting evidence against Percy. Once Ivy is gone, I will make my move. We might find ourselves on the road to freedom as early as tomorrow when we set off for London."

Tomorrow, Nicholas thought, seemed very far away at this moment, and freedom even farther.

"Tell me your plans," he urged. "I'm certain I can help, even if I have to summon all my naval contacts, past and present."

"I want to beat Percy at his own game." Delphinia's voice was quiet but determined. "I've kept a journal of our runs with newspaper clippings of shipping dates and names of vessels. My cellar is filled with casks of brandy I could not possibly have put there alone. I have two notes Mr. Warren sent me, one describing Percy's involvement in detail. Surely that is enough to convince the excise men of his deception. And despite the fact that Percy keeps a house in Martinhoe and has money with which to drink, gamble, and buy the services of women, he has no visible means of support. He is arrogant and boisterous, especially when he drinks. The constable is not fond of him. I do not think the men under him like him either, but they tolerate him. Still, I cannot expect them to risk their own livelihood by betraying him to the authorities. I am convinced I can find more proof, even if I need to set up the opportunity to do so by myself."

While Nicholas was satisfied she had considered her plan carefully, he was reluctant to let her pursue her intention to expose Wainwright by herself. Yet he did not wish to dim her enthusiasm. Instead he praised her ingenuity. "It appears you have thought of everything."

Her expression brightened with obvious relief at his acceptance of her plan. "I am glad you concur. I have tried hard to do so. I also have letters from James's creditors. He was always in need of money. I think he and Percy were planning this enterprise before he left. Since I was the one forced to endure the consequences of his activities, I still hope to find some evidence that James was the person who started this endeavor." She bit her lip, looking aggrieved. "When Ivy is safe, it will no longer matter what happens. If the authorities do not believe I am innocent, then so be it. I will go to the gallows with the rest of them. By then Ivy's fate will be secured, and Percy's smuggling venture will be ended," she added with a sigh of resignation.

And here he had been concerned about her independent streak

and wondered how she would adjust to life in London. He now understood the purpose of her rudeness had been to protect Ivy, as was everything else she had done. Yet while she possessed the boldness and courage to do what she must for Ivy's sake, he knew he would move heaven and hell before he would allow her to go the gallows for being forced to participate in the unholy venture.

"Ivy will not be happy until you are happy as well." He flashed her a severe expression that made her flush with recognition of his refusal to accept her choice to sacrifice herself. "Nor will I be. Such devotion deserves far better than the end you propose."

She shook her head and smiled. "Happiness is something I have lived without for a very long time now. It is the thing that is sacrificed first when one is desperate."

"You no longer need to forfeit your own happiness for anyone else's," he told her, speaking with an insistence he hoped would make her realize the truth of his words. "I am grateful you managed to find the courage to share this admission with me. It is no wonder you were unable to trust me, having been married to a murderer like James."

"I cannot say for sure that he committed murder. I did not see him push Annie. I saw her broken neck, her face white and ghastly looking, and he was drunk. That was my only part in it." She spoke frankly, but her tone was subdued. "When I first saw you lying at the bottom of the foyer stairs, it brought it all back to me. For selfish reasons I hoped you would not die. I did not want the authorities intruding."

"It is lucky for you I lived," he said mildly.

"I am ever so glad you did." Her eyes lingered on his for a moment. "And that you have stayed. Whoever would have thought it would take so long to get a carriage repaired?"

He started, uncomfortable with his own deception. "Certainly not I," he replied, giving her a smile that he hoped conveyed even a fraction of the love he felt for her.

Nicholas felt downright foolish when her smile broadened and she said, "No more lies, Captain, from either of us. I know the truth."

"You must think the worst of me." Chagrined, he took her hands in his gently. "I hope you can see why I had to delay my leave. How else was I to win your trust? If I had left when the carriage was ready, we might never have had time together."

"At the time, I had no reason to trust you." A new warmth came into her eyes. "But you have offered me such support."

"I intend to do more," he said firmly. "Who do you think Warren is?"

She hesitated reflectively. "I suspect he is a person of eminence who is collaborating with Percy. Otherwise, why would he refuse to meet me? I know the smugglers, though we do not talk. When I visited the cottage where Warren was supposed to live, I found only a

Frenchwoman. The next day the place was abandoned."

"I can inquire for him if you like," he offered. He welcomed even the smallest opportunity to remove her burden.

"No one here trusts strangers. They might think you were a preventive officer." Pulling her hands from his, she stood and walked across the room. Then she paused, gazing at him anxiously. "You must promise again never to reveal any of this to my father."

"You've nothing to fear on my account, but surely not all the local people are involved in smuggling. They have ears." He smiled wryly. "They must have tongues as well."

"They never speak of it to me. Perhaps Percy instructed them not to."

"I doubt Wainwright does anything for your benefit, unless it is also for his own. What became of the woman he was with the night of the murder? Is she involved in blackmail also?"

"They argued and she left during the night. She knew nothing of Annie's death." Her expression was earnest as she resumed her seat beside him. "What are you going to do now that you know the truth? What about your allegiance to the Crown?"

He took her hand and kissed it, stroking her palm with his fingers. "What of my allegiance to you? You need not fear betrayal on my part. My plans for you have nothing to do with what Percy has done. Trust me, Delphinia."

Her eyes were wary, but she seemed to relax in the face of her confession. "I will try. That is the most I can promise."

"I will not disappoint you. Of that you can be certain." God help any man who had dared to disappoint her in the past and now contributed to her further disappointment. From now on, he vowed, her life would be better. He would make it so. "What happens next?"

"Tomorrow night there will be a smuggling run behind the headland further west." She sighed ruefully. "As you know, the timing of the tides is so important. We have three chances in a month, with three landing points determined in advance. Our coves are close enough to one another so that if the preventive men are about, we put off the drop until the next night."

Nicholas asked the question he had been most curious about. "Do you not feel any fear about exposing the smuggling ring? The locals depend upon their cut. Do you not think they would blame you?"

Delphinia sighed. "I have decided not to identify the locals involved. The fact that they subsist on so little was the only way I could justify my part in it. They all have a trade, and they will get by without their work on the side. Since continental travel has been restricted by the war, Lynton has become a bit of a vacation spot." She smiled. "There's irony for you. Mr. Teasdale's inn might be full this time next year, with honest travelers rather than smugglers."

"At least they will earn something from tomorrow night's endeavor. I suppose they at least deserve that for their loyalty and the risks they have taken over the years." Trying to brush his own reluctant approval of their participation from his conscience, Nicholas indicated the sideboard. "May I?"

"Help yourself." Her tone edged with humor, she shook her head as he offered her a brandy. "None for me, thank you. I have lost my taste for it, I am afraid."

"I find that quite reasonable, under the circumstances."

Delphinia smiled gratefully and paced slowly across the room. He sensed she struggled before resuming a discussion of the subject she had been unable to avoid for so many years.

"I was reluctant to light the signal fire tonight, but I could not take a chance." Her serious expression was replaced by a lopsided grin. "To think I called it off because of you. Had I realized you were there, I would have waited and tried to gather more evidence against Percy."

"I regret having interrupted your activities." Replacing the brandy decanter on the sideboard, Nicholas returned to her side. He was not surprised that his sympathies lay with her, but he had not expected to feel such loyalty. While listening to her story, he had been captivated by her courage and determination to free herself from Wainwright's tyranny. Her bravery in the face of such cruelty made him determined to free her at any cost to himself. "I will come with you on tomorrow's smuggling run."

Her lovely countenance filled with alarm. "No, you cannot. Percy will see you for certain."

"I will not allow you to go alone." While her courage and stubbornness were a formidable combination, Nicholas knew neither was enough to protect her from someone as ruthless as Percy Wainwright. Their eyes locked until he feared she would refuse to concede. "I have no intention of announcing my presence, but you must trust me enough to let me follow you. I will not give myself away."

She appeared to consider his idea. "It is very risky. Your ankle is not at full strength. You need to be able to hide yourself well."

"You yourself have noticed how much the ankle has improved," he countered. "I was able to follow you well enough tonight."

After another hesitation, the doubt he had seen in her eyes was replaced with swift decisiveness. A bold conviction he had not heard previously strengthened her tone when she spoke again. "Do not follow too closely. Percy would just as soon shoot you as look at you, and not one of them will care."

"I intend to see him stand trial, if it is the last thing I do," he announced. "He belongs in Dartmoor, and now that the prison is no longer needed for French prisoners, he may actually end up there."

She looked at him with panic in her eyes. "I do not want this to be the last thing you do. I told Percy I thought he was being followed to explain why I called off the drop. He suspected it was you who had trailed him, but I denied it, saying only that I thought I saw someone from my window and was coming to warn him when I realized it was merely a shadow I had seen. It is imperative he not learn the truth. He is extremely dangerous."

"Dangerous to you also."

"But more to you," she insisted. "That is why you must do as I ask over the next few days and weeks."

Nicholas was only too happy to promise her anything she desired, knowing there was not, and had never been, any romantic attachment between her and Percy Wainwright.

"So what does the future hold for you?" he asked, hoping she might divulge some of her intentions.

"I will go to the local authorities when I return from London. We were fortunate our mild winter allowed us to resume activity in March this year. Usually storms force us to import goods on the north coast only in the summer months. The early start has given me time to consider my options." Her face clouded as she struggled with her emotions. "I will request that the authorities keep my identity secret so that exposing Percy does not ruin Ivy's chances of making a suitable match. I have to hope they will honor my request in exchange for information."

A branch clawed idly at the window behind Nicholas, startling him. This was the first time he had noticed the wind tonight, reminding him of the night he was lost on the moors. The rhythmic ticking of the mantel clock was the only warning that another day would soon dawn, ending a night in which neither of them had slept.

"I want to make it clear to you that whatever your future holds, I shall continue to serve and support you," he told her quietly.

"I hope you are still able to say that in May, when my cellar will again be full of either tea or brandy." She smiled, looking weary as she leaned back against the sofa. "By then Ivy will be on her way to a better life, and I will be free to act."

He returned her smile, catching her meaning and taking her hand at the same time. "And then you and I and the excise men will have a little tea party of our own."

* * * *

Nicholas followed Delphinia's instructions to the letter the following night. Deferring to her fear that Percy might have sent a spy after them, he remained a solid distance behind her. He felt privileged to witness such an enterprise, especially because it was illegal. Few gentlemen of his class were ever handed the opportunity to observe a smuggling run firsthand. How phenomenal it is, he reflected, that she trusts me enough to allow me this chance. How much we have both changed, and in so short a time.

This night they had a longer distance to walk, for the drop would be at Lee Bay, further than the run he had interrupted the previous night at Lynmouth. Tonight was less favorable than last night, Delphinia had warned him, for the wind was lower and the sky was clear toward the north. The few stars added an undesirable brightness to the night.

"You must stay out of sight, whatever you do," she had advised him before they left the house. "Remember I am as familiar with this terrain as anyone, and I will be safe."

The salty, brackish taste of the sea air pervaded his nostrils as Nicholas assumed his assigned location. He watched through dense shrubbery as the smuggling run unfolded before his eyes. The men had positioned themselves on land exactly as she said they would. He noted the vigilance and poise that was so critical to their illegal endeavor, particularly after the previous night when he had put an abrupt end to their watch.

Along the shoreline, moored deep in shadows that fused with solid rock, an array of small boats waited, hardly noticeable in the hidden coves and caves at the base of the cliffs. Nicholas watched with fascination as a foreign vessel of unfamiliar design, painted black with dark sails, emerged from the mists and moved steadily on the quiet ocean. The fore-and-aft rigged vessel traveled swiftly and silently on the current. No wonder smugglers preferred such a vessel. With grudging admiration, he noted its speed and grace.

"I will be watching for the signal from the spotsman on the ship," Delphinia had told him matter-of-factly. "He knows just where to look for me. There will be a flash from the ship which I answer with a furze beacon if the coast is not clear. Tonight, however," she had added, her eyes twinkling, "I trust there will be no need of a flare."

Somewhere on the cliff top, she was part of the land party, watching and waiting as the ship journeyed toward its destination. Nicholas could see no sign of her. He tensed in the darkness, the weight of uneasiness upon him. How could he be sure she was all right? The odds were that she was safely hidden among the gorse at the cliff's edge, as she'd said she would be, safer even than him.

The ship did not stop to unload its illegal cargo but continued to glide up the Bristol Channel. Nicholas heard the mournful toll of a bell buoy obscured in fog, warning sailors of the presence of land. In the dim starlight, he could make out the vague shapes of barrels being dropped from the sides of the vessel. The English boats had moved a few miles offshore, their movement almost imperceptible in the shadow of the ship. The French rig continued toward Bristol and returned into the mist, its clandestine rendezvous complete.

The flotilla sailed out toward the tubs, dragging them on board before rowing rapidly back to shore where shadowy figures waited to land the cargo. Nicholas was impressed by the speed with which the men switched from silence to action. In heavy overcoats, neckerchiefs, and sou'westers, their enormous boots sucking up the mud, they secured the boats on shore. Most wore beards that hid their identities. He wondered if Delphinia's Mr. Warren was among them.

"Don't you ever worry about being discovered?" he had asked her earlier.

"The whole community has a stake in our venture," she had replied. "The risk of our work being spoiled by an informer is slight. Besides, there is far more smuggling at Ilfracombe where only four excise men are assigned. It will take them a while to catch up with us."

Nicholas watched attentively as the surefooted crew hefted the small barrels. Half-ankers, Delphinia had called the flat-sided barrels designed by coopers for easier carrying, each holding a little more than four gallons. He could almost feel the strain as the barrels were slung together on ropes. These were the tub men at work, he decided. They performed the task with the quick, skillful motions of a job repeated many times before. When all the barrels had been paired on ropes, the men draped them over their shoulders, one in front, the other in back.

"The men carry the tubs for miles across the moors, because carts would draw too much attention," Delphinia had said. "When you walk beside them you can hear their labored breathing. Of course, it is worth it when tea sells for three pence on the Continent while it is twenty-five here at home."

All that exertion for a mere seven shillings a night. And they call this the free trade, Nicholas thought. What angered him most was that the smugglers were willing to make deals with the French. Our greatest enemy, he reflected bitterly. How quickly we forget the lessons of war.

From his own experience at sea, he knew that many excise cutters were commanded by the poorest seamen in the navy. They did not stand a chance against the bootleggers, who were clever and skillful and motivated by greed. The customs men had learned the hard way to be alert for tricks, inspecting cargoes for false-bottomed barrels and similar deceptions. When it came to contraband, Nicholas thought, there was always someone cleverer.

While he watched intently, the men began their arduous climb up the steep cliff. Several hundred feet of swaying rope ladder had been lowered over the edge of the precipice by men he could barely make out in the grass. The ascent was slow but steady, and at last all the barrels were removed from the shore. Fortunately, the wind remained at a lull for most of the night.

Few things were worse, Nicholas conceded, than being chilled to the bone with wet trousers while at the mercy of the sea winds. The heavy surf made wading difficult and miserably uncomfortable. Knowing how hard the work was, he felt sorry for the outlaws, in spite of the fact that they were committing a criminal offense.

He glanced around furtively, recalling Delphinia's words about remaining invisible amidst the scrub and gorse. He saw no sign of Percy Wainwright among the men.

Had he joined Delphinia at some point? The thought gave him physical pain. If the two had met up, Nicholas prayed Delphinia had the presence of mind to remain detached. At the moment he could think of no better place for Wainwright to be than in London's Millbank Prison, its cells infested with cholera. Had any man ever deserved less? Nicholas thought not.

He shook off the chill that enveloped him from the night air. In the throes of danger as he and Delphinia were, it was hard to imagine they would be in London by tomorrow. He would not rest until he saw her safely removed from the situation that had imprisoned her for far too long.

He rose to his feet cautiously. It was time to return to the house. The crew was ready to begin the toilsome job of lugging the barrels over the moor to Briarcombe.

* * * *

Delphinia remained upstairs as she always did while the men stacked the casks in the cellar. Nervously she waited at the top of the stairs, where she heard Percy barking orders below as he counted the tubs and supervised their placement.

Once they were all accounted for, he usually joined her in the library, but tonight was different. She noticed abruptly the downstairs had become quiet. Still he did not come. Checking the cellar door, she found it had been locked before she realized the job was finished. Although she would not expect any of the men to linger below, she was surprised Percy had vanished as well.

When she was sure he was nowhere about, she knocked on the drawing room doors. She was let in by Nicholas, who waited quietly.

"There's no sign of Percy anywhere," she said uneasily.

"Perhaps he was tired and headed home," he suggested.

His words failed to convince her. "He always stops by after a run. Where could he be?"

Nicholas stepped up beside her, his six-foot frame towering over her in a manner she found appealingly protective.

"I do not know, but I hope you can put this worry behind you long enough to sit with me so we might talk." He placed an arm about her shoulders. "There is a matter I would like to discuss with you."

Trying to vanquish her sense of foreboding, Delphinia was warming to the idea of conversation when the drawing room doors opened softly behind them. She leaped where she stood, clutching Nicholas's arm.

Percy Wainwright stood in the doorway, pointing a gun at them. For a second her heart stopped.

"Hello, Delphinia, my dear," he said in a scathing tone. "I had a good idea where I would find you, and with whom."

He studied Nicholas with a cold, blank stare. No, Delphinia thought, this cannot happen now, not when everything has started to turn for the better.

"Why don't you leave her alone, Wainwright?" Nicholas's voice was low and threatening.

Delphinia watched breathlessly, unable to move. She prayed neither would do anything rash.

Percy emitted a high-pitched, reckless laugh that echoed throughout the drawing room and up to its high ceiling.

"Without her, business would be far less profitable," he protested with mock sadness. "Believe me, we value her assistance. But right now the three of us are going to take a walk."

"Where are you taking us?" Delphinia demanded. Hysteria rose within her. She had to be calm. She needed all her wits to deal with Percy.

"For a stroll by the sea, my dear. Here, Captain, catch." He tossed a length of sturdy rope to Nicholas, who retrieved the coil in midair. "If you want to live a little longer, you will do as I say. You're going to bind Delphinia's wrists behind her back. Tightly now, and no games," he added severely. "I'm going to check to make sure it's done right."

Her heart pounding, Delphinia stood helplessly with her back to Nicholas. He gave her a brief, reassuring embrace before he grasped her fingers in his strong hands and tied the rope about her wrists. She felt him bind it securely, as Percy had ordered.

"Percy, what are you doing?" she burst out.

"Never mind. Let's see what kind of job the captain's done." The gun still in his hand, he grabbed her roughly and spun her about. His fingers examined the knot before he thrust her from him.

"You're not taking any chances, Captain," he muttered. "Good for you. Now let's go outside quietly. We don't want to wake the servants. I warn you, if you make as much as a single move, she's dead. Lead the way, Captain."

With Nicholas in front, Percy gripped Delphinia by the wrists, shoving her through the foyer and out the front door. As she stepped over the threshold into the cold night air, it crossed her mind very briefly to cry out for help. But what were the chances that Ivy or Sophy or, even less likely, Childers might hear? If they responded Percy might well shoot all of them.

She did not trust him in such a desperate state. She remained silent, wishing she could know what Nicholas was thinking as she followed him. Oh, please, she begged silently, do not try anything foolish. Percy will kill you, and I could not live without you.

"I knew you could not be trusted," Percy growled in her ear, as they made their way unevenly over the dark hollows. "Everything was fine until the captain came. Now there's hell to pay. I am not about to lose all we've worked for, I can tell you that, even if you would throw it away."

He is going to kill us, she thought wildly, or, if not me, certainly Nicholas. Should she stop in her tracks and refuse to take another step? She hesitated just long enough to earn herself a painful thrust from behind as Percy jammed the gun barrel into her ribs.

"No tricks, Delphinia. I warned you," he said sharply.

"Do you think you can get away with this, Wainwright?" Nicholas laughed with scorn. "You'll never get us to the coast in one piece."

"Then I'll take you there in dozens of pieces," he snapped. He returned his attention to her. "You see, my dear Delphinia, I had to ensure you were securely bound, but I didn't want to truss the captain that way. I don't want him to be found with ropes about him after he meets with his unfortunate accident."

Shaking his head in a deliberately ominous fashion, Percy turned to Nicholas. "It's very dangerous for strangers to walk the moors at night. Too bad you didn't learn the first time when you hurt your ankle. Now move and shut up, before I blow your head off."

Delphinia listened to his words with horror, scarcely believing he could intend to do as he claimed.

"Percy," she pleaded, hoping he would hear the distress in her tone, "please, if I have ever meant anything to you at all, let him go. He will not say anything to the authorities. He is on our side. You have to believe me."

"Why would I believe such rot? Really, Delphinia, I credited you with more intelligence than that."

They were following the path toward Moorcombe Marsh, with its treacherous fissures and bogs. Even in daylight the marsh was dangerous to navigate. Surely Percy could not be planning to take them through terrain with which Nicholas was totally unfamiliar.

Perhaps if she pretended to stumble she could kick her heels back and catch Percy's ankles, tripping him up and knocking his feet from under him. She would have to be careful not to lose her balance here. It would be only too easy.

As they turned downhill, she wondered if her tall stature blocked Percy's view and gave Nicholas an advantage. If she were to slide, Percy might not have a clear view of Nicholas. Still, any attempt to escape might only get her wounded.

Before she could act on her idea, she heard the slipping of feet on soggy moorland. Nicholas tumbled to the ground before her, his flailing arms knocking her off balance. With a cry she fell awkwardly on the slope, not knowing whether his fall was deliberate or accidental.

"Damn you, Hainsworth," Percy muttered from behind her.

Then Delphinia felt herself being struck in the ribs as a gunshot shattered the silence of the night.

Chapter Twelve

Engulfed in darkness, Delphinia let out an involuntary scream. Powerless to struggle with her hands bound, she attempted to use her feet to regain her balance. She felt no pain in her ribs and realized the shot she'd heard had not been fired in her direction. Panic swept over her at the thought that Nicholas might have been wounded.

As she struggled Percy was beside her in an instant, trying to subdue her. She kicked a leg out at him, missed by a yard, and was rewarded with a slap across the face.

Nicholas must have heard her groan, for she heard the scuffling of feet in the dark, followed by the thud of bodies hitting the ground. Relief that he was still alive mixed with fear at the sounds of their struggle. A night bird in the tree above them squawked and flew off in fear.

Delphinia listened to the men's grunts in the darkness, paralyzed with terror, wondering who had the upper hand. As Nicholas continued to wrestle with Percy, she looked around wildly for a glint of steel, hoping to find the pistol even though she did not know how she could retrieve it with her hands still bound. The night sky did not offer even a glimmer to help her locate the weapon.

Delphinia recognized a sudden groan of pain that was all too familiar and knew Nicholas had been hurt. Freezing in fear, she heard the thrashing of thorn bushes as Percy fled, the leaves rustling in the wake of his escape.

"Nicholas, are you injured?" she cried as she rolled onto her side, ignoring the soreness of her bruised rib.

"Only my pride," he muttered. He staggered to his feet. "You're not hurt, are you?"

"No, I'm fine."

He coughed loudly, kneeling beside her as he fumbled in the dark with the ropes that bound her hands and chafed against her wrists. "I can feel my jaw swelling a bit, but not as much as my ankle. I don't need any more injuries than I already have. Percy apparently had other ideas. Come, let's get you home."

Placing a muscular arm about her waist, he eased her into a standing position. She fought dizziness as she regained her balance.

"Wait," she said, feeling a sensation near her ankle. "Look."

Her foot touched something hard. A metal object glistened in the wet underbrush. In the glow of starlight from a passing cloud, Nicholas picked up the pistol Percy had left behind.

"A rather valuable find, I'd say," he muttered, positioning the gun away from her. "One never knows when it might prove useful."

* * * *

On returning to Briarcombe with Nicholas, Delphinia found that its inhabitants had continued their uninterrupted slumber under the moonless sky but for one. As they entered the front door, Ivy met them in the foyer in her dressing gown. She was pale and shivering more from fear than from cold.

"I thought I heard a shot. Has something happened?" She spoke in little more than a whisper until a frown gave her a new worry. "What's this bruise on your face? That wasn't there earlier."

Here was the confrontation Delphinia had feared most. Her throat went dry at the prospect of revealing her activities to Ivy. Would her sister ever understand? Delphinia looked to Nicholas for confirmation. He nodded to her as if leaving the decision to her judgment. Taking a deep breath, she turned to Ivy.

"Yes, something has happened," she admitted. "I am about to tell you something I should have told you a long time ago."

And I pray you will not hate me when you hear it. Please, Lord, let her find forgiveness in her heart.

Scarcely daring to breathe, Delphinia slipped an arm about Ivy's shoulders and led her into the drawing room where they sat side by side on the sofa. Almost mechanically she repeated her entire confession, fearful Ivy would resent the possible scandal her own sister's actions may have created.

When she had finished, Ivy stared at her in horror and disbelief. "I had no idea," she said in a soft voice. "All the time I have been sitting here reading copies of *La Belle Assemblee* you have been risking your life. I've been so intent on packing for London and making my farewells to the villagers and writing Mrs. Herbert with my plans I did not even realize all you've done for me. And all so I could have a better life than you have had."

Apparently overcome by the realization of her sister's generosity, Ivy lowered her head and burst into tears. Delphinia's heart lightened with relief. How much Ivy has grown up in the last few weeks, she reflected tenderly. All at once Ivy looked older and yet more vulnerable.

This, Delphinia knew in a heartbeat, was her chance. The opportunity she had always wanted for a relationship with her sister lay bare before her. She had an overwhelming urge to cradle Ivy in her arms, if the girl would let her.

"But that is what I want most for you." Speaking in a comforting tone, she pushed Ivy's hair back from her forehead, reaching an arm about her shoulders. "You must not blame yourself. Having you here was often the only joy I had. You were my source of hope. Without you I would have given up long ago."

"I cannot believe you did not. Oh, Delphinia."

Ivy shook her head in bewilderment. Impulsively she threw her arms about her sister. Delphinia embraced her as if it were the culmination of a long-awaited dream now realized.

"I never imagined anything like this," Ivy went on, releasing her from the embrace and taking Delphinia's hands in her own. "I am not sure I would have thought you capable of anything so sinister."

"I did not know you paid any attention to what I did." Delphinia was surprised. "What did you think I was doing?"

"It sounds too frivolous." A smile crept across Ivy's face. "I thought you had a lover of whom you could not speak."

Delphinia stared at her, aghast. "Ivy, you didn't!"

"The thought did cross my mind."

"I warned you not to read so much of the Minerva Press."

Delphinia wiped away a tear from her eye, catching sight of Nicholas as she did so. He sat unobtrusively to one side while the sisters unraveled their tangled emotions. His discretion was one of his most endearing qualities. Whatever must he think of it all? Delphinia had never met a man who showed such patience and understanding. A lump welled in her throat.

"To think you did all this for me." Ivy's eyes widened with wonder. "I-I've never felt so loved in all my life."

Her words filled the distance between them in less time than it had taken Delphinia to tell her story. Before either of them could weep again, Delphinia returned to practical concerns.

"In a few days you will be safe in London," she reminded Ivy. "We will preserve your reputation even if we cannot save mine."

Ivy frowned worriedly. "I'm afraid to let you come back here alone. Perhaps I should postpone my come-out for another year."

"You mustn't do that," Delphinia insisted. "Everything I've done was for your sake, to find you a place in Society."

Sadness tightened its relentless grip on her heart. How much happier they might have been if she had met Nicholas sooner, before James had come into her life, or even later, after she had exposed Percy. The timing seemed all wrong.

"I don't want you to take any more chances because of me," Ivy went on. "The position you are in frightens me."

"I only did what I had to do for our family, and what you would have done in my place." Even as she made the statement, she knew it was the truth.

Ivy spoke with difficulty. "I know you resented having Mrs. Herbert here. I hope you understand that I only spent time with her because we shared the kind of relationship I always wanted to have with you."

Delphinia sighed dismissively. "It is as much my fault as yours. I hope you see that to let you close to me would have meant giving away my secret. I could never have put you in danger by telling you the truth. But Father must never learn of this." Her voice grew strained as she added, "You must be a consummate actress, Ivy, not to let him find out."

Ivy sniffled noisily into the handkerchief Nicholas offered her. "It was you who told me I would be a great success in London because I had learned to dissemble so well." She blew her nose and smiled brightly. "This time I won't fail you, I promise."

Ivy's fervent vow surprised a laugh from Delphinia. "I know you won't fail me, just as you never have."

The sisters embraced tightly, releasing the restraint that had separated them, before Ivy said goodnight and retired to bed. Afterward, Delphinia turned her attention to Nicholas. He sat in an upholstered chair, looking tired but content somehow. He smiled at her in a most affectionate way, one that embarrassed her.

"Well, that's done," she said briefly, and took a seat.

"What a long night it has been." He laughed quietly. "It is nearly dawn, and London is only hours away."

Delphinia wrapped her arms about herself, gazing out at the night through the room's tall windows. Although there was nothing more than moors beyond the window, she feared the darkness, as if even the four o'clock sky held danger in its depths. Their impending departure weighed upon her like lead.

"I'm not sure it is wise to go away now," she murmured.

"You must," Nicholas said forcefully. "You are not safe here. I know you are worried about facing your father and aunts and your friends in town, but you are safer in their presence."

"What do you think Percy will do next? We cannot stop him from leaving the country." Intent as she was on bringing Percy to justice, the idea of his escape depressed her.

"I'm convinced he'll be back," Nicholas said thoughtfully. "The next drop after your return from London is already arranged. That means he'll have at least one more month of forked cargo. The lure of riches is too great."

"Won't he assume we will go to the authorities?"

Nicholas shook his head. "Wainwright knows we won't risk a scandal at this point. He preys on your fears, Delphinia. He knows that for the next month your life will focus on Ivy and the diversions of London." He studied her with a look of disquietude that frightened her. "I fear he will become far more dangerous after the next drop."

She reflected on the history she shared with Percy and shuddered. "I would not put any kind of cruelty past him."

"It amazes me no one's clapped irons on him before this." Nicholas rose and pounded his fist into the back of the cushioned chair, his sudden fury startling Delphinia. "He should have been arrested long ago."

"When you stumbled on the hill tonight," she asked, "how could you be sure he wouldn't shoot us?"

"I couldn't." A crooked smile played on his lips. "I took a chance that he would not hurt you. A very big chance. I dragged you down, hoping he would stumble as well and fire toward the ground. It was our best chance."

She shivered at the recollection of their encounter with danger. Were it not for the fact that Nicholas placed a higher value on her life than Percy did, she might be dead already . . .

"Maybe he thought over his plan," she suggested, "and realized it was unwise to kill us."

"I imagine he felt it was safer to get away while he could. Something tells me we haven't seen the last of Percy Wainwright."

The thought chilled Delphinia. She could not imagine facing Percy after the ordeal he had forced upon them.

"What kind of danger are we in?" she asked quietly. "I would not want anything to happen to Briarcombe."

Nicholas moved closer and sat gently beside her, entwining his fingers with hers. How large his hands were, and how strong.

"You cannot worry about fears that have no substance," he advised. "The best we can do is to proceed as planned. Ivy will need you in London. No one will notice the slight bruise you sustained tonight, and if someone does it can be explained away easily enough." He ran his finger with infinite tenderness gently along her cheek.

Anxiety filled her. "But where will you go?"

"I shall try to prepare for any contingency. Here is what we shall do. We will turn over all the information you have collected on Wainwright to my solicitor in London. We'll let the revenuers track down Mr. Warren. And we won't breathe a word of this to your father."

Her heart leaped. "What about your visit to St. Ives?"

"I have been giving that matter a good deal of thought, as I have your reputation." Sitting before her with one hand resting on his knee and the other holding her hand, Nicholas laughed softly and looked away, as if he felt suddenly shy. "This may not be the best time, but since you are to leave for London in a few hours, I might not have another opportunity."

For the first time since she had met him, Nicholas seemed at a loss for words. His awkward, laconic state was so rare that his silence alarmed Delphinia. The possible reason for his hesitation concerned her even more.

"What is it you want to ask me, Captain?" she asked.

"Please, Delphinia, no more titles. From now on let it be my Christian name always. It is hardly fitting to address a husband by his rank, after all, when one becomes a wife."

She stared at him in astonishment. "A wife?"

His green eyes gazed directly into hers, the tenderness she saw there making them slightly misty. "Your ears have not failed you, my dear. That is what I said. Do you need more time to think about it?"

"Does this mean what I think it does?" His wholly unexpected words left her feeling too dazed to think clearly. She could not seem to recover from the shock in a timely fashion.

"Perhaps I need to be more direct in my request. I am asking you to marry me, Delphinia." When he spoke, his tone was so exuberant that Delphinia realized he had failed to recognize her stupor. "I would not dishonor you by asking you to marry without your father's permission, of course."

"Oh, it is a tremendous honor!" she assured him hastily. Her thoughts reeled with the sense of dishonor that bound her to her past. "But how would your family receive me?"

"They will be less concerned with your past than with the grace and beauty you possess at present. I doubt they care a fig whom I choose as long as I choose someone. Your widowhood has been my good fortune, for it has given you a second chance at happiness."

She froze as Nicholas knelt before her, taking her trembling hands in his sturdy ones. "I am asking you to give me a chance to make you happy. I ask you to please consider my request."

How very like Nicholas Hainsworth, thought Delphinia. He would not attempt to plead for her hand with flowery declarations as he proclaimed his need for her. Rather he would present her with an option and leave it to her to make up her mind. His words were delivered in a tone of cheerful earnestness, but she could not help feeling he was offering for her prematurely. He had not yet been to London this Season. If he had, he might have found another woman more appropriate, one he might deem superior.

She had viewed herself as a liability for so long she could hardly bring herself to put her faith in anyone who would find her attractive. When men talked about being leg-shackled, she assumed they were referring to someone like herself, someone who had a history of misfortune, who had fallen from grace and was of no merit. Why would anyone of Captain Nicholas Hainsworth's eminence choose to tie himself to such a woman?

Slipping her hands from his, she rose and moved awkwardly across the room. "I appreciate your propriety in trying to save me from scandal, but I fear an engagement may simply create a greater one," she warned him.

"When will you realize, Delphinia, this has nothing to do with protecting your name? We are so right for each other. A betrothal seems destined, do you not think so?"

"I would like nothing more," she answered honestly.

Nicholas gripped her by the shoulders and turned her firmly about so she could see nothing but the hope in his eyes, a look that filled her with despair.

"I know it is difficult, perhaps impossible, for you to fathom, but I know you would love my home," he told her. His eyes were bright with enthusiasm. "I cannot describe to you the beauty of Tregaryan. If you saw St. Ives you would not be lonely for Exmoor. There is a tranquility that fills the soul. Instead of being windy and desolate, the harbor is sheltered and peaceful. You could trade gloom and mist for sunshine and mild weather. It is not an even swap exactly, for you have never been there, but that is what I have to offer you. I think it is a better than fair exchange."

She was filled with foreboding as it occurred to her that the comfortable security she had always known at Briarcombe would likely be gone once the local families discovered she had exposed their smuggling operations. Her throat went dry at the thought. She hesitated to voice her fear. She knew Nicholas wanted her to be happy in the wake of his marriage proposal, and she had no intention of disappointing him.

"I shall cancel my trip to St. Ives so we may proceed straight to London," Nicholas announced. "Sylvia will understand. She will even be delighted, once she learns why." He gazed upon her for so long a time, with something so akin to adoration in his eyes that it alarmed her. "No one could love you as I do, my dear. I hope you will always remember that."

"But Percy remains a threat," she protested faintly, "to you as well as to me."

"One does not always have to take the flagship to win the battle. We can defeat him yet, Delphinia." He folded an arm about her shoulders, as if the matter were settled. "With you as my second-in-command I would not expect to fail."

Somehow she could not share his mood of expectation. At present, she was so overwhelmed with fear and uncertainty about the future that she had not given herself time to stop and think about her own life. Inside her a voice of warning from the past arrested her hopes before they could take root. So many aspects of her life were yet unsettled, so many problems still to be conquered.

Yet she could not imagine a man to whom she would rather be married than Nicholas. His actions on her behalf had persuaded her he was a man of integrity who would stand by his promises. He lived by a code of honor that would not allow him to risk the reputation of any woman, even one such as herself.

She had not forgotten Percy's warning about the village gossip concerning her guest whose departure was long overdue, and Nicholas would never put her reputation at greater risk. He also had a mother whose wishes he wanted to satisfy. It was clear that a number of concerns had prompted his offer of marriage.

Delphinia bit her lip nervously. She could not bear the thought of disappointing such a wonderful man in any way. She had been isolated within her own small world for so long she was not convinced she could live up to his standards. What if she failed at marriage a second time? It would be disastrous, the very last thing she wanted.

Still, the possibility of her father's name being disgraced again because a gentleman had paid her a suspiciously lengthy visit concerned her deeply. Perhaps the best thing she could do under the circumstances was to accept Nicholas's offer. In doing so she would be making not only her father happy, but his mother as well.

She turned to him slowly, only a slight reluctance tugging at her conscience.

"I should be quite happy to accept your offer, Captain—Nicholas," she replied demurely.

* * * *

Several hours later, Delphinia was overwrought with worry as she tried to pack for her visit to London. She found fault with everything from her wardrobe to the cut on her cheek.

"I have been so preoccupied I have had little time to think about my clothing," she admitted to Ivy. "My clothes are all out-of-date and ridiculous. I am ashamed to wear such things. Everyone will think me a country dowd."

To her consternation, Ivy giggled. "You are more worried about this trip than I am. It is good to see you in such a state, Delphinia. Just as Nicholas said, this is a second chance for you."

Delphinia and Nicholas had confided the news to Ivy that morning that they intended to ask her father's blessing upon their marriage once they were in town. The very idea of Nicholas asking her father, the earl, for her hand filled Delphinia with trepidation. She had not been in contact with her father for so long that the request would come as a shock to him. She wanted him to know how upright a man Nicholas truly was.

Would her own father think she had behaved improperly in offering Nicholas shelter beneath her roof? The thought of being physically close to Nicholas, of being able to put her arms about him whenever the mood struck her, appealed to her. The impulse came far more often now. His physique was so masculine while his disposition was so kind. Delphinia found it hard to believe she had been so fortunate to receive a proposal of marriage from such a man.

Then she remembered the danger she faced from Percy's knowledge of her background. Oh, dearest Ivy, she thought desperately, it is so important to choose your friends wisely, and even more critical to find the right spouse. Otherwise one could pay forever, with a mistake as deadly as hers had been.

* * * *

"My only regret is that we are traveling in separate carriages," Nicholas told Delphinia shortly before their trunks were loaded into the waiting vehicles. "But as we are not certain what course of action will be taken following our visit, it makes sense to bring both. And our carriages will leave at the same time and travel the same route, so you and Ivy are in no danger, dearest, even if we are bound for separate destinations. At any rate, our routes will not diverge until we reach London."

"We shall not be separated for long," she said, adjusting her gloves as she paused in the hall. She reassured herself with the thought of his arrival in town perhaps even more than she reassured him. "You will visit us at our home in Park Lane. And Curzon Street is not so very far away, after all. Although your carriage will always be within sight of ours, Ivy and I will have no fear with Mrs. Adamsdale along as our chaperone."

She thought of their father's tenant and wondered if she and Ivy would be able to get a word in edgewise.

"But your mother," she protested to Nicholas. "I am so apprehensive about meeting her. I am intimidated already, and we have not even left Devon."

"It is a waste to worry," he told her as he stepped into the doorway, watching Stebbins advise Hobbs on how to load his toiletries case, "for you will not find her at home. Since she does not expect me in town, she has already departed for St. Ives to be with Sylvia and her family. So you are spared the pressure of meeting her right off. It is just as well. You have enough pressure on you at present."

With her life in turmoil, Delphinia was greatly relieved there would be one less person whose favor she had to win.

With Sophy in pursuit, Ivy dashed past them and outside, dancing with excitement, as the servants finished arranging the luggage within the carriages.

With his usual perceptive grasp of her emotions, Nicholas paused on the threshold before stepping outdoors. "I shall be outside," he told Delphinia, "whenever you are ready."

With a catch in her throat, Delphinia turned to take a final look around before leaving home, profoundly regretting that marriage was the farthest thing from her mind. Uppermost in it were the charges she would set in motion to be brought against Percy Wainwright when the time was right.

Chapter Thirteen

During their journey to London, Delphinia found herself so absorbed in recent events that she worried less about the trials before her than those that lay behind. Two months ago the idea of a marriage proposal coming from the most desirable man she had ever known, on the same night their lives were threatened, would have been unimaginable.

If what lay behind her was so dreadful, she pondered, how would she ever cope with what was to come? If Percy decided to seek vengeance upon her, her deepest fear was that he would not take out his anger on her, but on one of the two people she loved most in the world—perhaps even both.

She watched idly out the window as they rode, noting the passing landscape of trees and cattle with little interest. Nicholas's coach, as he had promised, was always within sight of hers. She saw it close behind each time they rounded a bend, for both were following the same path in case Percy had someone watching the roads as they departed.

The ride with Ivy and Mrs. Adamsdale passed uneventfully, as their chaperone chatted about her sons, making the time slip away without much chance for Delphinia to brood over her concerns. In a rare moment of serenity, she realized she knew perfectly well how to cope with catastrophe. She would face the future in as steady a fashion as she had every crisis that had befallen her. Her future could not be any worse than her past.

She managed to retain this positive frame of mind even as she dismounted from the coach in London, removing her bonnet as she stepped inside her father's home in Park Lane for the first time in years. The foyer floor was cluttered with bandboxes and trunks before the aunts had finished showering their nieces with effusive greetings.

"When will someone devise a faster method of travel?" Aunt Tilly complained. "We were so anxious for you to arrive we could hardly sit still. I cannot blame the horses, poor beasts, for they can only go so fast. That leaves you to blame, Delphinia, or is it Ivy's fault you were delayed?"

"We took care packing, as we did not want to forget anything essential." Delphinia glanced about the elegant entranceway of her father's home. Quickly she checked her complexion in the gilt mirror by the door, pleased to see how much the cut on her cheek had faded. Filled with sudden humor, she turned back to her aunt. "And yes, Ivy did bring nearly all her possessions."

"What if I decide to change my hair?" Ivy giggled. "Who knows when I might need my copies of *The Ladies' Toilettes?*"

"Or your Minerva Press novels?" Delphinia teased, as Ivy nudged her.

"Thank you, Delphinia," Ivy said hastily, "but now that I have arrived, I am sure I shall be too busy to read much."

Their banter ended abruptly with the firm closing of a door behind them followed by slow but solid footsteps. Delphinia did not need Ivy's exclamation of joy to recognize her father's imposing step. What surprised her, as she turned to greet him, was how the years had changed him, stealing his vitality and leaving wisdom in their wake. His hair was so much grayer, his walk slower than when she had seen him last. He seemed older and more vulnerable. The difference in his appearance tugged at her heart.

As he released Ivy after a fond embrace, Adam Herrick's eyes locked with Delphinia's. She saw no judgment there but instead an affection and interest she had not seen or felt since childhood. The expression on her father's aging face made the years disappear, as if the two had never parted. Without another thought, she rushed forward, throwing her arms about her father.

"Papa," she wept, burying her face against the lapel of his coat as she released the pain of her lost years.

"You have come home at last, Delphinia," he murmured, his aloof tone touched with irony, as always. "It is high time. Come, my dearest, tears are unladylike and will only prevent you from talking in a dignified fashion. We have much to catch up on."

* * * *

Delphinia found herself immediately caught up in activities related to Ivy's come-out. To prepare their niece for the myriad social outings they had planned for her, Aunt Tilly and Aunt Rose had arranged appointments with modistes for the first week Ivy was in town. Sophy had done her best to shorten the bodice of Delphinia's old dresses for Ivy. The result was passable by country standards, but the stitching was hardly that of a professional.

"In deference to Sophy's thoughtfulness I shall wear her creations about the house," Ivy said doubtfully. "But I am glad I shall have something a bit more stylish to wear when we go walking."

On only the second morning in their father's house, before she had even begun visiting shops, Ivy announced her intention to reorganize the old schoolroom into a sitting room she and Delphinia could share.

"I do not think your father would mind if you were to have the room renovated," Tilly judged, eyeing the outmoded wallpaper. "Indeed he must be softening, for as he's aged—as we all do—he has become most obliging at taking advice."

After her encounter with her father the previous night, Delphinia wondered how the earl would receive Nicholas's request for her hand. She hoped her father would trust her not to make the same marital mistake twice but instead be full of humility and appreciation.

Thinking about drapery fabric, she went downstairs after lunch in search of a current periodical when the clatter of horses' hooves on pavement drew her attention to the window. Peeking out between the lace curtains, she was thrilled to see an elegant maroon-and-gold barouche draw up before the house, a familiar seal on its side. She had flung open the front door and run down the front steps before the caller had alighted. Nicholas stepped from the carriage, smiling broadly upon seeing her.

"Nothing makes me happier than to see you are happily settled." Gently caressing her shoulders as he greeted her, he extended to her an arm within which she hooked her fingers as they continued to walk toward the house. "My carriage was behind yours the entire way until we reached London. I had instructed Hobbs to keep you in sight until we went our separate ways here in town."

"I am grateful for that. I am also glad to have the opportunity to talk to you in private," she confided, clutching his arm. "I fear I shall find myself in the company of chaperones for the next two weeks. Have you been able to take any steps toward bringing Percy to justice?"

"I have already spoken with my solicitor," he told her solemnly. "He referred me to a barrister, one he assured me will give sound advice as to how to proceed."

A sudden fear gripped Delphinia, sending a chill through her in spite of the morning sun. "When are you meeting with him? Am I to be present?"

She was greatly relieved when he answered in the negative. "I see no need to put you though what might prove a lengthy and nerve-wracking consultation. I shall meet with him Thursday to discuss our course of action. In the meantime, you ought to remain with Ivy, where your talents can be put to their greatest use."

She laughed shortly. "I am afraid my greatest talent might well be deception, but I will be only too happy to take your suggestion and stay here."

He paused with her in the shade of Hyde Park's greenery and gazed into her eyes with a look of earnestness.

"My biggest concern at this moment," he admitted with a smile, "is whether your answer to me is still the same."

"My answer?" A moment passed before she comprehended his meaning. "Do you mean to your question of marriage?"

He gave her a lopsided grin. "Is there any other?"

"Of course my answer remains the same!" Anxiety rushed through her. "You do not wish to withdraw the question?"

"No, my silly sweet." He gave her hand a quick, gentle squeeze. "I have come not to see you but rather your father. I wish to address my question to him, if he is available."

The request startled Delphinia. "So soon!" she replied with a sinking feeling.

"Yes, so soon." Nicholas laughed merrily. "I see no point in wasting time. A fortnight is not long, and there is much to accomplish while we are here. I hoped I might be fortunate to catch him on a day when he is not bound by Parliamentary duties."

"I believe he was in his study when I came downstairs just now," she said. "I talked with him briefly last evening. He had had a busy day, and I retired early. I had no chance to talk with him about you. About *us.*"

She had been alone for so long that the plural sounded strange to her. Releasing her hand, Nicholas flashed her a disarming smile that made her melt inside. She had never imagined she would ever be so fortunate as to win the heart of such a man.

"Then since you have no objection, I shall approach your father and ask him the question for which I most want an answer. First things first, after all." He laughed again and drew her arm closer within the warm folds of his coat. "If we have no other question answered within these two weeks, that is fine, but this is the one question for which I must have an answer."

* * * *

Since it appeared no one from within her father's house had seen them outside together, Nicholas waited until Delphinia returned inside before he lifted the brass knocker to announce his arrival. He felt none of her trepidation at the idea of addressing her father. A supreme confidence filled his heart at the thought of asking for her hand in marriage. The match was so right that her father could not possibly refuse him.

He was admitted by Fenwick, the butler, who requested his patience while he notified Lord Hartridge of this unexpected caller. In the interim, Nicholas studied the tasteful interior of the home. The earl's London residence was even more sumptuous than his country estate, as was customary. The cherry wood side tables, gilded chairs, crystal wall sconces, and paintings by Constable and Reynolds made the entrance a warm and inviting place, he reflected with anticipation, to wait for the chance to ask for the hand of one's future bride.

Fenwick returned within minutes and led Nicholas into the earl's study. Adam Herrick, the Earl of Hartridge, rose from behind a broad desk to offer a cordial reception.

"Good afternoon, Captain," the earl greeted him briskly. "Yours is a name I have seen before. In connection with your military prowess, perhaps?"

"That may be, sir," Nicholas replied modestly. "It was an honor and a privilege to have served under Lord Admiral Nelson."

"A stunning battle, unquestionably." The earl shook his head. "Unfortunate that it required the sacrifice of some of our finest."

"If only he had survived long enough to savor his victory," Nicholas agreed gravely.

"One can only imagine that Nelson is proud of his men, even in heaven." Lord Hartridge resumed his seat at his desk. "Please have a seat, Captain. How may I be of service?"

Nicholas took the seat across from the desk Delphinia's father had indicated. As he did so, he took in the essence of the study, much like his own in somber tones of mahogany wood and burgundy upholstery with gold accents. A sense of timelessness and ancient wisdom pervaded the books, globes, and prints. He noted the marble bust of Athena on the desk before him and, behind it, a portrait over the mantle of a woman he took to be Delphinia's mother. The resemblance was so vivid that Lord Hartridge must be reminded of his loss every time he looked upon his daughter. Now that he was actually in the presence of the earl his courage foundered, and the familiar elements put him more at ease.

"Sir, I have come about your daughter," he began.

"Which one?" the earl responded.

"Lady Delphinia, sir."

Nicholas hesitated. How could he begin to put into words the effect she had had upon him in such a brief time? He had neglected to consider the possibility that the earl would be surprised by his request. Delphinia was such a remarkable and desirable young woman, the likelihood had never occurred to him.

"I traveled in Devon recently and had occasion to meet your daughter when my carriage became stranded on the moors."

"A sudden storm, eh?" the earl inquired.

"Yes," Nicholas answered in surprise. "Such storms must indeed be as frequent as your daughter claims they are. I was incapacitated for several weeks, during which time she was kind enough to accommodate my fellow travelers and me at Briarcombe." He drew a deep breath and continued. "In that time I came to make the acquaintance of Lady Delphinia and discovered we are quite compatible. I have come to ask for your daughter's hand in marriage, sir."

Lord Hartridge studied him for a few seconds that felt like an eternity. He sat with his hands folded under his chin, his expression thoughtful.

"I must say," he remarked at last, "this is not what I had expected to hear during this encounter. Are you aware my daughter was married previously?"

"Yes, my lord," Nicholas answered carefully. "I am familiar with the circumstances of her marriage."

"And that knowledge poses no difficulty for you?"

"None, my lord. I love and admire your daughter deeply." He was careful to keep the source of that admiration from her father.

"Well, Captain," the earl said, raising an eyebrow, "I am happy for you. The question is, is she happy?"

Nicholas started. "I have every reason to believe so."

"This is the first I have heard of this." Adam Herrick frowned. "It is not like Delphinia to be fearful of talking to me. She generally speaks her mind, a fact of which I assume you are aware. For your sake, I hope you are."

The earl eyed him speculatively. The look made Nicholas smile in return. "I understand your daughter well, my lord."

"How fortunate for you, Captain." His tone was dry. "Perhaps it will give you a hint of the Herculean responsibility you are assuming."

"With all due respect, my lord," Nicholas ventured, "I wonder if she finds it difficult to voice to you her regret at having disappointed you the first time she wed. I want to assure you I intend to see she does not disappoint you a second time."

While he was sure Lord Hartridge wanted to determine for himself the character of the man his daughter had chosen, Nicholas hoped to convince the earl of his own sincerity. At the same time he wanted to seize the chance to mend the largest tear in Delphinia's relationship with her father.

After some consideration Adam Herrick spoke. "You have my permission to marry Delphinia. I'll even give you my blessing, if she tells me you make her happy. I would like to talk to her first to make sure she knows her own mind, though according to your estimation, it sounds as if she does."

Nicholas smiled broadly and shook Lord Hartridge's hand.

"I thank you, sir. Not to make a play on words, but you have a most engaging daughter."

The earl cocked an eyebrow and answered dryly, "Captain, I have two."

* * * *

Delphinia waited anxiously in the corridor outside her father's study. She had taken advantage of the comfort offered by the stiff-backed chair by the door to pass the time, until sitting became too tedious. She was beginning to grow concerned for the fate of the narrow oriental rug on which she had been vigorously pacing, when the door finally opened and Nicholas emerged. To her surprise, Lord Hartridge was right behind him.

"Father!" she said faintly, halting in her tracks.

"I have spoken at length with Captain Hainsworth, who has apprised me of your intentions," her father said in a frank but hearty tone. "I imagine you are waiting to hear my answer."

Her heart pounded until she saw smiles spread gently across each face in turn.

"Is this so, Delphinia?" her father asked quietly. "Have you indeed fallen in love? Never mind, I can see by your face it is so. I admit I am surprised. I thought after your first experience with marriage that you would have thought it too much a risk to try again."

"I never considered it until Captain Hainsworth came to Briarcombe," she replied.

"Then I am happy to give my approval, my dear, if you have given yours. I can see the captain has earned your trust."

A feeling of ecstasy swelled within her. She contained herself, conscious of her dignity, and expressed her gratitude with a brilliant smile that she hoped conveyed the happiness she felt. "Thank you, Father. Thank you so much. This time I shall not disappoint you."

"You never have, my dear," he said with some surprise in his voice. "It is only yourself you have disappointed. Rose and Tilly tell me you have been an excellent influence on Ivy. They said they would not have thought she was the same niece who left here nearly two years ago. I must say, I was impressed with her maturity when I spoke with her last night and this morning. Tell me, Delphinia, what have you done with her?"

"More than you might imagine, Father." She could not resist smiling at Nicholas. "She has matured, hasn't she?"

"The transformation is remarkable," Nicholas agreed, irony in his tone.

"I would say the transformation is miraculous," Lord Hartridge continued. "She has turned into a lady almost overnight. But her come-out must not overshadow your matrimonial plans. We shall plan a lavish fete for later in the Season."

Delphinia's heart raced. "But I had planned to return to Exmoor in another week and a half. There are matters that must be attended to," she said truthfully.

"What pressing matters are there at Briarcombe?" Lord Hartridge asked sharply.

"My family has some tin mining concerns in the area that require my attention," Nicholas replied, using Delphinia's fabrication as an excuse.

"And I promised the church I would bring spring lambs to several families on the moors," Delphinia added for extra measure. "I had not expected a betrothal so soon—in fact, never again. I still cannot believe it is real."

But the celebration became a reality later in the week, when the engagement was to be announced to a group of family friends. For the occasion, Delphinia hastily procured the talents of an ambitious seamstress who worked day and night to embellish what had once been a simple ball gown. By the time she had finished, the ivory satin dress was adorned with violets stitched to the bodice and hem and coordinating lavender ribbon.

The gown won Delphinia the favor of the ladies and the compliments of the men on the evening of the party. The attention of the well-wishers almost overwhelmed her, so unaccustomed was she to large gatherings in her honor. Among the guests were Lord and Lady Nettleton and Rowena Herbert, who were shocked by the suddenness of the betrothal but delighted by the news.

"I see you've been up to quite a bit since we left, eh, Nick?" Harry teased, nudging his friend.

Delphinia desperately hoped Nicholas's mother would be as happy as his friends when they finally met in a few months. Tonight, her greatest supporters proved to be her own maiden aunts. And to think I feared this reunion, she mused.

"We are so happy to see you again and to see how you've grown," Aunt Rose confided in a private moment during the evening. "We are especially pleased to have met your young man."

A trill of laughter and pleasure rippled through Delphinia at the idea of having a young man.

"I am grateful for the chance to redeem myself," she confessed. Feeling humbled, she took a deep breath. "I was so ashamed of having disgraced our family with my marriage."

"My dear, there has been no disgrace," Aunt Rose assured her with an earnestness that brought a lump to Delphinia's throat. "You are an accomplished, poised young woman preparing for marriage—to a distinguished naval captain, no less. Despite what you see as earlier transgressions, this fine young captain saw fit to ask you to be his wife."

"Proving he is a man of high standards," Aunt Tilly added truculently. "Life can be long and lonely, dear. You have a new chance for happiness, one you deserve."

Delphinia tried to stem the tears welling in her eyes. Their encouragement was harder to bear when she realized they did not know half of what she had endured these five years.

"If you ever had any doubt, you have already redeemed yourself in our eyes with this fine fellow." Aunt Rose gazed across the drawing room to the fireplace where Nicholas stood conversing with several acquaintances from the House of Lords. "And we have been most impressed with what you have done with Ivy. She has had a great education at your hands."

With so many guests in close proximity, Delphinia cringed at her words. Ivy's experience at Briarcombe during the past month had included the things she had least wanted her sister to see, but Delphinia had had no choice. She felt an even greater guilt when, several minutes later, Nicholas came to her side and managed to guess how distant her thoughts were.

"It will all work out, dearest, you shall see."

Although she would not tell him, her thoughts at that moment, despite the festivities taking place all about them, were on Percy Wainwright. She could not forget Percy's pledge to initiate plans for their own engagement upon her return to Briarcombe.

Chapter Fourteen

During her second and final week in London, Delphinia managed to coax up enough courage to consider venturing out to visit old friends. Her resolve sprang not only from the realization that she would not have another chance to renew acquaintances for some time, but was also prompted in part by Ivy's reluctance to go anywhere without her. Delphinia felt deeply touched by her sister's uncharacteristic shyness.

"I don't know where to begin," Ivy lamented late one night in the privacy of their sitting room. "I did not have the opportunity to make many friends in town before I left the schoolroom, and now Father expects me to find a husband. It is just too daunting, not to mention unfair!"

"Finding a husband is the very last thing you will be expected to do, at least right away," Delphinia reassured her. "Father is so pleased with my engagement he wishes the same for you. By the time you are asked to make a decision you will know every lady and gentleman in town." She squeezed Ivy's hand. "Don't forget, you have already met two young men who seemed quite pleasant the night my betrothal was announced. That is two more than you knew when we arrived."

"Yes, but I wish they had not looked me over with such a careful eye," Ivy complained. "I shall have to pay attention to every detail. I did not worry half so much at home."

Tears welled in Delphinia's eyes when Ivy referred to Briarcombe as home. Drawing confidence from Ivy's faith in her, Delphinia summoned the nerve to post several letters to friends. The sisters began their social ascent by accompanying Aunt Tilly and Aunt Rose when they visited ladies who, like themselves, were elderly and somehow less intimidating. Although Delphinia felt more nervous than Ivy, the encounters gave her the impetus to arrange a call upon one of her oldest friends with whom she had renewed her friendship at the engagement party.

"You remember Margaret Hillsberry," Delphinia reminded Ivy as she assisted her sister with the creation of a new hairstyle, the old one having been deemed too youthful. "She has a younger sister named Rosamond who is also making her come-out. Maybe Rosamond is someone with whom you could share confidences when I'm gone."

"I wish that day would never come," Ivy brooded.

Delphinia laughed, a deep rich sound that rang solidly even in her own ears. "Is this the same sister who, two months ago, could not wait to be rid of me? It hardly seems possible."

Her self-assurance was elevated further upon their visit to Margaret's, where she learned the true depths of her self-control. She encouraged Margaret to talk of her own life, giving herself time enough to talk only about her future with Nicholas while revealing little about her past. She was moved to discover Margaret had also had her share of hardship, having lost an infant just six months earlier. What Margaret had not revealed, Delphinia learned the next day from another friend, was that her husband had followed the example of the Prince Regent and taken mistresses, if one were to believe the rumors.

"What a busy week this has been," Ivy remarked at home that night. "Once you and Nicholas are gone, I shall have to find someone else to share my evenings with at Covent Garden and Drury Lane. And I have heard so much about the Fashionable Hour at Hyde Park. I wish we could go together."

"I am not quite ready for Hyde Park." Delphinia quelled the concern the recollection stirred within her. "I carefully chose the friends we called on this week because I knew they would not be judgmental. But for you, this is just the start."

"Perhaps when you and Nicholas are man and wife you will not mind going again," Ivy said wistfully.

If it ever comes to pass, Delphinia worried. She could not easily dismiss her old fears, although she knew both Ivy and Nicholas saw them as having little substance. She merely smiled at her sister. "I'm sure I won't mind then."

"Perhaps the lives of your friends have not been so different from yours after all," Ivy suggested. "They might not be as judgmental as you think."

"We all seem to be given a different set of challenges we must learn to cope with," Delphinia said thoughtfully. She sighed at the weight of her own difficulties. "Mine shall come tomorrow when I face the custom officials."

"Nicholas will be with you," Ivy reminded her. "I know that whatever happens, he will bring you home safe and sound. You are so fortunate to have found him and won his love."

"No one could have been more supportive and devoted than he has been to me." Delphinia leaned back in her chair and closed her eyes, fixing his comforting image in her mind. "Just the same, I shall not sleep a wink tonight, nor will I until this is over."

* * * *

The lack of sleep did not keep Delphinia from being completely awake and on edge when Nicholas called for her the following morning. She had lain awake, searching for a method of diverting her aunts. Recalling their recent visit to the National Gallery, she decided to tell them she was to make a business call with Nicholas at the custom house and then go on to the gallery. They might not care to visit again so soon and would send Mrs. Adamsdale as a chaperone instead. Their father's tenant would be less curious about Delphinia's reasons for wanting to visit the custom house. She might even choose to remain in the carriage.

And it is true, she conceded, that Nicholas has business at the custom house. I just wish it did not concern me.

Her assumption had been true. Her aunts had declined going along as chaperones. She and Nicholas commented only on local landmarks in the presence of Mrs. Adamsdale as they rode through the elegant streets of Mayfair and then on to busy Piccadilly and the Strand. Even small talk proved too burdensome for Delphinia as they passed London Bridge.

The slowing of the carriage and the silence after the steady jingle of the bit and bridle told her when they were approaching their destination. The carriage came to a complete stop on Lower Thames Street, where she had a clear view of the Tower of London looming before her. She shuddered and realized how fortunate she would be if she did not end up there.

"The original custom house burned down two years ago," Nicholas said to her privately as they alighted. "I wonder if this one was built on the Thames as a warning to smugglers who travel the river."

Although his effort to steady her nerves with casual conversation had failed, Delphinia appreciated the attempt. She held his hand tightly as they stood before the newly built custom house, her knees nearly giving way. Three and a half stories high, the imposing structure was fronted with tall windows.

"I wish it had never been rebuilt," she confided in an undertone. "I would not be surprised if the original were destroyed by a vengeful smuggler."

"The barrister to whom I spoke was most pleasant and suggested we speak directly with a Mr. Wetherall," Nicholas said quietly. "His job here is to seek out smugglers."

"What did he think would happen to me?" she ventured in a strained voice.

"He could not say with any certainty. I am confident that after today we will have a better sense of what the future holds."

The gravity of his tone frightened her. She suspected he knew more than he was willing to admit in her presence.

"You are pursuing the wisest course, Delphinia," he said in a gentle voice, looking directly at her. "I will be with you the entire time. Tell the truth. What happened to you should never have taken place. The preventive men ought to be grateful to you for coming forward."

Perhaps they would be grateful for the opportunity to seize a smuggling accomplice who had been gullible enough to deliver herself to their office. Trembling, Delphinia clutched Nicholas's sleeve as they walked past the gas lamps and wrought iron railing through the portals of the custom house.

* * * *

After a brief wait Jonah Wetherall received them in his second-floor office. For once Nicholas did not mind using his influence and credentials to hasten their entry, for he knew Delphinia was tormented by fear of recrimination and needed to reveal her knowledge before her courage failed her.

"Good morning, Mr. Wetherall," Nicholas greeted him. "Lady Delphinia Marlowe and I have come today regarding a very serious matter. This lady possesses firsthand knowledge of a smuggling enterprise on the north coast of Devonshire."

Nicholas decided to use a more familiar reference to Delphinia whenever he alluded to her throughout the conversation. He hoped the title would put her on an equal footing with the customs official. Wetherall listened politely to his introductory speech, a look of amazement and deep curiosity altering his features.

"I hope you will give Lady Delphinia the chance to tell her story," Nicholas concluded. "There are heinous men at work who deserve to be behind bars, at the very least."

Wetherall turned to Delphinia. "Please tell me of these men and how you know of their smuggling efforts," he encouraged patiently.

Looking almost physically ill, Delphinia seemed relieved by his kindness and appeared to collect herself.

"I will start by telling you what I know about Percy Wainwright," she said haltingly. "He is a wastrel who blackened his own name with lewd behavior and reckless living, all of which earned him a huge collection of vowels on which he never made good. That was before he left London and became a blackmailer."

Nicholas listened intently as, with slow and painstaking accuracy, she related the details of her background, just as she had to him, omitting nothing but the emotional aspects. She faltered only when she described the death of the young woman who had perished under mysterious circumstances. She presented details of James Marlowe's debts, journal entries describing specific smuggling runs and cargoes, her notes from Mr. Warren, and her full knowledge of Percy's smuggling activities. Her voice seemed to grow in strength and conviction the further she delved into her experience.

"If you send the authorities to my home in Exmoor before two weeks are out," she concluded quietly, "you shall find a cellar full of West Indian tea and French brandy, for our next drop will take place shortly."

When she had finished, Wetherall appeared stunned by the disclosure. Nicholas reflected solemnly how humiliating it must be for a woman of Delphinia's breeding to find herself in the position to be forced to reveal such valuable information. He wondered if the significance of her confession might not be worth something toward her future. He was prepared to bargain for her life, even with his own if necessary.

"Because Lady Delphinia has been so cooperative in coming forward, at great risk to her own reputation and that of her family, would it not be possible to make some sort of agreement that would ensure her safety?" he inquired smartly.

"I can offer no guarantee as to the judgment of the courts," Wetherall warned.

"Surely these considerations must be addressed," Nicholas insisted in a severe tone. "Her father is a very influential man in Parliament who has been wronged by no action of his own. Lord Hartridge has many friends–I see by your expression you recognize the name. There are many who would prefer that his reputation remain unsullied by this incident. Lady Delphinia has risked her life in order to save our nation a fortune in revenue. If scandal were to result, who knows how many others would fear to come forward with knowledge of similar activities? It is to your benefit to protect the innocent in this situation, is it not?"

Wetherall looked contemplatively at each of them in turn. "You are absolutely right, Captain," he conceded. "This information is essential to putting an end to this smuggling ring of which Lady Delphinia knows."

"I will help in any way I can," Delphinia volunteered. "If this evidence is not sufficient, I can give you the dates and locations of future drops. Surely that will be enough to convince you how dangerous and determined these men are."

Nicholas saw Wetherall's eyes bulge at her words. "And you have actually participated in these runs?"

"As I told you, they have blackmailed me into serving as a lookout and providing them with storage space in my home."

Pain sliced through Nicholas as he watched her struggle to hold back her emotions. Her fear grieved him, even though he knew nothing he might have done could have spared her this moment.

"Do you think there is a chance we could penetrate their ring at the next drop?" Wetherall asked.

"If you are careful," she said warily. "I could suggest a precise hiding place where you will not be spotted. You see, there are few on the coast you can trust. Those who are not active in the operation will never betray the rest."

"I can attest to that," Nicholas added. "I have seen with my own eyes how clever these men are."

"Do you think they can be stopped?" Delphinia asked Wetherall.

"It will be difficult, but this information from you will make our job considerably easier, and we will give it our best effort," the custom officer told her. "We must beat them at their own game, which is difficult to do because they are not men of honor, as we are. Often if they know the preventive service is on their trail, they pack up and go elsewhere."

Nicholas saw Delphinia's face fall with disappointment as she said,

"And I know so little about Mr. Warren. I have tried to learn more about him, but without success."

Nicholas glanced at the spot on her cheek where her bruise had faded considerably. He felt tempted by the memory of the incident with Wainwright to insist the preventive men go to Devon and arrest the man immediately, but he knew that patience was required in order to prove Percy's guilt.

Taking up a notepad, Wetherall studied her solemnly. "I assure you, Lady Delphinia, we will do whatever we must to ensure your anonymity as well as your safety, since one depends upon the other. Now let us address specifics regarding the upcoming run."

By the time they left the customs office and a plan had been developed to bring Wainwright to justice Nicholas was encouraged to note that Delphinia seemed relieved if somewhat subdued. He slowed his pace as they walked downstairs, wanting to talk privately before returning to the carriage and the awaiting ears of Mrs. Adamsdale.

"I hope you feel as proud of yourself as I am of you, Delphinia," he said gently. "Such a confession required tremendous integrity, which I always knew you possessed. Your demeanor in that office was admirable."

"Thank you. I at least have the consolation of knowing I have done the right thing." She smiled weakly, but he could not ignore the doubt in her voice.

"Then why do you look so grim? Wetherall will never create a scandal, knowing who your father is."

"I have such a terrible sense of foreboding. I cannot describe it, but it is always with me. I don't think it will go away until I've returned to Briarcombe and find everything as safe as when we left it." Appearing as if she might cry if she were forced to look at him directly, she averted her gaze, her expression melancholy.

"Do not fret more than is necessary. Your worry is most likely due to the fact that you shall be returning to Briarcombe a day before I will," he said slowly. "It is to our disadvantage that we have a set of dual concerns. I feel it necessary to remain here to ensure that the custom house takes prompt measures to ensure that Wainwright is brought to justice. Your concern is with Briarcombe. Will you not consider delaying your leave a bit longer?"

She shook her head. "I feel it best that I return promptly, as I told the staff I would."

Nicholas released a sigh of regret. He knew that while Delphinia was enjoying her visit to London more than she had expected to, she had genuine reason to worry about Briarcombe in their absence. Having spent time reflecting on her concerns over the past few days, he had decided that since he planned to leave less than twenty-four hours after she would, there was very little time for them to be apart, diminishing the risk of their plans going awry.

"Very well then. Your nervousness is understandable," he rejoined, "but I am convinced it will disappear in time, once we are husband and wife and you no longer have anything to fear."

He knew from her expression that his words had failed to reassure her. Frustrated at his inability to ease her worries, he attributed her fears to the ordeal she had endured for so long. But why could she not find relief in the certainty that the end was in sight for the bootleggers?

"It is a fear I cannot name. I don't know what it is." She paled as she spoke. "Maybe it is just this day and being here at the custom house. I will be so relieved once we have returned to Exmoor and Percy is captured, and we can put this behind us."

"Come, let us step into daylight again." Taking her arm, he escorted her out to the sidewalk, deciding to attempt to lighten her mood. "I am sure Mrs. Adamsdale has a great deal more to tell us about her sons."

* * * *

Delphinia was surprised how quickly the rest of the week passed once her visit to the custom house was behind her. Within a few short days she had packed her belongings again, and the carriage that had brought her to London was ready for the return trip to Briarcombe. She made her farewells to her father, Aunt Tilly, and Aunt Rose inside the house, but it was Ivy who walked her to the carriage and climbed inside with her, remaining with her until the last possible moment before the carriage would set off for home.

"Promise to write me every day," Ivy urged. "And I know I need not remind you, but do be careful, Delphinia."

"Try not to think too much about it," Delphinia begged, "or you will not be able to enjoy yourself here. Remember, Nicholas will be with me."

"Yes, of course." Ivy smiled, a look of relief overspreading her face. "I feel as if I have grown up overnight, and it had little to do with coming to London."

"You have grown," Delphinia said tenderly. "That is why I do not worry about you as I did. I know that when the time comes, you will choose more wisely than I. Whatever else happens, Ivy, never, never compromise yourself or your standards."

"Aunt Rose and Aunt Tilly will not let me," Ivy quipped.

"Nor will your friends Lady Nettleton and Mrs. Herbert, I am sure. I am leaving you in safe hands." Delphinia drew a handkerchief from her reticule, handing it to her sister whose eyes needed it more than her own. She did not hesitate to pull Ivy close to her. They embraced each other tightly. "Why is it that when we had all the time in the world to be together it did not matter," she murmured, "and now that I am going we cannot bear to be apart?"

With a sob Ivy let her go. "When will I see you again?"

"I will be back before the Season is out." But even the sound of her calm voice did not convince her.

Ivy's sobs stopped suddenly, replaced by a shaky smile. "To think how abominably boring I found life at Briarcombe until so recently. There was a time I never wanted to see it again, or you. And now I cannot imagine being apart from either!"

* * * *

The ride back to Exmoor began pleasantly enough. Mrs. Adamsdale was a companionable chaperone who kept Delphinia's anxious mind occupied with talk of her sons, the older one who had done well for himself in London, and the "loyal one" who fished on the boats out of Polperro. Delphinia listened to the woman's casual chatter and jumped at the chance to respond, thinking she had never appreciated small talk more in her life. Mrs. Adamsdale could not know how much the conversation had contributed to keeping her spirits from sagging.

From the carriage window she saw springtime had come to the moors in the places where twisted broom and tussocks of dead grass had given way to bright patches of color. The landscape resembled a patchwork quilt in vivid greens and browns where the earth had been turned over and planted.

The cry of curlews over distant marshes told her Briarcombe was not far off. Mrs. Adamsdale had finally nodded off and snored softly in slumber, lulled to sleep by the gentle rocking of the town coach.

The sun peered intermittently through high clouds that massed above them and scudded rapidly overhead before the light finally disappeared. During the late afternoon drive, the earth turned bleak and mottled. Shadows retreated across the moors, as if frightened away by some unseen terror.

As the miles rolled away behind them and the hedges gave way to open moorland that brought her closer to home, Delphinia felt as if she were going to her doom. Her spirits fell the closer she came to Briarcombe. She felt bereft without Ivy's warm presence and was surprised to find she missed London as well. Now that she had been to town again, she began to miss all the activities she loved so.

If only she could stem this feeling of dread. She should be so happy. Her future prospects were brighter than they had ever been. She and Nicholas had made arrangements to end Percy's tyranny that had kept her captive for so many years. Ivy looked forward to a future of happiness and good fortune, and Delphinia was engaged to marry the man she should have married five years ago instead of James. What could possibly go wrong?

How much she had not wanted to leave Exmoor, and how much she wished now she might have stayed in the house on Park Lane. She dreaded going home, not knowing what she would find. She stared numbly at the granite crags in the distance, monstrous and timeless.

The nagging fear that her wedding with Nicholas might never come to pass chilled her.

It was totally illogical, of course. He had professed his love for her repeatedly during their fortnight in London, and she had never doubted his sincerity. But now that she was alone he seemed as far away as a dream that was briefly entertaining but was soon lost in the routine of daily living. His absence smarted worse than any blow. If only he were riding with her, she felt sure her worries would ease.

Nicholas seemed far away in London, and although he would join her early the next day if not before, she was going to Briarcombe alone. It was by her own insistence that she had come on ahead. She felt a great desire to be home and reassured that the house was just as she had left it and that nothing of consequence had transpired in her absence.

Twilight had come and gone by the time the manor house inched into view on the crest of the hill. A feeling of relief washed over her at the sight of the familiar lantern by the door. The house seemed solid and secure, as if time had stood still since she had left. For a moment she was able to relax until she reached the front door.

Bidding a quick farewell to the sleepy Mrs. Adamsdale, Delphinia jumped from the carriage, without the aid of the footman, almost before it had come to a full stop, so relieved was she to be home. It was just as she had left it. She was through the front doors within seconds and greeted by Sophy, who hovered about in waiting.

"Sophy, you don't know how glad I am to be home and to know that everything is just as it was when I left," she said warmly, relief coursing through her as she turned to allow the housekeeper to help her remove her cloak as she pulled off her gloves.

Delphinia sensed ominous news awaited her when Sophy did not reply right away, a look of distress on her face. "Miss, there's been some trouble," she began quietly.

Before Delphinia could question her, the drawing room doors opened wide. She turned to see the cause of the motion. She swayed on her feet at the sight before her, her mind refusing to believe what her eyes told her must be real.

In the doorway stood her husband, the man she knew should be dead. On his face lingered that too familiar grin, and his hand held a glass of brandy. She would not believe the truth until the deep, taunting voice that had haunted her in nightmares called her name.

"How have you been, Delphinia?" James Marlowe asked with delight. "I've been wondering when my dear wife would return home."

Chapter Fifteen

When Delphinia regained consciousness, she was lying on the sofa in the drawing room. Someone must have carried her here, for she could not remember lying down. Her hands felt warm until she realized Sophy stood over her, rubbing them in her own as if she were comforting a child, her face pinched and frightened.

Delphinia blinked. Surely she could not be in Exmoor. The feeling was so different from when she had left for London. She vaguely recalled a cry of alarm and the feel of hands grasping her when she fainted, but she had been in such a state of disbelief she barely remembered whose hands they were, except she knew they were not James's.

James. Her shock flooded back. The warmth and security of Sophy's touch vanished at the memory of her arrival. How was it possible James had returned? He was supposed to have perished on board a ship to America.

Delphinia closed her eyes again, unable to stop the tears that insisted on falling. Of all the people she would love to have seen again in this life James was the absolute last. Yet he had greeted her at her own door.

The idea sickened her. She curled herself back into the sofa, afraid to get up. A mixture of anger and fear coursed through her. How dare he return to destroy her life now that true happiness was so close? The worst was they were still married. She could hardly contain her fury. She realized how quiet the room was but for Sophy's sniffling.

Delphinia opened her eyes quickly to be sure James was not in the room with them. Seeing no sign of him, she took a deep breath and sat up slowly, letting her legs dangle from the sofa until they touched the floor.

"Are you all right, my lady?" Sophy asked anxiously.

"Just confused, Sophy. What happened here?"

Sophy's lips tightened. "Mr. Marlowe came back while you were away. Childers and Clennam tried their best to keep him out, but he wouldn't listen to any of us."

"I'm sure he wouldn't. I know you did your best." Planting her feet firmly on the rug, Delphinia found her strength returning slowly, which she considered a fortunate happenstance. Facing James again would require every ounce of strength she possessed.

As she regained her senses she still felt lightheaded, but asked Sophy to show James in and to leave them alone. He was annoyingly long in coming. When he did, he entered the room slowly, as if time meant nothing to him. Indeed, perhaps it did not. She stood behind the sofa, placing a distance between them as he paced before her.

"I wanted to give you sufficient time to get over your shock," James said sarcastically once they were alone. "Otherwise I would have been by your side. I've missed you, Delphinia."

"It shows in your loyalty," she retorted scathingly.

"Here, let me pour you a drink," he offered with a smile.

Trying to stop her heart from pounding, Delphinia watched as he helped himself to a brandy, a habit of Percy's she had grown to despise. This had to be a trick of fate. She stared hard in disbelief. There it was, the grin he flashed her when she was in the heat of anger. The black hair, piercing blue eyes, and weak mouth were all aspects of James with which she was intimately familiar. This vision before her was a horrifying reality.

"No. I don't want anything to do with you. All these years I believed you were dead," she blurted. "I had a letter saying you were drowned at sea."

The loathsome grin turned humorous. She hated the sight of him, knowing he enjoyed seeing her shock as she attempted to adjust to her new reality.

"I don't suppose you're going to tell the truth, but you never went to America at all, did you?" she asked bitterly.

"Oh, there was a wreck," he admitted. "Percy's cousin Georgina drowned in that storm, with another man traveling under my name. As far as you and the law were concerned, James Marlowe was dead. It was the best thing for me."

And the worst for me, she thought. She could hardly comprehend the fact that he was still alive, much less that he had assumed a new life in that time.

"I never went to America as I'd planned," he continued. "I went to Portsmouth for a time before sailing to France. I came back a year ago, after being abroad for four years, making new contacts for my business venture." He looked at her expectantly. "The one you have helped me with."

"What business venture?" She stared at him, an awful awareness dawning. "You are Mr. Warren, aren't you? It was you all that time. You were Percy's partner, directing the whole operation from the background." Her thoughts spun with the realization of his deceit. "No wonder you never wanted to meet me in person."

"You might not have recognized me, actually. I had a beard until I moved back here."

She gazed at him in horror as he gestured around the room. "What do you mean, moved back here?"

James shrugged. "I've come home again. Eventually I grew nostalgic for my homeland and for you. We are still married, after all."

The reminder made her heart beat faster with dread, as did the same old sarcasm in his voice that she was used to. Her fury that he had the legal right to trespass at Briarcombe in her absence nearly choked her.

Her head reeling, she pieced together what must have happened. Percy had not escaped after all, but had gone to James and told him Nicholas knew the truth about their enterprise. And James had responded with the ultimate hold he had over her, the fact that she was still his wife. As her husband he had every legal right to remain in her home, where he was still the master.

"That explains the Frenchwoman I met in your cottage," she reflected. "Naturally she would have been frightened by my appearance. She knew of your illegal operation."

"You terrified Antoinette by coming so unexpectedly. That could be a bit sticky. She is still under the mistaken impression that she is my legal wife. I never had the heart to correct her." He laughed coarsely.

She stared at him, dumbfounded. That he was married to another woman should not have surprised her, though it had. He had never had a heart at all. Would his second marriage have any impact on her engagement to Nicholas? Most likely James's second marriage would be declared illegal, but the first would not be affected.

Slowly the extent of his deceit dawned on her. As long as James was alive, she would not be free to marry Nicholas. The room swayed as panic seized her. James would never agree to divorce her. Even if he did, the resulting scandal for Nicholas could cost her not only his respect but that of society. It struck her that it was no longer safe for him to return to Briarcombe.

Her heart pounded fearfully as she felt her world crumbling around her. She found she could not catch her breath. Somehow she had to find a way to steady her nerves.

Rising to her feet, she took a deep breath and walked about the room, seeing nothing as new realizations continued to dawn on her. "Percy knew you were alive, and he lied to me as well. He helped to hide you. What do you want, James? Why have you returned now?"

"I've come back to claim what is rightly mine." His tone had turned cold. "I understand from Percy that you have a new friend. That's not very discreet when you already have a husband, is it?"

Reality overwhelmed her, and she reached for a table to keep from swaying on her feet. James's return threatened all her dreams that had taken shape in London. She was furious at James for deceiving her and at Percy for his treachery.

"You cannot do this, James."

"My dear, I just did," he said smugly.

His confidence in the face of her possible ruin helped Delphinia pull herself together. As her strength and determination surged within, she vowed silently not to let history repeat itself. She would find a way to be with Nicholas in spite of James's plans. If she could marry him, she would at least find a way to protect him from the dangers James and Percy posed to anyone who threatened their ill-gained fortune.

"I suppose our servants have told everyone in town by now," she surmised, thinking of the pending plans of the excise men.

"For the time being, I'm telling no one. Your servants, my dear, seem besotted with you. I doubt they're likely to reveal anything that might betray you."

That was a relief. If only she could get word to Nicholas and ask his advice. He might be only hours away by now. She needed a clear head. She wanted to sit quietly, preferably alone, but at the moment that was not an option.

"What do you expect from me, James?" she demanded. "I am your wife in name only, and that is how it will remain."

"From now on you will take orders from me," he instructed curtly. "If I hear of any further dalliances with the captain, I will bring a charge of adultery against you."

He would not dare, Delphinia told herself, for it meant he would have to reveal his own deception. His smuggling endeavors demanded he remain invisible, as if he were still dead. If only he were. Feeling her throat go dry, she forced herself to stop trembling and quiet the terrors within. The person she trusted most was not here with her. It was up to her alone to find a way to preserve all that she held dear before James and Percy could destroy those she loved.

Until now James had maintained his stance by the door. Perhaps, she surmised, he knew she would scream if he tried to touch her. Now he moved closer to her, his voice low.

"I expect your continued participation in our operation. You have no choice but to continue to help us, Delphinia."

"No," she said fiercely. "I will help you no longer."

The drop was less than a week away and must go on as scheduled. Even if it resulted in scandal to herself, it was the only way justice would be served. Afterward, James and Percy would be on their own and likely sent to prison for their crimes against the Crown. She never took her eyes off him as James stepped slowly to within inches of her face, his gaze as steady as hers.

"You know," he said, with a laugh so careless it chilled her, "I wouldn't want to see the lady of the house meet with an accident. That would be most unfortunate." He paused, his voice a menacing whisper when he said, "Consider yourself warned. You are to remain in this house until I tell you otherwise."

Unable to face him further, Delphinia turned her eyes away, breaking the stare they exchanged. In her mind she saw only her father's revolver, tucked between a pair of lace gloves in the bureau drawer where she always kept it. She had slept with it under her pillow before she thought him dead. Now she would have to live that way again.

"I do not want you seeing your friend again. Is that clear, Delphinia?" he asked as easily as if he were inquiring about dinner time.

"Perfectly clear, James."

Holding her head high, Delphinia slowly opened the drawing room doors and went up to her room in silence. She tried to retain her presence of mind despite her trembling, letting her guard down only after her door was closed and locked. It was only a matter of hours until Nicholas would arrive.

Until then, she told herself, her father's revolver would have to suffice if she were in need of help.

* * * *

Delphinia lay fully dressed upon her bed without turning down the blankets, one hand draped across her forehead. Her immediate concern was what would happen when Nicholas arrived at Briarcombe. Percy had attempted to kill him once. This time, with James's help, he might succeed. She was sick at the thought.

She refused to consider the possibility. Still in a daze, she could not begin to fathom what this would do to their relationship. Even if they were to escape the danger Percy posed, would he want to continue the attachment, knowing she had a husband and an unscrupulous one at that? She drew strength as she remembered the depth of the love he had professed for her while they were in London. Their only option might be to run away to a foreign land where neither would be recognized.

"A husband is for always," her mother had once told her. "When one marries it is for life."

Her mother had been correct, she realized. She should have made a wiser decision initially, for now she was burdened with James's legacy.

Now it was too late. A husband was for always. But she did not want this one. She pulled herself back from the temptation to succumb to self-pity, knowing it was more prudent to focus on the problem of having James in her home where she was now a prisoner.

She compared the life before her with the civilized drawing rooms of London. After her visit with Ivy and the freedom she had enjoyed there she could never tolerate the limited existence she foresaw with James. How could she write her sister every day, as she had promised, without revealing this change in plans? If only she might see Ivy happily wed. She might not be allowed out of the house, even if a betrothal were to happen.

She felt relieved and grateful that Ivy was away and still looking forward to marrying after what Delphinia had shared of her own experience. Not only was she happy for Ivy's absence, especially now that James had returned, but having shared her own stories of marital woe with Ivy, her sister now understood the pitfalls of a bad marriage and would choose wisely and more carefully than Delphinia had. She was especially glad that Ivy believed happiness was possible with the right man. Yet it made her wistful to think that when she had found the right man at last, the wrong man had returned.

Her reverie was interrupted by a quiet knock at her door. Sitting up at once, she slipped her hand under the cambric pillowcase, fingering the steel beneath it.

"Who is it?" she called, unable to keep the tension from her voice.

Delphinia was startled when the door swung slowly inward to reveal James standing there. She stood at once, her defenses rising. Somehow James must have found the extra key to her room.

"This is not your room," she informed him coldly. "Did you forget? Your belongings are down the hall in the room at the top of the stairs."

The room Nicholas had slept in so recently, she thought bitterly.

"The hour is growing late." James smiled at her intently. "I thought I might help you undress for bed."

He had taken no more than two steps into her bedroom before she took the revolver securely in hand. She clutched it fiercely, cocking and aiming it at his heart. Only her desire to see Nicholas again kept her from pulling the trigger.

"I can take care of myself," she said in as threatening a manner as she could muster. "Do not make me use this. Is that clear, James?"

He backed out of the room slowly, his eyes locked with hers, the smile never leaving his face. "Perfectly clear, Delphinia."

* * * *

Nicholas signed his name in the register at the Stag Hunters' Inn in Brendon after a long and uneasy ride from London. He had shortened his stay considerably, remaining in town only a few hours after Delphinia had left. In that time he paid a visit to the customs office to ensure they would pursue Delphinia's confidences promptly. He then visited briefly with close friends to apprise them of his impending nuptials before returning to Exmoor. He owed them that courtesy, he decided, even if they would have to wait to meet his betrothed. He would not think of asking Delphinia to meet acquaintances in his circle while she was so fearful of events at Briarcombe.

Silently he cursed the bad luck he had encountered on the trip. His journey to Devonshire had been beset with misfortune from the start, when he had forgotten a piece of luggage containing a sapphire necklace he had removed from the family vault in London as a special present for Delphinia. He might not have opted to return for it had he been able to predict the many other delays he would face.

The new wheel came loose on the carriage, making him question Melcher's abilities as a wheelwright. One of the horses, his favorite at that, lost a shoe, causing more time to be lost while they detoured to a stable to have him properly reshod. Finally, terrible rains in Wiltshire made him decide to seek shelter for the night rather than proceed in such a downpour.

Nicholas inquired casually at the desk at the inn in Brendon and was relieved to hear that the area had been quiet in recent days, without incident of any kind but for Farmer Black's cow taking down a fencepost that needed repairing. Noting that it was after ten by the walnut clock on the mantel, he decided it was too late to call at Briarcombe. He sent Stebbins upstairs to his room to unpack for the night, thinking he would call on Delphinia first thing tomorrow.

Just for tonight, could he be satisfied with the innkeeper's statement that Exmoor had been quiet of late? He did not want to take any chances. There was no possibly way to predict with any accuracy what Percy would do next. It had been too many hours since he had seen Delphinia, and he missed her more than he would have thought possible to miss another soul. No, Nicholas decided, I will not wait. He was anxious to reach Briarcombe and reassure himself Delphinia was safe.

But he would not risk taking a carriage. This time he would go on horseback.

* * * *

Delphinia sat beside the library fire, threading a needle by candlelight as James watched her. In her lap was a pair of James's socks, well worn and odorous and, unfortunately for her, full of holes.

"Darn these," James had instructed, tossing them to her as she had entered the room, angry at finding him there.

She had thrown the socks toward the hearth and missed.

"Have Antoinette darn them," she had muttered.

James had stepped toward her so suddenly she started. He yanked her roughly by the arm and ordered, his voice quiet but barely controlled, "I told you to darn them. It will give you something to do instead of thinking about your *friend* all the time."

As she rose from her chair prepared to issue a retort, he pushed her backward, almost knocking her over in the process.

"I will mend your socks," she conceded violently as she resumed her seat, knowing his physical strength gave him the upper hand. She had come downstairs to assert herself, hoping her presence would remind James that she was still the mistress of Briarcombe. If Nicholas were to return tonight, she would wait for him downstairs where she would be aware at once of his arrival.

As she picked up her needle and threaded the cotton through its eye, she wished that with every jab of the instrument she might be stabbing James in the eye. No, he was already blind to reality. The heart would be better except he had so little heart that a puncture was not likely to do significant damage.

As if her evening were not unpleasant enough, Percy Wainwright soon joined them by the fire. To her chagrin, James had invited Percy to move into the house as well. And to think the Nettletons and Mrs.

Herbert seemed like bothersome guests, she reflected dismally. She wished they were here now.

Listening to the clink of the men's brandy glasses was such an irritation to her she focused on her darning. She stitched mechanically, uncomfortably aware of James's eyes on her most of the evening, as he consumed more than a moderate amount of smuggled brandy.

"You've changed, Delphinia," he commented at one point. "You've become far more independent than I remember. I'm not sure whether or not it is a change that flatters you."

Delphinia stared at him defiantly. "It matters not what you think of me, James, for you cannot hurt me anymore."

He looked at her shrewdly and stretched his legs out lazily, striking his foot against a table in his annoyance. "I could press you further on that point, but I shall let it go for the moment."

"Where's that beastly dog of yours?" Percy inquired.

"Where he is safe," she retorted, keeping her eyes on her work. After James had kicked Brutus the day before she had assigned Agnes the responsibility of keeping her mastiff in the kitchen and caring for him there, a spot where James was not likely to go.

"James doesn't like him either, I see," Percy said dryly. As he swirled the brandy in its glass, the amber liquid gleamed in the firelight. "You know, you might be a bit more civil and stop behaving like a captive bride."

She glared at him, the needle tight within her grip. "How would you expect me to feel?" she shot back, her tone reckless. "You cannot keep me here against my will forever. I have a voice, and I will use it. What do you think you will do with me then?"

The fire crackled and threw out embers, startling her with their proximity. The firelight made James appear more sinister as it cast shadows across his chiseled features. "That, my dear, is the very question we have been debating."

James was staring at her, his expression inscrutable but decidedly indifferent to her pain. The look made her blood freeze in her veins. She wished she had said nothing.

She saw Percy's gaze flicker in James's direction. "You told me you had reconsidered," he said in a voice almost too low for her to hear.

"If you doubt my ability to secure our future," James retorted, "perhaps you are the one who ought to go elsewhere."

Delphinia was alarmed by the unprecedented tension between the two men. A knock at the door drew her attention.

"Come in," James roared, slurring his words.

Childers appeared in the doorway, looking years older than when she had left for London, Delphinia thought sadly.

"You have a caller, madam," he announced stoically, turning to her.

"Captain Nicholas Hainsworth is here from London."

As James rose to his feet, Delphinia caught her breath and dropped her mending. She stood as well, but not as quickly as Percy, who laid his hands on her shoulders and pressed her back into her chair. She clutched the chair arms, too numb to react.

"Show him in at once," James ordered. "Don't keep the man waiting."

Perhaps two seconds passed before Nicholas appeared, his tall frame filling the doorway. Delphinia's heart leaped at the sight of him. Nicholas's eye caught hers briefly before he turned his gaze to James Marlowe. In Nicholas's face she saw both astonishment and suspicion. Although he could not possibly have guessed the identity of the man before him, the fact that a stranger had called was enough to let him know something was amiss.

"I've been hoping to meet you, Captain," James said languidly, not bothering to extend his hand. "I'm James Marlowe, Delphinia's husband. Husband of the woman you had hoped to marry."

Delphinia choked back her pain, her eyes never leaving Nicholas as she waited to see his reaction. His emotions were unreadable.

"That's impossible," Nicholas said slowly. "If you're not dead, you damned well ought to be."

"Actually, I'm very much alive." James smiled at last, staring at Nicholas as if sizing him up. "Yes, Delphinia, I can see how the good captain is more suited to you than I am."

"Your sympathy is downright touching, James," Percy said with a cutting smile.

"That, however, doesn't change the fact that I am still your husband," James continued, looking to Delphinia, "now does it?"

She wished it did. He was not the husband she wanted. Speech would not come. She remained rooted to her seat.

Nicholas looked at her steadily, his face unchanged as he quietly asked, "Are you all right, Delphinia?"

"As well as I can be," she managed, rising. She shook off James's hand as he grabbed her arm to prevent her from running to Nicholas. "James has been alive and in hiding all these years."

If only she could find a way to communicate with Nicholas. She wished desperately that she might warn him to depart before they harmed him.

Nicholas slid his gaze from James to Percy. "Well, Wainwright," he said, "this is very much like the last time you and I met here, when I told you to leave her alone."

"Alas, you can't tell James to leave his own wife alone, now can you?" Percy laughed condescendingly. "Fancy that. It's a crying shame for you, old boy."

"There is no way you shall win, Marlowe," Nicholas told James, his tone quiet but steady. "If I have to go to Prinny himself, I'll see to Lady Delphinia's divorce."

"On what grounds?" James said scornfully.

"On grounds of desertion, to start."

James shrugged. "That never won anyone a divorce. And I did not desert her. I have been away for a time, without realizing my dear wife believed me to be dead."

"He has committed no crime," Percy spoke up, his tone smug.

"I think he has committed plenty," Nicholas countered.

James chuckled. "You'll have to prove it first."

"I take back my words," Nicholas said with an icy smile, glancing from one to the other. "You both ought to be dead."

"You know, that has a decidedly malevolent ring to it," Percy replied. "It sounds rather like a threat to me."

"You'll stand trial at the assizes for this." Nicholas stood squarely in the doorway, not budging an inch.

"That sounds like even more of a threat. I won't have any of that in my house." James stepped forward in an authoritative manner. "I am the master now, and you are not welcome here, Captain. You are forbidden to enter this house ever again. If I see you on the property I'll have you brought up on charges of trespassing or worse."

Their eyes locked. The blaze in the hearth crackled in the tense silence. Nicholas's gaze wavered, settling at length on Delphinia. Her throat constricted with fear. What was he thinking? His expression was cautious. She looked at him with desperate longing, hoping he could feel the pain in her soul.

"I'm sorry to have disturbed you, Marlowe," Nicholas said cuttingly. "I shall do as you say. Goodnight, Wainwright." He looked back at her briefly before he turned toward the foyer. "Good-bye, Delphinia."

"Nicholas!" she cried out with a sob, her arms restrained by Percy. She had seen no sign in Nicholas's face that he would find a way to turn this situation in their favor.

She tried in vain to free herself as James planted himself in the drawing room doorway, watching as Nicholas departed.

"Show him out, Childers," he instructed.

With a sinking heart Delphinia heard the front door close softly. She was left with silence until James's harsh laugh echoed throughout the library.

Chapter Sixteen

Delphinia stumbled from her bed the next morning to find her bedroom door locked. Even when she attempted to use her own key, the knob would not turn. Her heart sank. James must have put a chair or other instrument beneath it to make escape impossible.

She rattled the doorknob until she decided he must intend to keep her captive in her room, denying her access to the rest of her home. Maybe he locked her in because Nicholas had returned. Dread overtook her at the possibility.

She dropped back beneath the covers in frustration, wondering miserably what future lay in store for her beloved. Alone with the emptiness that surrounded her, she took the only positive step she could. She reached beneath her pillow to make sure her father's revolver was still within reach. Reassured by its presence, she sat up and gazed at the treetops beyond her window, where the sun's rays fell upon a world now forbidden to her. Fate had played a cruel trick in taking away her hopes just as spring had enlivened the land.

Delphinia wished desperately she could have given Nicholas a sign to stay away from Briarcombe and keep himself safe. He had been equally unable to share his emotions with her. Surely he had not revealed how he felt in his final words. They had consisted only of good-bye and her name. She closed her eyes wearily, the weight of uncertainty too much to bear. She had grown so accustomed to the deceitful methods of James Marlowe and Percy Wainwright that she had known no other manner of behavior until Nicholas had entered her life. And, she realized with an aching heart, she had known Nicholas for too brief a time to judge his sincerity with any degree of accuracy.

Would he come back for her? Until now, his conduct toward her had not been tested by adversity. Did she dare to hope that even at this moment he might be plotting her release from this prison? Or would he seize the opportunity to set his life to rights and abandon a woman with a dubious reputation?

Tired of guessing at puzzles without solutions, Delphinia slumped back against the pillows. Feeling listless, she thought she heard a knock at the door but dismissed the idea until a voice called out to her.

"Breakfast, miss." Sophy's warm yet strained tones penetrated the locked entrance.

Before Delphinia could invite her housekeeper inside, the door opened and closed quickly to admit Sophy. At the sight of her Delphinia bolted upright, swinging her legs over the side of the bed. Sophy inclined her head toward the door, making Delphinia suspect James was prowling the corridor.

Nodding her understanding, Delphinia eased herself back into bed.

She watched as Sophy placed the full tray she carried on the nightstand.

"Thank you, Sophy, but I don't think I can eat all that." Delphinia smiled weakly. "I'm not feeling very well today."

"You must keep up your strength, miss," Sophy replied. "Here, let me set up this tray for you."

As she spoke, the housekeeper fumbled distractedly with her pocket. Her pudgy fingers emerged abruptly with an envelope that she thrust forward. Delphinia accepted it with trembling hands.

"From Captain Hainsworth," Sophy whispered, bending low and tucking in the sheets as she spoke. "One of the stablehands gave it to Childers. I'd have put it on your tray, miss, 'cept I was afear'd Mr. Wainwright would see it."

Delphinia tucked the note swiftly beneath the bedsheets.

"I shall do my best to eat what I can," Delphinia said with a meaningful smile. "I can't thank you enough, Sophy."

Beaming as if she were thrilled to have been entrusted with even a small part in the drama that was unfolding around her, Sophy bowed and left the bedroom, closing the door protectively behind her. As soon as the housekeeper had gone, a key turned in the lock, confirming Delphinia's suspicions about the presence of someone in the hall. But she was too emboldened to worry further about the matter. As the footsteps died away she tore open the envelope and read Nicholas's familiar handwriting.

"My dearest Delphinia," he had written, "be assured of my undying love for you, and never doubt for a moment that I will see you safely out of this dilemma. If you are able to get away, meet me at Watersmeet this afternoon between one and three. If you do not come, I will know you are not in a position to slip away. Have faith. Remember our plans. Yours eternally, Nicholas."

How could she escape, if even briefly? Glancing out the window, Delphinia thought of her staff and, in particular, of Effie, the tall young maid who fed the chickens and who always wore her familiar bonnet of blue, claiming the sun marred her complexion.

Looking back at her nightstand, she noted that Sophy had omitted her traditional morning juice from the tray. Had she done it intentionally, planning to return in case her services were needed? If so, how clever she had been. But even if she hadn't planned it, it gave Delphinia a perfectly legitimate excuse to summon her housekeeper.

New hope sprang up within her. She would have a chance to communicate with someone who could help. Suddenly the world beyond her window no longer seemed beyond her reach.

* * * *

Delphinia attempted to behave in a casual manner as she made her way across the moors, just after one o'clock that afternoon. She pretended she was on her way to a neighbor's cottage, imagining she carried eggs in the basket over her arms instead of a few eggs that actually concealed the pistol Percy had dropped the night he had tried to force Nicholas over the cliff. Its diminutive size made the pistol a better fit in the bottom of the basket than the revolver that remained beneath her pillow, now underneath Effie's head.

If she ever lived to tell Ivy of this adventure her sister would hardly believe it. With a smile Delphinia thought of the maid who rested right now in the bed she had vacated. They managed to deceive Percy brilliantly when Sophy brought the maid upstairs, claiming Effie was in training. Once they had gained access into Delphinia's room it was easy enough to switch identities with matching disguises. She hoped Effie was enjoying an afternoon spent in comfort.

The maid's blue cotton bonnet hid Delphinia's features effectively until she reached Lynmouth. There she lowered her face discreetly so she would not be recognized by the villagers.

She followed the lane until it wound down the steep climb toward the spot where the East Lyn River was joined by Farley Water and Hoaroak Water. She walked deep into the cool valley with its covering of shrubbery, watching the river cascade over gray rocks, splashing into pools and continuing its downward flow among ferns. The isolated location looked like nothing so much as the trysting place it was to be when Nicholas arrived. Delphinia waited, listening for the sound of humanity over the rushing water.

Nicholas was beside her almost before she realized he had spotted her within the sheltered grove. He parted the branches behind which she hid and seated himself beside her on a rock. At a distance she might not have recognized him in Stebbins's clothing. But when he finally stood near her, his face only inches from her own, there was no mistaking the familiar tingle of anticipation that always coursed through her at his presence.

"You managed to get out," he said softly, catching her hands as she reached out to him. A look of relief dissolved the tension that had been on his features when she first saw him. "Have they harmed you in any way?"

"No, I'm fine. If only we were the couple we pretend to be," she whispered in a fervent tone. "Life would be so simple."

"Remember we are among traitors and thieves," he replied quietly. "We will have plenty of time for each other when this is all over." He paused. "I hope I have not been a fool in allowing you to go through with this plan to expose Percy and James rather than encouraging you to escape while you are able."

Delphinia shook her head. "I can't run from Briarcombe now, even while I have the chance. If my deception is discovered Percy and James wouldn't hesitate to harm my staff in ways I dare not consider. And you and I have come too far toward our goal of exposing them to give up now." The reminder of their plight sobered her. Tears filled her eyes despite her joy at seeing him. "I did not know what to think when you left last night. Did you have any idea that James had returned?"

"Childers told me the moment I arrived. He said James had confined you to the house." Gently he brushed her wet cheek with his finger. His tone turned savage as he continued. "I would have killed James had I remained in the same room with him another minute."

"I doubt anyone beyond the staff knows he is back. He seems to be hiding out at Briarcombe. The heavy rains of late have kept the servants in, so they have not had a chance to gossip. I can only think he must be afraid of discovery at this point. I think he just wants to get through this next drop."

They strolled farther into the brush away from the occasional passing villager who glanced in their direction even though they knew they couldn't be seen within the protective greenery. Nicholas shook his head, an expression of bewilderment clouding his handsome features.

"How can it be? How is it possible he escaped revelation all this time?"

"Apparently Percy's cousin was traveling with a man who took James's place on board ship unexpectedly and gave Briarcombe as his last address. When the ship went down, James was believed to have died." She smiled bitterly. "And the authorities notified me of his supposed death."

"I should have thought to check the ship's manifest, knowing his reputation," Nicholas berated himself. "From what you have told me, this is just the kind of trick your husband would pull. Had I thought twice, I might have spared you this shock."

"You could not have known." Delphinia gazed earnestly at the beloved face before her, trying to gauge his emotions while hiding her despair. "This means I am still married."

"I spent this morning giving my solicitor instructions to work on solving this dilemma." Nicholas took hold of her arms and held her firmly so he could gaze directly into her eyes, leaving her little doubt as to his intentions. "If there is a way to spare your reputation, he will find it for us."

Relief flooded through her at his reference to the two of them as a couple in spite of the difficulties she had caused him. He still wanted to marry her. His loyalty was almost too heartrending to be believed.

"I was so afraid you would no longer wish to marry me," she murmured, trembling as she spoke.

"What I wish is that James was in the ground like he should be," Nicholas said fiercely. "He is sailing too close to the wind on this. He's taking a great risk by remaining in this area."

"It is too difficult to lie to James and Percy anymore or even to pretend that I want to go on aiding them in their smuggling ring." She felt her frustration rising. "They don't trust me. They don't believe anything I tell them now. I don't know how much I can endure."

Nicholas startled her by gripping her shoulders and addressing her in passionate tones. "It will go easier on you if you can play your part without raising their suspicions. Never give up, Delphinia. Think of the plans we put into motion in London. Say nothing to either of them about our visit to the custom house. Remember what Wetherall said. We have to beat them at their own game. The fact that one has allies does not necessarily make a victory. The French and Spanish combined failed to defeat the British. I saw it with my own eyes. I want to see another victory here."

Clinging to the hope in his voice, Delphinia tried to emblazon his words upon her heart. She gazed into his clear green eyes, drawing strength from the sincerity she saw there.

"We need to try to anticipate their next move if we can," Nicholas went on. "Have you any idea what they are thinking?"

"I wonder if they might be planning to leave," she hazarded with a frown. "I think they are looking ahead and deciding what they are going to do when this run is over. What might James and Percy do to us?" She turned to him anxiously. "Should we tell the authorities that James is alive?"

"No," he said tentatively. "Not yet. You must do nothing to make them suspect anything has changed. I'm thinking not only of your reputation but your safety as well. How have they treated you?"

She emitted a sigh that wavered as she tried to disguise her fear. Her heart along with her courage swelled at the realization of Nicholas's concern for her safety. She would not let him down now. "They have locked me in my room, keeping me at a distance most of the time. I am a most unwilling partner, but I try to hide my revulsion from them."

"Be especially careful now, Delphinia, with the drop tomorrow night. My conscience will not permit you to return if I believe for one moment that you are not safe with James or with Percy."

"That is why I sleep with a revolver beneath my pillow."

The moment the words had left her lips she regretted it. The savage look Nicholas gave her made her suspect James and Percy had far more to fear from him than she did from them. She spoke up before he could express his concern.

"Let me assure you I know full well how to handle my weapon. Since Percy has moved back in, they spend their nights carousing. I feel rather safe locked away from them as I am." She smiled in spite of her fear. "I also know enough to protect myself by holding my tongue. Truthfully, I suspect they have less need of me now. It is the staff I must protect at this point."

She was relieved to see resignation finally settle in his features. Although Nicholas had struggled as he listened to her describe her trials, he appeared to be satisfied with her handling of the situation.

"Remember that the excise men will be present and watching at the drop," Nicholas reminded her urgently. "You must try to endure another day and night, and then it will be over."

"But still I shan't be free," she said wistfully.

Nicholas drew her close to him within the security of the surrounding trees. At that moment she did not care whether James or anyone else saw them together. All that mattered to her was the feel of his strong grip on her arms.

"You must trust that when the time comes we can work this out. I love you, Delphinia. Even though it is best for your sake that I stay away from Briarcombe at the moment, I will never leave you alone through this."

Her heart leaped at his words. She knew she would be willing to endure a far worse fate if it meant she would be with Nicholas in the end.

"I don't know when I can get out to see you again," she admitted, her voice breaking. She chose not to tell him the manner of her escape. "I should return before James and Percy become suspicious. I need to see to the servants' safety as well."

"If I do not see you before then, I will see you at Lynmouth tomorrow night. In case they change their minds about taking you with them, you must find a way to make yourself essential to their plan." Holding her hands tightly, he studied her with anxiety in his eyes at this new worry.

"I will make sure I am there. There are servants enough to ensure that. But how will I find you?" she asked with despair. Her throat was tight from holding back tears, but she would not disappoint Nicholas by letting them fall and revealing the weakness that clutched at her insides. She made a stab at humor. "You do have a tendency to lose yourself on the moors, you know."

"I shall be the one waiting in the wings to take you away from all this," he whispered. "I promise. Pretend it is merely a play, and we are acting out our assigned roles. Until tomorrow, my Delphinia."

With a brief kiss that made her reel with its determination and intensity, Nicholas released her and turned away abruptly. Tomorrow loomed before her like a cloud that was impossibly out of reach as he disappeared into the dense shrubbery beyond the grove.

She quickened her pace as she headed for home, the May sunlight warm on her shoulders in contrast with the cold dread in her heart. She would try to hold the memory of this moment close during the upcoming hours, when she would need sustenance most.

* * * *

Delphinia remained fully dressed in her room upon her return, once again wearing her own clothing, her spirits still high because she had been able to return home without incident. She hoped her afternoon escapade had gone unnoticed, for she was surprised and suspicious when James allowed her to come downstairs to dinner that night. She was relieved when he gave no indication that he suspected anything unusual in her behavior. After talking with her kitchen staff to ensure all servants were safe, she had returned to her own room to reflect on her next move.

She must have dozed off, for it was after ten o'clock when she awoke and saw the late hour on the mantel clock. She felt in her bones that something was wrong. The house was too quiet. By now the servants must have gone to bed. She had expected James and Percy to drink during the evening, but the downstairs rooms were silent. James had been surprisingly sober at dinner, distracted even, more than she had ever seen him. To see him in such a grave state unnerved her and made her suspicious.

Intending to explore the library for a reason for their silence, Delphinia tried her bedroom door gingerly, surprised to find it unlocked. Opening the door, she peered into the corridor cautiously and, after determining it empty, stepped beyond the threshold of her room. The sudden appearance of James coming around the corner as she headed for the staircase startled her.

"Change, and quickly," he instructed tersely.

"Change for what?" she asked dumbly.

"The drop has been pushed forward by a night. It's tonight instead."

She stared at him in astonishment. "Tonight! Why?"

He did not answer. Instead his eyes darted up and down the corridor. "We're leaving shortly, and you are coming with us. I don't trust you to stay here alone. I want you with me where I can keep an eye on you."

Panic seized Delphinia. Nicholas and the preventive men were not expecting the smuggling run to take place until tomorrow night. There was no way she could possibly reach anyone on such short notice. They would be twenty-four hours late.

Of all reasons for James to want her to accompany him to the drop, lack of trust was the last she had expected. Who could guess what plans James had for the interim? There was not even time to get word to Sophy. She put up a faint argument.

"But—the moon—we might be seen—"

"I have bigger worries than the moon, Delphinia. There is little time. Now hurry."

Hurrying was the last thing Delphinia intended to do. She had to stall as long as possible while she found a way to get word to the servants to warn Nicholas. But they were asleep, she realized in dismay.

Her heart sank when he gripped her arm and all hope disappeared.

"Come, I'll take you to your room. And don't worry," he added darkly, "I shall wait outside while you change. But that is the only privacy you shall have, I assure you. I don't intend to take my eyes off you until tonight is over."

Chapter Seventeen

Why is it, Delphinia reflected, that life never seemed more precious than just before its end? She had never been more certain, as she and James waited on the moors for the incoming schooner, that his intention was to do away with her by some means before the night was through.

They had crossed the moors quickly and waited now in the dark until it was time. James hid in the grass in the shadow of a rock, a rifle at his feet, while Delphinia sat hunched beside him.

"Why did we come here so early?" she complained. "The ship is not due for nearly another hour."

His haste had left her no time to get word to anyone, even the servants. She had to hope someone would wake, guess the worst, and take action to notify Nicholas in her absence. The hope was a slim one.

"We came so you wouldn't have a chance to tell anyone our plans." James rolled onto his side in the darkness and looked up at her. "I do not have reason to trust you any longer, Delphinia. It's very sad when a husband cannot trust his own wife."

She glared at him scathingly. "It is sad when one is wed to a hypocrite," she rejoined tartly.

She knew she should hold her tongue, but what did it matter now? She had nothing to lose. Gazing out at the cold ocean, she wondered how he would perform the deed. Would he push her over these rocks once the run was completed, or would he shoot her first and dispose of her body in the churning waves?

Either was preferable to being his wife and having him force himself on her, she thought resolutely. Whatever happened, she knew she would never see Nicholas again. Her throat tightened with the acceptance of her fate. She resolved to remain as brave as possible under the circumstances, as he would want her to.

She closed her eyes and smiled, raising her closed eyes to heaven, grateful to have had the chance to know him. She hoped her life had had meaning, certainly for Ivy and maybe for Nicholas. At least her life had been a lesson for Ivy as to what not to do, and now she would die before Nicholas's reputation could be tainted by the scandal.

"I can think of better ways to spend our time here together." His voice was cold and casual. "It's unfortunate I made you remove your skirts. Trousers are so burdensome."

Another thing for which I am grateful, she thought with relief. As James leaned his face toward her cheek and brushed it with his lips she recoiled very slightly, not wanting to upset him further. With her back pressed against a rock she had nowhere to go. In the dark she saw his silhouette rise to a sitting position before her. She lifted her knee instinctively, prepared to use it against him if necessary. He drew back at once, but she saw a glint in the cloud glow and felt the cold sensation of metal against her temple. He held the pistol at her head.

"It would be so easy to do away with you now, after having my way with you one last time," he threatened in a low tone.

She glared at him defiantly. "Do not even consider it," she retorted.

He appeared to dismiss any discussion of her wifely duties at present, for even in the darkness she could sense the change in his mood as he fell silent and turned toward the sea. In that instant she realized how her sense of self-worth had increased, so much so that even James seemed to recognize her independent spirit. What a stroke of misfortune, she reflected, that she had found her inner strength when it was too late for help to reach her.

"What I have left is promised to Captain Hainsworth," she said with satisfaction.

"Then it is too bad he shall never be with you again."

She ignored the sarcasm in his tone. This, she thought with a sinking heart, is confirmation of what I have known all along. This was the plan that explained James's recent sobriety and contemplative attitude. He had been considering murder and had decided it was the best course of action. The worst part was that James was correct in stating she would never be with Nicholas again.

No one would come for her, nor would they look for her within the next twenty-four hours with the drop not expected until tomorrow night. The thought made her feel physically ill.

As if to erase any doubt James laughed quietly in the darkness, this time not even bothering to reach for her hand.

"I regret this, Delphinia," he said, his smile taunting her in the dim light. "Knowing you has been a truly enriching experience, one that has changed my life."

As well as her own, she thought. Forever.

* * * *

Nicholas looked out the window of the Stag Hunters' Inn through raindrops that pelted the glass with increasing intensity. In the yard below he watched Stebbins consult with the grooms while the ostlers hastened to greet a lone traveler dismounting from his horse.

Moving his attention indoors, Nicholas returned his gaze to a table by the hearth where a letter from his mother waited for an answer. He had looked forward to announcing his upcoming nuptials to his mother especially, but James's return had spoiled that. At the moment, he found himself unable to concentrate on anything but Delphinia and the danger in which James's presence had placed her.

As he contemplated the best way to handle the situation, he looked back at the window. He felt inexplicably apprehensive tonight. Even the brandy he had poured himself had grown stale. He found he could no longer enjoy the taste of it because it had come from the inn's store, and who knew where it had originated? Smuggled in from France like the majority of England's spirits were? When he considered the damage the lure of smuggling had done to Delphinia's life, and how the desire for wealth turned men's hearts hard, he felt ill.

Money advanced one only so far. What was it worth if it did not solve one's problems? Even if Nicholas were as rich as Croesus he could not necessarily solve Delphinia's problem in a fashion that would satisfy her. He knew well she would not risk a scandal that might mar her father's reputation and harm her family name further. Just as he knew she would walk away from him before she'd bring scandal to his name.

A crack of thunder outside his window caused him to jump. What did smugglers do in a rainstorm like the one he had encountered upon his arrival in Exmoor nearly two months ago? He had never thought to ask Delphinia. Judging by the grim appearance of the night sky he decided it was fortunate the drop would not take place until tomorrow night when, hopefully, there would be fairer weather.

Two sets of footsteps on the stairs outside his room drew nearer, capturing his attention along with his curiosity as they approached. There was a sharp rap on the door before the landlord announced himself. Nicholas opened the door at once and was startled to see Wetherall standing beside the innkeeper, an enigmatic smile on his face. The man who had just arrived in the innyard had come to call upon him.

"Gen'l'mun to see you, sir," the proprietor said, a wary look on his face. "Just arrived from London."

"Good to see you again," Nicholas greeted Wetherall, adding to the landlord, "Mr. Wetherall is an old naval friend I haven't seen in years. I am not surprised he would arrive in a gale such as this."

Nodding his satisfaction, his doubtful expression making Nicholas suspect he was not entirely convinced, the innkeeper bowed his head and left them alone. He might require watching, Nicholas thought, when they were so close to success and his loyalty was questionable.

"I am an old naval friend of sorts, aren't I?" Wetherall agreed after the footsteps had died away.

"But not the sort that is welcome around here," Nicholas warned. "The innkeeper is probably suspicious of you already. I was not expecting you until tomorrow. Have a seat by the fire and warm yourself."

"Thank you, Captain. It's a raw night to be abroad, especially on the moors." Rubbing his hands together, the preventive officer perched on the edge of a stiff-backed chair beside the hearth. "I purposely came to town early. I wanted to get accustomed to the area before we begin our business."

"A wise move, and one that probably explains your effectiveness at catching smugglers." Nicholas reflected on his decision with approval. He kept his voice low, constantly aware he was in one of the most active smuggling regions of England.

"I have been in touch with the local authorities in Devon that Lady Delphinia recommended," Wetherall confided. "Trustworthy men. They have been alerted and are prepared to apprehend this gang of smugglers tomorrow night."

Nicholas listened attentively but worried about Delphinia's safety. The fact that the revenuers would be on the scene meant gunshots would be fired and bullets could miss their mark. When he considered the possibility of losing her, beads of sweat broke out on his neck.

"And what of Lady Delphinia?" he demanded. "I have only been able to see her once upon my return. Wainwright does not trust her after her journey to London. He will undoubtedly keep her with him during tomorrow night's run."

"We shall take every precaution to ensure her safety, but, of course, there is always a risk. Lady Delphinia has involved herself in a dangerous business, a fact she knows very well." His tone sober, Wetherall paused to glance at the rain-streaked windowpane. "I have tomorrow to acquaint myself with the coast. Since I am your old maritime chum no one will think it odd if we go for a sail. If the weather is fair, that is. I'd like to see the shoreline from the water and get a clear view of the cliffs in daylight."

"It's certainly too nasty to study the area now," Nicholas agreed.

"It was the storm that delayed me getting here. A very tough night, Captain, as I am sure you can appreciate." Wetherall sighed. "But I defer to your nautical experience. You have no doubt seen worse."

"I arrived in worse." Nicholas smiled. "So what is the plan for tomorrow night?"

"We must catch them in the act," Wetherall announced. "If we cannot view the coast tomorrow I'll lie low until nightfall. No point in raising anyone's hackles just yet." He smiled briskly. "It's the leaders I want, this mysterious Mr. Warren and Percy Wainwright."

Nicholas realized the excise man had no idea the other leader had been identified as Delphinia's husband, still believed to be deceased. Taking the unappealing brandy, he contemplated his earlier decision to remain silent for the time being. Wetherall's words prevented an immediate reply.

"I want to see Briarcombe firsthand," Wetherall added. "I should like to view the location of the storage entrance and see where the men enter the house to store the barrels. I don't think we need disturb Lady Delphinia, but if this downpour lets up, perhaps I might have a glimpse of it tonight." He winked. "Darkness is the perfect cover. We're playing by the rules of their game now."

The suggestion lifted Nicholas's spirits slightly. "I think that's wise. The men will most likely be imbibing, so we'd probably not gain entrance, but we can view the outside. I'd like to go with you, actually. I've been a bit uneasy all evening. A bout of the jitters, I imagine."

"Nothing to fear, Captain." Wetherall spoke cheerfully. "The local men are as anxious to catch them as the preventive service is. We're closing in on them now. I don't doubt it for a moment."

"I wish I could be as optimistic as you." Nicholas paused, a nagging worry surfacing. "How are we to leave without arousing suspicion if we call for our horses? The people here might know about tomorrow's drop. They could alert Warren and Wainwright."

Wetherall considered. "Excellent point. We'll tell the ostlers we're eastward bound. We'll ride off in that direction and turn back once we feel it's safe."

How were they to know beyond a doubt when it was safe? There was no way to ensure they would not be followed. Yet they had to reach Briarcombe tonight. Nicholas knew that doing so would put his own fears at ease. The ruse was not ideal, but they had invented it on short notice, and it would have to suffice.

"A worthy plan," he conceded, rising. "One we can all live with, literally."

Forcing himself to be satisfied with the solution, Nicholas took his greatcoat from the pegboard on the wall, noting Wetherall had never removed his. He felt grateful his companion in this venture was prepared at a moment's notice, knowing he himself must be as well.

* * * *

A misty light from the clouds cast its reflection on the landscape before them as Nicholas and Wetherall directed their horses west toward Briarcombe. The heaviest rains had done them the favor of subsiding, making riding more tolerable.

"Better to be out now in case the deluge gets worse," Wetherall said, pulling the brim of his hat lower over his eyes. "A carriage would have called attention to itself. Traveling by horseback like this makes us look more like local riders, don't you think?"

Although Nicholas appreciated Wetherall's efforts to fill the silence, the journey had not made him more inclined toward speech, unable as he was to quell his concern for Delphinia's safety. As they neared the manor house he glimpsed the familiar lantern by the door, but this time there was no candle in Delphinia's bedroom window, as there had been the night he arrived. He wondered if she had already retired.

Riding closer, he saw the downstairs rooms were dark. He was surprised by the quiet. He had expected to hear the sounds of revelry and carousing. The silence that greeted them was more ominous than reassuring.

"I don't like the look of this," he told Wetherall. "It's too quiet. Stay out of sight. I'm going to knock. Hopefully I shall be able to rouse Childers rather than Wainwright."

Or James Marlowe, he thought anxiously. Dismounting from his horse, he hurried to the door and seized the knocker with a fierce grip. Despite the late hour, he was not about to give up.

When there was no response within, Nicholas tried the door and found it locked. He headed toward the back of the house, making his way inside by smashing a window in the hall near the servants' quarters. He was alarmed to see Childers's relieved expression as he made his way into the kitchen and discovered the butler to be one of three servants lying bound and gagged on the floor.

Nicholas lost no time ensuring the servants were physically unharmed before untying them. Childers breathed heavily, letting out a gasp as Nicholas released him from his bonds.

"Where is your mistress, Childers?" he demanded.

The aged butler shook his head, looking confused. "I don't know, Captain."

Nicholas's heart stood still. "What do you mean? Where is she?"

"Usually there's little that wakes me, Captain," Childers confessed, "but I was unable to sleep tonight, worrying about our mistress. I found Brutus whining and scratching at the door. On my way to check on the house an ill-bred fellow I've seen in town seized me, brought me here, and tied me up as he had the others."

Nicholas broke in, fearing the worst. "Have you seen Marlowe and Wainwright?"

One of the other servants spoke up, rubbing his throat. "I heard their voices outside. Heading for Lynton, Captain, toward the cliffs. They've been gone perhaps an hour or more."

Childers peered at Nicholas, worry evident in his rheumy eyes. "I regret we could not have done differently, Captain."

"I want you to stay put, but send Clennam to fetch the authorities. Not local men. Go only as far as you must to find a town where the excise men are welcome. Take Delphinia's horse. Have them dispatch men to the coast at once. And Childers, check upstairs to ensure the other servants have slept through this and are safe." He laid a brief hand on Childers's shoulder. "I only hope there's time. There should be. You have done well, Childers, rest assured."

He turned to see that Wetherall had followed him indoors and found his way to the kitchen.

"What's the word?" the excise man demanded.

"Delphinia's not here and neither is Wainwright," Nicholas related tersely, giving him a full account as they turned back and made their way outside. "I don't know if we've time to make it to the coast or not. It's a long ride, and the night is not young."

Running back to his mount with the excise man and stepping swiftly into the stirrup as his hands gripped the wet, slippery reins, Nicholas turned the horse toward Lynton. What was it Delphinia always said about not having enough time?

"I fear they've outsmarted us again, Wetherall," he confessed shakily.

"Not if we give it our best, Captain," Wetherall promised.

Chapter Eighteen

Although the horses were swift and pounded the turf in a heavy gallop, it seemed to Nicholas that their hooves were weighed down by lead. With a curse he spurred his horse on, heedless of the wet moorland. Any hope of success he and Wetherall might have was a question of timing. They might already be too late. The smugglers had been so clever he would not be surprised if one of them kept an ear to the ground listening for hoofbeats, expecting the excise men.

What struggle could they possibly give, two men against twenty? What would happen to Delphinia if they were not in time? He could not fathom the idea of losing her, and he knew in his heart that if he didn't get there in time he would. He rode as hard as he could with Wetherall in close pursuit.

Nicholas felt as if they had been riding forever, but he knew it must have been no more than twenty-five minutes before they stopped and tethered their horses in a wood a safe distance from the cliffs. From there they hurried through the dense underbrush to a point Delphinia had designated near the shore.

"It is because of me that her life is in danger," Nicholas berated himself breathlessly as they ran. "Wainwright knew he could not trust her. We must hurry. There is only a small span of time in which they are on the beach. We may not be in time."

"Idle words," Wetherall said dismissively. "We have them, you shall see."

They took their places silently near an oak grove. Through the tree branches Nicholas could see several shadowy figures at the top of the narrow road that led down to Lynmouth. Bootleggers. His heart turned over as relief mixed with fear. They had not come too late. But where was Delphinia?

"We could not have arrived at a more opportune moment," Wetherall said softly. "Now we must hope the local authorities arrive soon. Are you certain Childers can be trusted?"

"He is one of the few locals who is entirely trustworthy," Nicholas assured him.

"It's the leaders we want." Echoing his earlier sentiment, Wetherall did not take his eyes from the scene before them. "As soon as we hear horses we'll split up. You know who you are looking for. Keep an eye out for Wainwright. You take the left flank. I'll take the right."

* * * *

From where she crouched, Delphinia watched the smugglers carry out their operation with their usual methodical precision. Her legs were so stiff beneath her they had developed cramps. To her right Percy addressed James who knelt beside her on the left.

"I don't like this, James," Percy said in a near whisper. "Don't like it at all. It ain't up to snuff."

"We're in the clear," James retorted.

"Perhaps you ought to reconsider this plan," he persisted. "Sailing so close to the wind like this, you'll regret it, take my word."

"I'll take your word for nothing," James growled. "I shall take your share of the drop if you don't cut line."

James dragged Delphinia to her feet and placed a pistol squarely at the small of her back, the rifle in his other hand.

"It isn't right, James." This time Percy spoke with more emphasis. Was it desperation Delphinia thought she heard in his voice? She noted the rifle he held low by his side and shivered. With four weapons between the two of them she saw little chance of escape. "She's been square with us, I tell you. You can't do this."

"I can do anything I please," James snapped. "As fond as I am of Delphinia, I cannot trust her to keep her mouth shut once we have gone. We no longer have a use for her. Sometimes you forget I am in charge here, Percy. I don't need your advice."

"Sometimes I think our operation worked better before you came back," Percy said shortly.

Delphinia winced as James removed the gun from her back and waved it wildly at Percy. "Sometimes I think it would have been better to blow your head off rather than let you have a stake in this," he said, the deep, ominous quality that Delphinia knew so well returning to his voice.

Percy did not have a chance to respond. The shouts of men resounded abruptly through the valley. Voices seemed to ring from every direction. The men's cries shattered the stillness, paralyzing Delphinia where she stood at the cliff's edge.

"Damn! It's the preventive service," James muttered under his breath. "They've found us."

* * * *

The sight of the local constabulary arriving at the cliffs in a tumult of noisy confusion failed to ease Nicholas's tension. They announced their appearance with the beating of horses' hooves along with their shouts and cries. Nicholas watched in dismay as the men on the beach scattered. From his secure spot on a scree-covered slope, chaos appeared to break loose before him. Wetherall had penetrated the brush to Nicholas's right and must now be watching as well, he assumed.

On the steep cliff road up from Lynmouth, the men staggered under their illegal weight, many of the tubs they carried falling from their shoulders and breaking. The odor that rose from the beach was evidence in itself of their unlawful acts, Nicholas thought with triumph.

"It's every man for hisself!" cried one of the smugglers.

Where was Delphinia in the commotion? Nicholas gazed about

frantically in all directions. Then he saw her, her hat blown off. Her hair streaming about her shoulders. She was running along a far hill with James alongside her. Their awkward movements told him James was holding her captive.

Nicholas jumped to his feet, feeling the weight in his pocket. Before he had a chance to draw his pistol, he saw Percy Wainwright emerge from a hollow in the cliffs. Percy had not seen him, watching the activity to his left as voices indicated the excise men were coming closer. Nicholas had no time to lunge at him now. He had to reach Delphinia. He was at a disadvantage, not knowing the moors as the natives did.

Percy plunged into a valley and disappeared from view. By now Nicholas had his pistol in hand, expecting a shot to be fired from any direction. When none came he glanced up at the cliffs, only to find Delphinia and James had disappeared.

* * * *

From the precipice where James had taken her Delphinia could see only darkness below. The surf pounding on the rocks echoed loudly in her ears, almost drowning out the sound of the preventive men. Yet she knew they could not be far. They were well concealed within the caves and curves of these cliffs.

Roughly, James grabbed her by the wrist and tried to drag her closer to the edge. She retaliated by falling to her knees and throwing herself with as much force as she could against a man twice her weight. Fighting was her only hope now. As he pulled her along the ground, she dug her heels into the turf, but the earth beneath her feet was soft from the rain and offered no resistance.

"James, don't do this," she begged in desperation.

"I won't let them take me, Delphinia." His eyes held a wildness she had never seen before. "I've always run. I'll keep running."

"But you won't get away," she said plaintively.

He stopped and appeared to consider her words.

"If I go," he vowed, "you're going with me, I swear it."

She closed her eyes against her fear. "All my presence will do is slow you down, James, when all you want is to be away from here. You know it as well as I. Won't you reconsider and let me go at last?"

"Not a chance, love." The bitter desperation in his tone filled her with dread. "You are my best hope of escape."

* * * *

Nicholas scrambled through the briars and gorse of the hillside, his pace slowed by the unfamiliarity of the territory. Why had he not remained on horseback? His mount did him no good tethered out of range.

He slipped in the mud and wet gorse and rose again for a desperate final ascent up the cliff where he had last seen James running with Delphinia. High above him, they had looked like runaway lovers. He wished he were the one fleeing with her instead, taking her to safety far from Exmoor.

Then, like a scene repeated in a dream, Percy Wainwright appeared from nowhere, his back to Nicholas. His gaze was focused on the pair on the cliff top above them. Percy had not noticed Nicholas standing behind him as the blackmailer raised his gun and aimed it carefully.

Breathless in the dark silence, Nicholas heard Percy curse under his breath. "Good-bye, Captain."

Wainwright had mistaken James for Nicholas. Before Nicholas could make a move Percy had raised his rifle, pointed and fired. The figure on the cliff paused. The shot had found its mark. After a second's hesitation, James Marlowe stumbled and fell forward, pitching headlong over the cliffs to the sea below. On the precipice above, Delphinia fell to her knees.

Nicholas wanted to run to her immediately, but he could not resist informing the criminal of his error.

"Wainwright," he called softly.

Percy turned abruptly, his expression ghastly in the pale light. Now I know what it means to have seen a ghost, Nicholas thought, as Wainwright said, "What—you—"

"I'm afraid you have killed Mr. Warren," Nicholas informed him in mock apology.

For once Percy was speechless, obviously too confused and shaken to react. From behind them, Nicholas heard a pistol cocked. Nicholas turned apprehensively to see Wetherall standing next to him, his gun pointed at Wainwright.

The constable joined them within seconds. Nicholas did not wait while the man seized Percy, clapped irons on him, and took him into custody amid Wainwright's protests. Instead he hastened to the top of the cliff where Delphinia had risen to her feet. She stumbled in his direction, falling into his arms with a cry as she reached him. He held her close, stifling her sobs in the shoulder of his greatcoat.

"It is over," he said soothingly. "Warren is dead, Percy has been captured, and our whole future lies before us. Cry all you want now. If I have my way, you shall never shed a tear of unhappiness again."

He held her lovingly, languishing in the contentment of holding her in his arms where she belonged, feeling at that moment the deepest, most tender affection he had ever felt for anyone. After a few minutes, she managed to stop her tears but for an occasional hiccup. Slowly she lifted her head to survey the scene around them. Along the beach and on the road broken casks oozed their illegal cargo. A number of men were being led away in handcuffs.

"And now I am going to take you home to Briarcombe," Nicholas told her gently.

Clutching the sleeve of his coat, she looked up at him with anxious eyes. "But what shall we say about James?"

"What is there to say, my dear? Wainwright is claiming James was alive, but he is having trouble convincing Officer Wetherall. It seems James's disguise was too successful." Nicholas smiled at her as he reflected on the irony. "One day a body will wash up on shore and be identified as that of Mr. Warren, the mysterious drifter who passed through Exmoor. James Marlowe was supposed to have died at sea three years ago. He has fulfilled his destiny at last."

He took her hands in his, stroking them with his fingertips and watching her tears fall silently.

"So, in answer to your question, my love," he said tenderly, "we shall say nothing. People will believe what they know about Mr. Warren, which is very little. Percy can say whatever he wishes, but there will be few to hear since he will be behind bars."

He smiled, enjoying the relief that filled her violet-blue eyes and seemed to wash over her as easily as the waves lapped the shore.

"As for your staff," he continued, hoping to offer her further reassurance, "they care for you so deeply I am certain they will choose to protect you just as you protected them. Did you not put their welfare before your own, after all? Your staff believes you to be in danger. Now that you are not, you can return to protect them."

* * * *

A half-hour later Delphinia was safely ensconced at home again almost as if the events of the night had never occurred. Sophy, Effie, Childers, and Clennam bustled about seeing to her comfort, asking only if she was safe and whether or not their gentlemen guests would be returning.

When she answered in the negative, informing them that Percy had been taken into custody and that his friend was dead, they accepted it with discreet surprise, refraining from asking her to elaborate. A wave of gratitude swept over her along with an amusement she had never expected to feel again. They were so loyal to her and knew her ways so intimately that no other words were needed.

Yet there were words yet to be exchanged. After Sophy and Effie had seen her comfortably settled with a second cup of tea while Nicholas checked on the status of the remaining servants, Delphinia requested that they close the doors so she might address them privately.

"I wanted to thank you," she began quietly, "for all the loyalty and support you have shown me during this ordeal." She paused, unable to find words appropriate for the devotion they had displayed. "You have been privy to all that has gone on in this house in the absence of my father, who wisely or otherwise left me in charge. I want to assure you that no matter what happens in the coming days, I intend to protect you or die trying, if it comes to that."

Delphinia gulped deeply and released her breath after delivering her promise, knowing there was little that could compensate for such dedication on the part of her staff. To her surprise Sophy and Effie exchanged a glance before throwing their arms about her, forming their own circle of protection.

"Lord, miss, after all ye've done for us, it's you who needs the help now," Effie assured her in a tone of sympathetic concern.

"And we're here to offer it," Sophy promised, tightening her grip. "If anyone is to die trying, miss, it'll be us, not you. This shall all blow over like the clouds after a storm. You'll see. Never you mind. It's time you got some rest and let us do the protecting—" Here she winked at Effie. "—though I don't think you'll be able to rest for very long, if the good captain has his way."

* * * *

Within the week, Nicholas and Delphinia returned to London. Delphinia was delighted when her family greeted her with joyous celebration and merry festivities. After the fear and pain had begun to subside, she found herself more than ready to prepare for a life of happiness.

Upon receiving her son's letter with news of his betrothal, Callendra Hainsworth had made the journey back to town from Cornwall, impatient to meet her future daughter-in-law. From the shelter of a potted palm in her father's drawing room during one evening gathering, Delphinia carefully watched the expressions on the faces of Nicholas and his mother as they passed by, unaware of her presence. She felt awkward in her secluded spot, unable to announce herself before they entered into conversation of a private nature.

Delphinia tensed with consternation. What was she to do? Fearful she was partaking in the questionable act of eavesdropping, she realized she had waited too long and now must give them a private moment together rather than disturb them. Her hesitation allowed her to hear their reflections of the first evening the three had spent together.

"I could not be more pleased if I had selected her myself, Nicholas," Delphinia overheard Lady Greymore tell her son. "You have made a wise choice. She is a jewel worth waiting for."

"I am glad you give me credit for my fine taste, Mother," Nicholas replied.

"I think it is I who deserve the credit," she objected. "If I had not issued you an ultimatum, you might not have had the sense to ask for her hand when you did."

Filled with jubilation and a peace she had never expected to experience, Delphinia waited until they had moved a suitable distance away before she emerged from her enclosure. While Aunt Tilly and Aunt Rose were deep in conversation by the windows with Lord and Lady Nettleton, Delphinia took Ivy aside and asked her to serve as witness at their wedding. After Ivy had recovered from her excitement, the sisters chatted quietly in a corner beneath the palms until Nicholas joined them.

"Whatever will become of Percy?" Ivy asked curiously.

"Transportation is too good for him," he replied. "He will go to the gallows for crimes against the Crown."

"And James was never identified?"

"His body was apparently washed out to sea," he said. "Percy told the truth, but the authorities did not believe him because he had lied so many times before. As far as the rest of the world is concerned, James Marlowe died three years ago."

"And may he remain that way," Delphinia murmured.

"He was thwarted by his own scheme," Nicholas added.

Delphinia let her gaze travel about the room, preferring to look ahead to her future rather than behind to her past. "Ivy, you are upstaging all the girls here. There are so many young men, and all of them want to dance with you!"

"I am too smart for most of them," her sister declared.

"It is fine to be smart to a point," Delphinia cautioned. "But if you are too smart you shall frighten them away. Remember that men do not like bluestockings."

"Then that is all the better," Ivy announced carelessly, "for it means I shall end up with the bravest of them all—the only one brave enough to tolerate me."

"And have you met a man with flair, as you had hoped?" Nicholas inquired.

"All the men in London have flair," Ivy said emphatically, "but I am not sure I care for it now that I see it in practice. Those who have flair often have not the brains or the money to support themselves. No, I am going to wait. Delphinia's experience with marriage makes me want to choose very carefully."

"My first experience, that is," Delphinia qualified, tapping Nicholas teasingly with her fan.

She was pleased and surprised to find Ivy reconsidering her prospects, as she admitted, "There are several men who might be possibilities. I shall try to choose before the Season is out. Until then, I shall enjoy myself."

"I must warn you, men grow bored with games," Nicholas said.

"It is not likely, however, they shall grow bored with Ivy," Delphinia reminded him.

"Delphinia is right, Nicholas. I have all the time in the world." With a coquettish smile, Ivy lifted her fan demurely as a strapping young man smiled at her from across the room. "There is a most definite possibility."

Delphinia watched as Ivy stepped discreetly aside to allow her admirer a chance to address her in private. Delphinia turned to Nicholas with a smile of deep affection.

"My mother adores you," Nicholas confided exuberantly. "By the way, these ivory gloves are charming. They remind me of an image I had of you when I was delirious. You were wearing the very same gloves."

"My mother gave them to me. I always loved them. They were the only ones I had left after I moved to Exmoor."

"You shall have hundreds of new pairs when we are wed," he promised.

They fell silent as her father and Nicholas's mother strolled onto the terrace, their expressions thoughtful.

"I wonder if she is warning your father how contrary I have been about marriage," Nicholas reflected.

"I have not acted as a real daughter in years." Delphinia felt wistful suddenly. "So many emotions have come between Papa and me."

"Now you shall have a chance to catch up on those lost years."

"I confess I do not look forward to leaving London ever again."

"This time when we leave we shall be going home to St. Ives as man and wife," he reminded her. "I am afraid, my dear, that you shall have so much time on your hands you'll be bored. I hope Tregaryan will provide opportunity enough to keep you occupied. Inasmuch as you say you do, I do not think you hated smuggling altogether."

She considered. "It was an adventure. But I only betrayed the Crown because I was forced to do so."

"I am glad to hear it." Nicholas smiled at her. "I would not want to wake some night to find you sneaking down to the sea dressed in gentlemen's clothing—probably mine."

"You would have to be delirious indeed to picture such an event," Delphinia teased.

Then, tucking her gloved hand in the crook of his elbow, she walked with him toward the terrace, glancing through the doors toward the horizon. She was pleased to see that the view ahead was quiet, the way she liked it, without a storm in sight.

LaVergne, TN USA
08 April 2011
223434LV00001B/47/P